THE **M**PIRE

A NOVEL BY T.L. JAMES

TRINITY

Text Copyright © 2010 by TL James

Published by PHE Ink
9597 Jones Rd #213
Houston, TX 77065
www.PHEink.com

PHE Ink and the portrayal of the quill feather are trademarks of PHE
Ink.

James, TL, 1971
The MPire: Trinity: a novel by TL James. – 1ˢᵗ ed.

Summary: *Mallory Haulm survived his greatest enemy – his father.
However, can he survive his Trinity – The Family Business, the Son of
God and the Holy Hell Raiser?*

ISBN: 978-0-9824475-3-6 – Print
978-1-935724-48-3 – eBook

{1. Death – Fiction. 2. Four Horsemen – Fiction 3. Family Saga –
Fiction 4.Austin, TX -- Fiction}

LCCN: 2009912152

Edited by Charisse Smiley and Jean Holloway

Genre: Speculative Fiction/Science Fiction/Family Drama

Printed in the United States of America

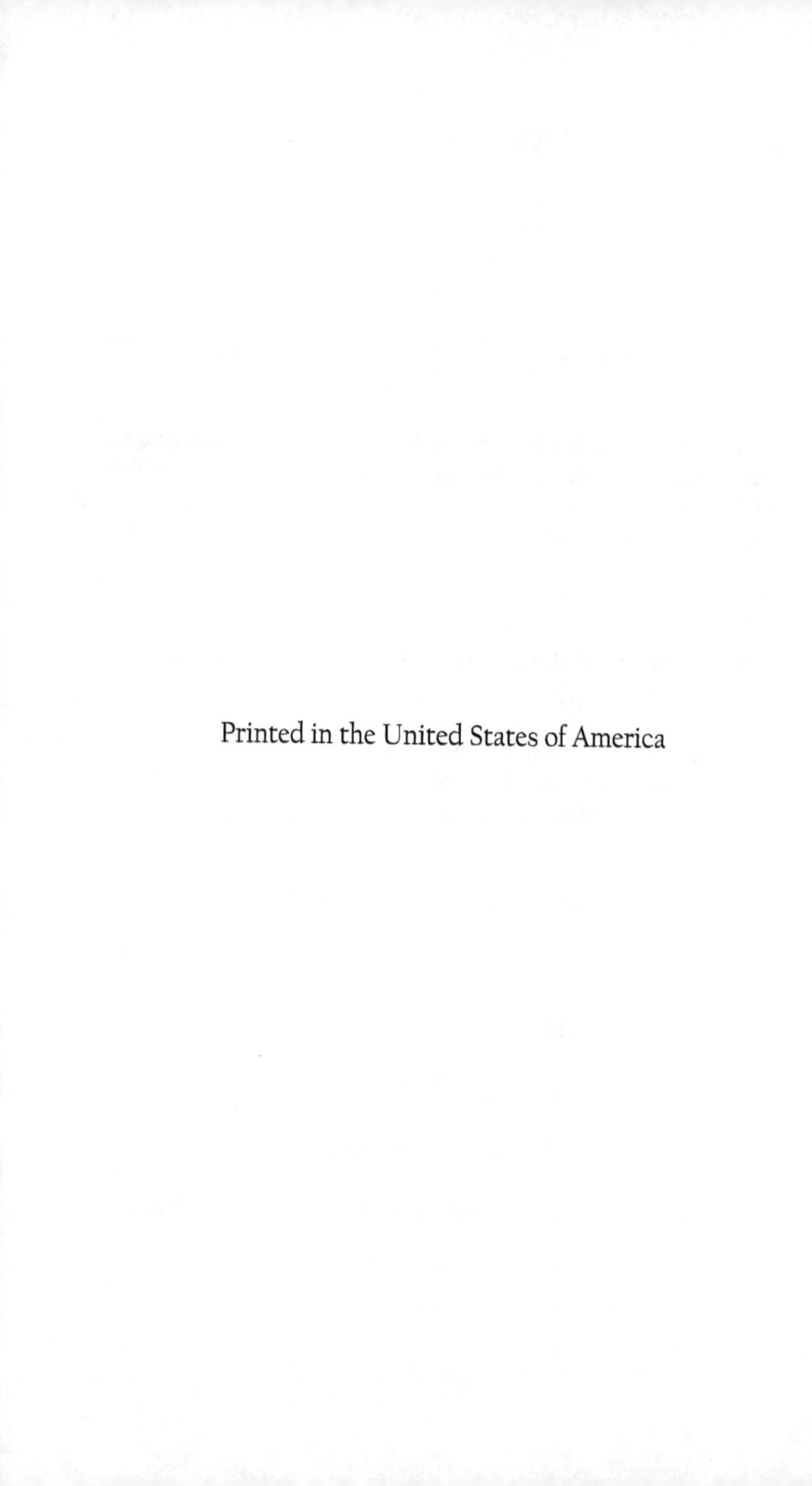

Printed in the United States of America

God is good...

...ALL THE TIME!

TRINITY

CHAPTER ONE

"Mallory, stop bitching about that got damn wedding. You're gonna give me a complex." There was a knock on the door. "I'm starting to think that you don't love me." Silas rushed to open it.

Brielle was standing in the doorway, studying a piece of paper. She looked up in confusion. "I'm sorry. I think I have the wrong penthouse," she said softly.

"Okay." Silas went to close the door, but noticed that she kept studying the paper and looking at the address on the nickel plaque on the door. "There is only one penthouse here. The others have been converted into a big closet. Who are you looking for?" He said.

"Mallory Haulm."

"He lives here, but his clothes live in the rest of the building. Come in." He stepped back and allowed her to enter. As she walked in, she noticed her painting hanging on the wall. It took her by surprise. "You like that painting, too? I'm not into art, but I love this one. It depicted him perfectly, right down to those sexy green ass eyes."

"Thank you. He was a great subject."

"You painted this?" She nodded. "You're Elektra or Brielle? Oh yeah, you can come in..." He escorted her into the living area. "You're the one disrupting the peace in my house. Mallory!" He yelled.

"Your house?"

"I guess I should say our house. I did make him move in with me. Mallory!"

"Pardon my ignorance, but who are you?"

"I'm Silas." Her confusion remained. "His lover...his boyfriend. He didn't tell you?" She shook her head no. "That son of a bitch. MALLORY!" He screamed.

Mallory slowly strolled in while reading the velvety invitation inviting him to the Essence Awards. "Hey, I found the invitation. Are you ready to go?"

"Mallory, you have a visitor." He looked up and saw Brielle standing next to Silas. "You never told her about us. You sat up all night bitching about that wedding, but you never told her about us."

"I tried. Really, I did." He slowly walked toward her. "Why are you here?"

"I..." Her voice cracked. "...wanted to speak with you."

"Speak?" Silas snickered. "Oh, hell nawh!"

"Sile, come on. She's just here to talk, aye?" She nodded.

"Mallory Towneson Haulm, you better be glad that I'm confident!" Silas walked over to the kitchen to grab the dog leash. "...and I'm well aware that she can never satisfy you like I have. So feel free...talk."

"Silas..."

"Silas what? What are you gonna say? I'm overreacting. I have to watch these bitches come out of the closet for your ass. First, it's Paulette, now it's Brielle."

"Stop, Sile...she's not a bitch."

"No offense. Yeah, she is. Look. I'm leaving so you two can talk. Congrats on your wedding." He grabbed the dog and attached the leash to her collar. "Oh Mallory, don't accidentally fall in her pussy 'cause I'll accidentally put more than my dick up your ass."

"That's not necessary."

"It needs to be spoken for the record." He headed toward the door and stopped. "On second thought..." He turned around and walked toward the couple. "You walk the bitch." He threw the leash at Mallory. "And come back with my dog!"

Mallory slapped the invitation on Silas' chest. "Get dressed! We're going to be late." He snatched the leash and grabbed Brielle's hand.

On the elevator ride down, Brielle didn't utter a word or make eye contact. The door opened, but neither one of them moved. They stood in silence. Finally, the dog pulled at the leash and started the movement out of the elevator. After several paces, Brielle composed herself enough to start the conversation.

"So explain Silas..."

"Oh, he's just being an asshole because he's not as confident as he would like to think."

"No, Mallory. Who is he?"

He paused then sighed deeply. "You know who he is... don't make me say it."

"Why didn't you tell me?"

"I tried to tell you."

"When, Mallory?"

"Brie, I tried to tell you that night you kicked me out of your house."

"You offended Chad!"

"Whatever! He should not have been in our bloody bed. I tried to tell you at Sasha's birthday party, but you and Chad were so engrossed in each other. That was disgusting to watch, you know."

"Okay, Mallory."

"And I wanted to tell you last week at my party, but you sprung that got damn engagement on me! Was that supposed to be my birthday present?"

"I sprung! I didn't know until that night."

"That damn Chad, who does he think he is?"

"He's a man who found someone who makes him happy and he wants to make a commitment to her."

"Bullshit, Brie!"

"Don't start with me, Mallory."

"You're mine. MY SOUL MATE! I might have given him permission to fuck you, but not to marry you."

"You're a bastard. I'm not going to argue with you about this." She walked away from him. He sat on a bench and released the dog to roam free. He looked up and she was blocking his sun. "You're right. We're soul mates. We do belong to each other. One soul...one connection."

"I've been saying that. I don't see why you can't see that."

"Explain something to me. If we are so connected and we belong to each other, why are you with Silas? Seriously Mallory, we lost that connection. We don't make each other happy."

"I don't make you happy?"

"For the few moments that we are together, yes. But, once the sexual emotions are gone, no. I worry about you being with someone else, not fulfilling your needs. Be honest with me, I don't make you happy..." Mallory started to answer. "...for the long run." He looked down in agreement. "I want to be happy. Don't I deserve that?"

He sighed. "And you're going to tell me that Chad can do that?"

"Is Silas doing that for you?"

Mallory allowed a faint grin to grace his face. "Okay. So I take it that you accepted his little proposal?" She nodded. "Well, great. Go...get married. I won't get in the way."

"Thank you, but that's not what I'm asking for."

"You didn't ask for anything."

"Mallory," She kneeled down and grabbed his hand. "You remember the promise you made to me?"

"The eternal promise...I made to your father. Yes, I remember."

"You loved my father... Well, I was thinking... since you loved him like a father...you could take his place."

"In what?"

"The wedding, Mallory." She sat on the bench.

"Are you smoking crack? Not only do you want me to accept the fact that you're marrying Chad of all people, you want me to go to your little damn wedding, walk you down the aisle and give you away?" She nodded. "Why would you want to torture me like that?"

"Can you think about anybody else other than your damn self for a minute?"

"NO! What if I sabotage it and fuck up the entire wedding?" He sat back and started fidgeting.

"Even in your worst, you would never hurt me like that." He rolled his eyes. "You promised your life...that no man, woman, or spirit would harm me. That includes you."

"WELL, I LIED!"

She laughed.

He stood up and helped her to her feet. He wrapped his arms around her and kissed her forehead. "Only for you...'cause I love you. I want you to have the best."

"Thank you." She kissed him.

"Don't you have to clear this with Chad, first?"

"He'll understand. This is a deal breaker. You're the only person left who was close to my father." He kissed her back briefly. "So, I should make the invitation out to Mr. and Mr. Haulm or..."

"Just Mallory Haulm and Silas Luxapher."

"Luxapher? As in Lucifer...as in Satan?" He nodded. "Mallory, you're the one smoking crack. You're dating the Devil, now?"

"What?"

"You like living life on the edge, don't you? Millions of men are out there and you can only find the devil to love."

"He's harmless."

"And Matthew?"

"Is out of the picture."

"So you're going to tell me that Matthew, God's son, is okay with you sleeping with the Devil? He just relieved you of your agreement and promise of not denying him. He's just fine with relinquishing his greatest love to Satan?"

"Silas talked to him about that."

"Silas talked to him...what, over tea and crumpets? Oh, Mallory...have you lost all connection to the organ between your ears and allowed the organ between your legs to do all your thinking? Is the sex that good?" He rolled his eyes again. She rubbed her face hard. "You're in a dangerous love triangle. You have created a serious situation for yourself."

"I can take care of myself."

"You can take care of yourself, huh? You are psychotic."

"Brie, that's not fair. I'm not judging in your desperation with Chad. I really love him. He's good to me and our relationship is based on more than just sex. There's trust and respect. He makes me completely happy."

"Fine...fine. Just be careful." She sighed, while wrapping her arms around Mallory's waist. The dog returned and growled at the couple.

"She's her daddy's little bitch. Bloody hellhound, keeping tabs on me. I think that's why he bought her." He hugged her tightly and kissed her on the forehead. "I'll be fine. I'm well aware of the situation and I'm in complete control. Don't worry about me. You just tell the minister not to ask that bloody little question about anyone not agreeing to the marriage."

CHAPTER TWO

The guys gathered at the Haulm's executive club for Chad's bachelor party. Bailey and Marc planned the perfect party; complete with Vodka and Gin fountains, margarita machines, steak station, seafood buffets and dessert bars. There were showgirls, cigarette girls and exotic dancers. There was a main stage in the center of the room and the VIP table on the stage. There were semi-private rooms created with three sheer walls for couples who wanted to be exhibitionists. Bailey and Marc spared no expense for this party. In fact, the family teased Marc about hosting a 'Mallory-type' event. For once, Marc didn't mind the teasing. Everyone was invited and accounted for, except Mallory and Marek.

"Congratulations Chad! You're getting locked up." Marek wrapped up his phone conversation with Chad. "Don't do anyone that I wouldn't do."

"Hey, I won't! I'm not doing Stacy...you don't do Brielle." Chad snapped back.

"That's a low blow, muthafucka. Bye, bitch!" Marek hung up the phone.

"Congrats, boy. Where are the strippers?" Marc patted him on the back and found his spot at the VIP table.

"Hey, guys!" Silas rushed in looking extremely frustrated.

"Hey, Silas! Glad you can make it." Marc slid his chair over to Silas and patted him on the back. "So is it official?"

"Yep! She's pregnant." Silas huffed, "She finally got her I – A – N! Fucking triplets."

"Are y'all done?" Chad asked.

"I'm done. She don't never have to worry about me fucking her ever again."

"Lucky you! Not all of us have a replacement." Marlon said, "Well, I can't speak for Marc."

"Where is your booty buddy?" Bailey slapped Silas on the back.

"I don't have patience for your bullshit tonight, Bailey. Please?" Silas snarled out.

"What's wrong with you?"

"I'm just annoyed right now." Silas picked at the nuts on the table.

"Is it Mallory?" Marc asked, sliding over a bucket of popcorn.

"Who?" Silas paused. "Oh, no! Mallory is fine. We're good. I just umm..."

"Sounds like you need a drink," Bailey advised.

"Yeah. Give me a drink. Uhmm...Grey Goose and orange juice."

"You want a screwdriver?"

"Bailey, don't ask me got damn questions like that!" Silas shouted out. "Just get me Goose and juice, please." He covered his face.

Looking confused, Bailey walked away toward the bar.

"Is Mallory coming?" Marc asked.

"No. He's at home working on a campaign." Silas lightened up a bit. "You know, he had me installed as a full emperor."

"No, shit!" The guys at the table congratulated him.

"Yep, full status." Silas smiled. "He's campaigning for the board to approve an Inaugural Ball."

"Damn shame. He never worked that hard at HIC." Marc grabbed a handful of nuts and slid back in his chair. Marlon looked at Marc in disgust. Everyone knew that Mallory was a workaholic and that Marc pigeonholed him to certain duties. No one would speak out against him, except for Silas.

"MARC, YOU'RE A GOT DAMN LIE. You know good and got damn well that Mallory works hard. Shit, you just caged him. I don't. I'm the perfect employer."

"OKAY, OKAY!" Marc held his hands up in surrender. "Granted, he works hard. But don't you get tired of him asking them damn questions? Why are you buying this, why are you spending that?"

"First of all, he doesn't ask me questions about my expenditures. He understands that it is for me to spend and him to justify. It's not like we're gon' run out of money. The Federal Reserve is on the third floor of the building. We just print more money. Besides, his world is my oyster." Silas began to digress. "I could eat some raw oysters right now." Silas looked around for a waitress.

"What makes you the perfect employer?" Marlon asked, before flagging the waitress over to the table.

"We have the perfect relationship. I fuck him, pat him on the head and give him the keys to the empire."

"You need to cage him. He'll fly away with your empire." Marc retorted.

"He can fly away with my empire all he wants, but it's my world that he's flying in. Besides, he's content. And if he is content with me, he's not fucking with you. Isn't that was you wanted, Marc?" Silas shouted in aggravation.

"Fine. Calm down." Marc raised his hand in defeat.

"Here's your drink. How're you hanging?" Bailey handed Silas a glass.

"I'M NOT!" Silas shouted. "I'm bricking out this world and if Jack and the boys DON'T BRING THEY ASS ON..." He calmed down a bit when he saw his crew saunter in, surveying the party. "Oh, that's why they late. B-Coup! That son of a bitch. I can't stand bitches who wanna be me so bad they mimic every move I make. I AM THE TOP DOG! He ain't nothing, but a bottom bitch and he needs to stay that way. Fucking athletes. They think they the shit all the time." Silas downed his drink, "Time for Poker."

"Y'all playing Poker?" Bailey perked up.

"Yeah! But not your kinda poker game." He winked at Bailey. "But I would love for you to join me." Silas smiled and then briskly walked toward his crew.

"What the hell was that? And what's bricking?" Bailey asked.

"I don't know, but I do think he's talking about basketball." Marlon answered back. He quickly pulled out his phone when he felt it vibrate in his pocket.

"Is that Jackson Moon that plays for Houston? Kobe Justice and Tate James?" Marc picked up this beer. "Dayum! That's Burrell Cooper."

"Shit! That is! He pulled the league out of the shitter when the players boycotted. I respect him for that. I think he's a free agent or thinking about retirement?" Bailey said before sipping his drink.

"Nawh, I think I read that he was waiting for the best contract to come in. I wonder why he's meeting with Silas."

"That's a rumor in the making," Bailey retorted. "Satan and contracts?"

The family partied ways for their own individual entertainment. Bailey and the brothers tried hard not to monitor Silas, but his promiscuous behavior brought on a lot of attention.

The crew settled at a small table in the corner, laughing loudly. One guy was even bold enough to sit on Silas' lap. As time passed, they all slipped into the back room. Bailey noticed one guy sneaking a kiss while pulling Silas by the hand.

Meanwhile, in the back room, Silas and his boys got ready for Poker Night – 5-card draw, winner talks all. The thing that Silas loved about this game was that the winner takes all and Silas takes the winner – and the losers too. The men gathered around the table and one guy shuffled the cards. Silas pranced around the table on the hunt before stopping behind Burrell. He pulled Burrell's seat back and then hopped up on the table in front of him. He motioned for him to unzip his pants.

"You not gon' let me play tonight, Sile?" Burrell said with a hint of fear in his voice.

"Nawh, you a sore loser," Silas replied with a straight face. The guys all laughed. Silas adjusted his position, allowing the Burrell to pull out his dick. "Besides, I like how you dick-me-down."

Burrell sucked his teeth and arrogantly retorted, "You didn't bring your bitch for that?" Burrell went to jump up from his seat, but Silas pushed him down. A faint feeling of fear struck him when he saw a lighting streak of anger flash in Silas' eyes.

"Nawh, I was thinking that you were gonna bring Evan. Since he ain't here, you can do the honors." Silas leaned forward and whispered in his ear. "Are we having an identity crisis again?"

Burrell leaned in and whispered, "No...we square. Sile, I promise, I'm good. Don't do this. Not in front of my bo— your boys. I got you anytime...just not here... not right now. Please?" Burrell respectfully lower his head a bit and was relieved when he felt Silas pat on the back of neck, dismissing him from embarrassment that Silas intended to inflict.

Not hearing the whispers between the two, Moon chuckled and said. "'I guess you should've brought your bottom bitch, B-

Coup." Moon stopped shuffling the cards and shouted. "Sile, where is Kirby or that other dick queen you got?"

"You know Kirby ain't in the picture no more! And Xander is taking the bar exams this week – that's my favorite." Kobe snatched one of Silas' arms and slammed his body on the table. "But I heard that Silas got him an upgrade. He got him a RISTA-CRAT now!"

"That's right. A bloody rista-crat from across the bloody pond!" Burrell finally got up from his seat and grabbed Silas' other arm. They both were successful at trapping Silas. "You're settling down, Sile. This might be your last night to play with us. You won't be able hang out with us like you are use to, right?"

Silas tussled one arm free and grabbed Burrell by the neck. He kissed him hard and then bit his tongue until he drew blood. "Nothing will stand in the way of me hanging with MY boys. Remember that!"

"Damn!" Burrell licked the blood off his lips. "Tate, when you finish working his rise, lock the door. Moon, you on first! I'm finishing his ass off tonight." Then he leaned down and whispered in Silas' ear, "If you trying to settle down like me, this might be yo' last night."

"We'll see about that."

As the party died down, Silas slid out of the back room and joined Bailey and Marc at their table. Silas noticed that Marc was drunk.

"Hey, you disappeared?" Bailey inquired.

"I'm not into female strippers."

"You had a lot of friends here, huh?"

"Mmm...just associates dropping by to pay their respects." Silas looked around and noticed people staggering out. "I guess this party is officially dead."

"Yep, I have to take Chad home. He's not a drinker and he's fucked up. You need to take your brother-in-law home."

Silas frowned at Bailey and then looked at Marc.

"I...can't go...home like thisssss. Cllllaire will be an-angrrrry." Marc slurred, barely sitting on the stool.

"Where's Marlon?" Silas asked while trying to hold Marc up on the stool.

"He left. His wife called and he booked it out of here."

"Bitch. Alright, I guess you're going home with me, Marc."

"Do I have to tell you that there's no freaky sneaky allowed?" Bailey asked.

"And we were doing so well. I still have no patience for your shit, Bailey. Besides, I can only fuck one Haulm at a time. And Mallory is more than enough." He grabbed Marc by the arm and hoisted him up. "Come on, brah. Mallory's going to love this."

Marc barely walked out of the elevator by himself. He leaned on the door while Silas fumbled with the keys to get into the penthouse. Once inside, Marc stumbled down the foyer stairs and knocked a table down. "Shit!"

"Don't worry, that was Mallory's antique table."

"I don't feel like his shit tonight."

"Please...Mallory's dead to the world." Silas flicked on the track lights. "After he takes his V&V cocktails, he's out like a light."

"V&V?"

"Valium and Vodka...three 30 mg. valiums and an 8-ounce glass of Vodka." Silas helped Marc on the couch and walked into the kitchen. "Hungry?"

"How can you eat this late?" Marc got up then stumbled to the island and sat at the bar.

"I worked up an appetite. I can't sleep on an empty stomach."

"Just make me some coffee." Marc's head flopped on the counter.

"Coffee? Damn, I hope I can remember the password," Silas typed in a few passwords before he got the machine to work. Finally, the coffee machine came on. Then he programmed it for two cups. "Cool! Mallory has been trying to crack the code for this machine. I have to change it every two days. I should just take it out." He changed the subject. "There were some fine ass men there tonight."

"I wouldn't know about that, Silas," Marc slurred out.

"Oops. Forget who I was talking to."

"Were there now?" Mallory emerged from the darkness and wrapped his arms around Silas. "And you had to bring one home?"

"Yeah, baby! So we can share," Silas turned around and kissed him softly. "Why are you up?"

"We ran out of Vodka."

Silas removed Mallory's robe and continued kissing on his neck. "So you need me to put you to sleep the ole fashion way?"

Mallory grunted.

"Can I see my toy?" Silas dropped to his knees, tugging at his pajamas so he could kiss the tip of his penis.

Mallory grunted again. "Mmm, that feels so good. I smell coffee?"

"Two words...Sandra James. Remember your regret about that night you went to that Confessional Coffee house?" Silas wrapped his hands around Mallory's massive shaft, licking between his fingers.

"Nevermind!" Mallory braced himself against the counter awaiting Silas oral abuse when they heard a thump on the table. Mallory grabbed him by his braids and pulled his head back. "You had to bring him home?"

"Marlon bailed on him."

"He has a house to go to."

"He needs a place to crash for the night."

"He needs to go home."

"Have a heart."

"I have a hard-on and I don't feel like dealing with his bullshit, Sile." Mallory shouted. Silas pushed him up against the table and continued his exploration. Moments later, Mallory heard Marc grumbling. "Help me put him in the guest room." Mallory grabbed one side of Marc's body, Silas grabbed the other, and they dragged him to the guest room. "Watch his head, baby..."

"I am."

"No, the other head. I don't want his neck broken."

"Should we take his clothes off?"

"No! I don't need to be accused of anything. And I don't want to have to vouch for you. I know that your little dick is itching because there's a new ass in the house." He dropped Marc on the bed. "Come upstairs, Silas."

"Alright." Silas covered Marc up and kneeled down to kiss him on his forehead. "We'll talk when he leaves for work," Silas joked.

"Silas, I can still beat yo' ass down." Marc mumbled.

"Good night, brah." Silas laughed and closed the door. When he turned around, Mallory was standing there, waiting for him. Silas strolled up and wrapped his arms around him. He softly kissed his lips and asked, "Why don't we take a stroll down to Hell and find us a cozy cove and let the souls watch us as we make love."

"Watch?" Mallory protested a bit.

"You like an audience."

"You're the exhibitionist." Mallory kissed his lips. "Sounds awesome. I'm ready."

Throughout the night, Marc awoke to strange sex sounds. He tossed, turned, and tried burying his head between the down pillows. After a while, it stopped. He vaguely heard the door close twice and then the sex sounds started again. He slowly crawled out of bed and walk into the bathroom. As he washed his face, he heard Silas raise his voice and slam his fist against the wall. He knew that Silas possessed a bad temper and Mallory was no stranger to an evil side. Seconds later, he heard sobbing and Silas apologizing profusely. He walked out of the guest room just when Silas and his guest walked out of the bedroom. The guest looked at Marc angrily.

"Who is that, Silas?" Kirby squealed out.

"Kirby, you're too much of a drama queen. He's no concern to you."

"You bring me here and make love to me..."

"I have never made love to you. The only reason we fucked in this room is because he was in the room we normally use. You see we didn't fuck in the bed. We were on the floor."

"Silas, why?"

"Why what, bitch? This is why I hate calling you!" Silas held his hands up. "I should've call Xander."

"I thought you loved me. I was everything to you until you got with this Mallory." Kirby puffed up his chest. "What if I tell Mallory about everything you're doing?"

Silas grabbed Kirby by the neck and slammed him against the wall. "Then you will not live to take your next breath. I'm sick of your threats. And frankly, the sex is not that good anymore. You can leave now." He pushed Kirby down the stairs and watched him fall down the entire flight, landing at Marc's feet. Marc stepped over him and walked to the kitchen. Silas grabbed Kirby's shoes and roughly escorted him out the door. He walked back into the kitchen to see Marc sitting at the island. "Hungry?"

"You worked up an appetite again?" Marc asked sarcastically.

"Your point?"

"So that wasn't you and Mallory fucking the whole time?"

"You wouldn't have heard us. We weren't on Earth."

"Hmm. I take it he doesn't know about your extra activities and I guess you want to keep this a secret."

"And you know I don't do blackmail or threats." Silas warned.

"No...no, just agreements."

"What do you want, Marc?"

"Keep Mallory away from HIC permanently." Marc announced without blinking an eye.

Silas huffed. "Done. Anything else?"

"Scrambled eggs, bacon and fresh brewed coffee would be nice." Marc answered with an evil grin.

CHAPTER THREE

"Mallory, where is my driver?" Silas shouted.

"In the shop. You broke it, remember? I think it will be ready tomorrow." Mallory shouted back from upstairs.

"I'm leaving today."

"I know. Use my clubs. They are in my office closet." Mallory jogged downstairs toward the kitchen.

"Mallory, have you used these clubs?"

"No. I like them to be clean, but you can use them this time." Mallory interjected. "Don't use my cute putter."

"What's a cute putter?"

"You know, 'Itchy feet' the one." He grabbed two bottled waters, one for him and the other for the dog.

"Mallory, you bought a putter because it was cute?" Silas screamed out. "Prissy!"

"You love prissy. Oh and be careful not to get my Louis bag dirty." Mallory finally made it to the office while Silas was frantically transferring his gear into Mallory's bag.

"Mallory, do you have a dick?"

"Silas, did you not feel it last night?" He pushed Silas on the sofa and straddled him. "Why are you so nervous?"

"I don't know. We have been having these retreats for almost five years and today I feel nervous and sick."

"I'm sorry, baby. I asked if you wanted me to go." Mallory gently massaged his shoulders.

"No. That's okay. I'll be fine."

"So when is he due in?"

"In six hours. He said that he had to make a stop in Houston... probably to see my sister."

"Well, I will be out of here in two."

"I'm sorry. I was hard on you about hiding us from your family and look at me. I promise this year, I will tell him about us."

"I understand that it's hard. Shit, if Malcolm didn't have that heart attack, I would probably still be with piss-ass. You just owe me, again." He raised his face.

"I just got you a new plane a month ago. What do you want now?" Silas flipped Mallory on the sofa and he started kissing him.

"Mmm ...more of my Xavier!" The doorbell rang. "Oh, I forgot Marlon is coming by to get Shit."

"Mallory, her name is Tanic." He lifted himself up to allow Mallory to get the door.

"He answers to Shit." He slid from under Silas and jumped up from the couch. He lowered down to command the dog's attention.

"She, Mallory, she."

"Whatever. He's coming to get the hellhound." Mallory picked her up gingerly, walked toward the door and opened it. "Hey Marlon, her stuff is on the kitchen table." He handed the dog to Marlon and quickly hopped back toward the office. "Oh, her name is Tanic. And she doesn't eat dog food, so I cooked some chicken breast with rice and corn. She's doesn't like heat, like her daddy, so keep her in the AC as much as possible. And she is not fixed, so be careful."

"Okay." Marlon put the dog on the counter and opened the Tupperware container. He pulled out a piece of the chicken to sample it. "And he seasoned it for you, too!"

"Marlon!" Mallory shouted from the back. "Stop eating the dog's food."

"Damn...okay!" He took another piece and then closed the lid. Marlon grabbed the puppy and placed in her special travel bag. As he whisked off to open the door, a tall, dark man was standing at the entrance. It was Michael Luxapher. Marlon was petrified. Michael never spoke, but volumes of disgust shouted through his dark, sunken eyes. Cold chills ran down Marlon's back as he moved aside and allowed Michael to enter the penthouse. Marlon rushed out to the elevators.

Michael promenaded around the living room, inspecting Silas' penthouse. He was pleased. As he picked up knick-knacks and glided his hand across the mantle, he heard voices from the back.

"Oh, shit, Xavier! That feels so good," Mallory screamed out.

"Sssh! Ride this dick, bitch!"

"Oh, fuck! Xavier Haulm! Harder, baby, HARDER!"

"OH SHIT, SHIT! I'M EXPLODING!" Silas let out a loud cry as he climaxed. "Got damn Mallory Luxapher...you're the best."

Mallory bragged between breaths. "I know. You feel better?"

"Much...better." Silas let out a deep breath.

"Let's take a shower and then I'll head out. Aye?"

"Start the shower and I'll go lock the door. I have a feeling we're not finished." Silas finally rolled off the couch and on to his knees.

Mallory grabbed his pants and walked up the stairs into the bedroom. He shouted down. "I wouldn't worry about your Daddy. Shit, if he doesn't like me, fuck him."

"I'll be pissed. That's my ass you're giving away." Silas shouted back as he walked toward the door, closed and locked it. As he walked back toward the stairs, he spotted his father sitting in the kitchen. He stood frozen. He heard Mallory shouting, but he couldn't respond.

"This will work out. What can possibly go wrong?" Mallory chirped.

Silas was petrified. Michael stood up and took a few steps toward Silas.

"Xaaaa-vier, the shower's ready and so am I-IIIII..." He sung loudly, but Silas didn't respond.

His eyes were fixed on his angry father.

"XAVIER!" He shouted as he ran down the stairs to check on him. "What are you doing that you can't...answer...me?" He practically ran into Michael. "Michael?" He paused. "Um...how are you doing, sir?"

"Saully, may I have a word with you?" Michael asked sternly, not taking his eyes off his son.

"Yes, sir." He looked at Mallory. "Daddy, I want to say..."

"Alone!" He shouted.

"Daddy...anything you have to say to me you can say in front of Mallory."

"You lied."

"Technically..."

"You LIED!" He shouted. "Saully, if you have to lie about a relationship, it's not worth it!"

"IT IS worth it. I wanted to tell you in person so many times. I'm in love with Mallory."

"In love? In love? With a bottom feeder?"

"What?" Mallory shouted.

"Daddy, stop calling him that!" Silas moved closer to Mallory, using his body as a barrier between his father and Mallory.

"A bottom feeder?" Mallory questioned.

"You're not good enough to be in the presence of my dog...let alone the presence of my son."

Silas pressed his body against Mallory to deflect his next obscene comment. "Daddy, stop. He's perfect for me. I love him and he loves me."

"I don't need you to protect me from this bloody motherfucker!" Mallory pushed Silas aside to confront Michael.

"Mallory, stop." Silas grabbed his arms to reassure him. "I'll handle it."

"Do you think I am God?" Michael pushed Silas to confront Mallory. "Do you think I will tolerate your boorish behavior?"

"Do you think I give a bloody fuck? What are you going to do?" Mallory shouted back.

"There is a fate worse than Hell. Unlike your Heavenly Father, I take personal pride in doing my own wet work."

"Daddy, stop!" He turned back to Mallory. "Baby, just go take a shower. I'll be up there in a minute. Just go, please." Mallory reluctantly walked backwards toward the stairs. "Daddy, this is not necessary."

"You lied. I told you about them damn Haulms and you defied me."

"No, I didn't. I never told you that I was not going to see them. I specifically told you that I would keep my eye on them."

"Is this the phantom leader that's running the company? Is he the one running the boardroom while you're tramping off around the golf courses and having fuck fests with men?"

"Mallory is just consulting, I'm still the leader. He's a better businessman and he is just helping me out so I can get adjusted."

"Yeah, he's helping you out of your empire. Are you that helpless and stupid?"

"You are shitty!"

"Don't take that tone with me."

"How dare you take this attitude with me? If you want your precious little empire, FINE! Take it back. I never wanted the bitch! But don't judge my business decisions because you're not happy with whom I'm sleeping with. Shit, you sound just like them damn Haulms."

"Watch it, son! Poppy is not here to protect you."

"Get out, Daddy. How dare you use that name in front of me? You will not stand here in my motherfucking house and insult me. Get the fuck out!" He screamed and pointed toward the door.

"That was out of line, Saully." Michael raised his hand in surrender.

"You're out of line. I'm the next emperor and I make my own decisions. And if I want to fuck him and his whole got damn family, then that's my choice."

"Operative word...next, son. There is still the Inaugural Ball."

"You need to leave now." Silas walked out of the room.

"Michael? He's not to blame." Mallory slipped down the stairs toward Michael. "He told me that you were open-minded."

"About his sexuality...not his choice of partners." He stepped into Mallory's personal space. "I don't know you and I don't trust you. I don't want you with my son."

"That will be difficult to accomplish now because we are together."

"Then, I have a problem. I have to weigh my son's happiness over my contempt for you."

"You just said that you don't know me. How can you hate me?" Michael couldn't respond to that question. "I love your son."

"Of course you do. You love his power, his fortune and his empire."

"I don't give a fuck about the empire. It's your son. If he was broke..."

"You wouldn't have noticed him."

"I don't need his power or money. I have my own."

The room began to darken. Mallory looked around to see shadows growing across the windows. The air in the room began to stifle him. He looked up and Michael appeared to be three times taller than before - towering over Mallory.

Michael spoke in a deep tone that burned Mallory's ears, "Mallory, there is a fate worse than death and Hell. I could spend eternity torturing you for trapping my son's heart and making a fool out of him. I can make you disappear and I will find him new piece of ass in the blink of an eye. Do you want that?"

Mallory broke eye contact with him.

"You break this relationship off with my son and he better not be heartbroken."

Just as Mallory blinked, the room returned to normal. Silas walked back into the room and noticed the two talking. Michael turned toward him with a smile.

"Saully, I don't want to fight with you. Why don't you get ready and I'll let you spend the next eighteen holes telling me how good Mallory is." He patted Mallory on the back.

"Okay?" He looked at his father strangely. "I just need to grab my bag."

Mallory stood paralyzed in front of Michael. "You have a year...from today. I have taken your father down before; you're just a piece of cake to me."

Silas walked back into the room with Mallory's bag. He took Mallory by surprise when he kissed him. Mallory was trembling, but Silas didn't notice. "I love you, baby," he said as he leaned over and whispered in Mallory's ear. "Whatever you said to him, thank you." He and Michael walked out of the penthouse.

Michael waited for Silas to reach the elevator before he turned to Mallory and threatened, "He better not find out about our little conversation. My contempt does trump his happiness."

CHAPTER FOUR

It was the evening of Chad and Brielle's wedding. Mallory quietly snuck into the Groom's dressing area where Chad and the rest of the Haulm men congregated and prepared. They were all dressed in deep navy, long tail tuxedos. Everyone wore navy vests except for Chad, who had on a platinum vest.

Feeling a little queasy, Chad had a difficult time tying his Windsor knot. He was extremely nervous about the day's events. He had been vomiting all day and couldn't manage to keep anything in his stomach. The twins, Mattock and Maddox, were teasing Chad about Mallory's latest absurd statement about giving Chad permission. His older brother, Bailey, tried to provide comfort, but was doing it poorly.

Although he tried to support him, Bailey felt that marriage was a trap or a prison. His plan was to stay the ineligible bachelor. Mallory was his idol for the longest time until he broke his heart and switched teams.

"Uncle My, where is Uncle Mal?" Maddox asked.

"He's protesting. He said that he can't be a part of something that he doesn't condone." Uncle Myron answered.

"What is there to condone?" Bailey asked.

"That's just one of his pet peeves. Take his dog, his truck, or his last dollar, but don't take his wife. He'll pull his shotgun out for that."

"Mallory and Brielle were never married," Chad pointed out.

"He feels that any contact with a significant other is inappropriate." Uncle Myron saw the tension building in his son's face. "Don't worry, son, we're with you."

"I don't understand why he is so upset with this wedding. She's not his wife." Bailey finished dressing and flopped into a chair. "Daddy, does it have anything to do with the rumors about him, Uncle X and Aunt Felicia?"

Marc and Marlon walked in slowly.

"We don't bring that up." Uncle Myron quickly shut down the conversation.

"I hate family secrets." Bailey sulked further in the chair.

"It ain't your family that's keeping the secret." He smacked him across the head.

"What's going on?" Marc asked as he headed straight to the mirror.

For ritualistic events that involved the entire family, the horsemen always had to distinguish themselves from the rest of the family. The brothers and Uncle Myron were dressed in all black long tail tuxedoes with their signature color ties that differentiated themselves; Myron – war red, Marc – pollution green, Marlon – famine blue.

"Just wondering where Uncle Mal is?" Bailey frowned up at his father.

"I worry about him sometimes. It's the strangest things that set him off. He was angrier than Mallory. Hell, Mallory said that it was okay." Marc said.

"No he wasn't." Bailey teased. "He gave Chad permission."

"Do you get the permission in writing?" They all laughed.

"I can't believe that bastard." Tito said fighting with his cufflinks.

"Don't worry about that faggot. Mallory ain't shit. We got your back, brah," Bailey commanded.

"Why is she marrying me? Clearly, I'm not Mallory." Chad said.

"That's probably why." Marc said as he walked over and easily placed the links in Tito's shirt. "Mallory and Brielle haven't been together in a while."

"He's happy with Silas," Marlon said.

"Do you think she will be happy with me?" There was a long silence. "Guys?"

"Yeah! Sure! Real happy! Off her ass happy!" They all shouted.

"This is crazy. I should call it off."

"You better do it before Mallory gets here." Marc teased as he walked over and tried to help Chad, but he refused. "You might need his permission for that."

"I can't believe he said that to me. 'I give you permission'," he said in a mocking tone. "Fuck him!"

"He was cocky for saying that shit...and he said it like he meant it." Bailey reclined in the chair and started playing with a large cigar.

"He gave me permission," Chad repeated under his breath. "Fuck it, I can't do this tie. I'm calling it off."

"I did give you permission," Mallory seethed as he emerged from the backroom of the Groom' dressing room and walked toward Chad. Mallory was dressed in all black as well with a black tie accented by silver pinstripes. Although his tuxedo was the same, he appeared to be more distinguished than the other horsemen. Mallory possessed that effect with his entire horseman ensemble. He snatched the tie from Chad's hand and threw it around his neck. He adjusted the wide end longer than the narrow end, forcefully tightening the two ends together, choking Chad. "If I didn't, you wouldn't be here complaining."

"Fuck you, Mallory." Chad mustered all his strength to stand up to Mallory. "She loves me. I would have married her with or without your got damn permission."

"You probably would have, but would she?" Mallory turned Chad around to face the mirror. He wrapped his arm around his neck and began tying the knot. "She loves me. She will always love me just as I will always love her." Chad went to move, but Mallory snatched him back in place. "She will. Just face that fact." He took a deep breath. "Just like I have to face the fact that she moved on and has fallen in love with you. You make her happy and she shines when she's around you. I've never been able to do that." He patiently brought the wide part of the tie around and tucked it in. "I have to let her go. Thus, giving you permission to marry her." He finished the knot and Chad inspected it. It was tied perfectly. "Perfect. Just like you and her."

"Are you ready for this, man?" Bailey asked.

"Are you? Think about it for a minute," Mallory asked.

"Yes." Chad answered with a quiver in his voice.

"Okay, because Haulm men never divorce." Mallory said.

"I thought that was only for you horsemen?" Maddox inquired.

"Hell nawh! Why should we be the only ones to suffer that marital bliss?" The horsemen shouted. "No divorce and no separation."

"You can separate, but it will cost you." Mallory sat by Bailey and took his cigar. He placed it in his mouth and dared Bailey to say anything to him.

"How much is it costing you, Mal?" Bailey asked and pulled out another cigar.

"Ten grand a month and a new car every four years. And an anniversary gift." He snatched that cigar from Bailey too.

"Can I separate from you?" They all laughed. "I just want the plane." Bailey shouted as he snatched the cigar back.

"Silas spoils you like a fucking gold digger," Mattock complained.

"How do you know?" Mallory asked.

"Tabitha interns at LTC...admins talk and she listens."

"And reports back like her Uncle Marlon." Mallory glared over and Marlon looked down. "I'm not a gold digger. I just appreciate the finer things and it's great for once to have someone appreciate me on the same level. Believe me, it's not all about the sex. I love his companionship."

"And his empire...he works there too." Marc added.

"I just consult..."

"On a twenty four-seven basis." Marc and Marlon said in unison. "Jinx. You owe me a Dr. Pepper."

"That's why you gave Towneson Financial to me?" Chad asked.

"I didn't give you shit. I let you run it. Don't get confused. Towneson Financial and Brie are two different things." He stood up and walked toward Chad.

"Don't start that shit up again." Uncle Myron commanded.

"Mallory? Is Mallory Haulm in here?" The wedding coordinator peeked through the doors.

"Yes?" He answered.

"The bride is asking for you."

"OHHHH!" They all teased.

"Chad, are you ready? Not just for today...for life."

"Yes!" Chad answered with confidence this time.

"Okay...I'll end with this. Brielle is my heart. And if you hurt her...just remember I'm Death and I fuck the Devil. Between the two of us, I will make you suffer." He walked out throwing both cigars at Bailey.

"That motherfucker. That's why I don't mess with any of Mallory's bitches. I don't care if they're fine as hell. Shit, you have to live up to the expectations he left behind and listen to his threats."

"He doesn't bother me. Amanda and I are cool," Marc mumbled thinking about his situation with Amanda.

"That was some cold shit." Maddox said. "He didn't kick your ass for that?"

"We will never know," Marlon said.

"And it will be about two days after you see the Devil wearing an overcoat before I tell."

"It will be 42 degrees in Hell before you catch me wearing any kinda coat!" Silas walked in and Chad started to hyperventilate. "Shit, I'm hot in this damn tux."

"Hey, Silas. You just missed Mallory." Marc announced.

"His faggot bitch ass." Bailey's comment stopped Silas in his tracks. He wanted to respond to it, but decided to ignore it. He looked over at Chad.

"What's wrong, Chad?" Silas asked after he noticed Chad hyperventilating in the corner.

"Mallory's queer ass came in here fucking with him...threatening him and shit. Fucking pillow- biter."

Silas paused again and shot him a look that stopped him in his tracks. Marc decided to get up and stand between him and Bailey, patting Silas on the back on the way to protect Bailey from his mouth. Not taking his eyes off Bailey, Silas walked over to Chad.

"What did he say to get you worked up?" Silas picked at Chad's tie.

"He's Death and you're the Devil and if I hurt Brie, y'all will make me suffer."

He placed his hand on Chad's shoulders. "Chad, listen to me…just you and me talking. I love Mallory with all my heart, but he can be an obnoxious pompous ass." He laughed. "Marriage is hard enough without some pompous ass shooting idle threats, especially from one who can't handle his own wife. Hell, I can't handle mine. So how can I threaten you?"

Chad lightened up a bit. The others were trying to listen in. Silas grabbed Chad and guided him into a private room.

"Look, if Mallory loved her as much as he says he does, he would be standing here - not you. And if Brielle loved him more than you, she wouldn't have accepted your proposal." He grabbed Chad's coat and assisted him in putting it on. "Be good to her…love and cherish her as much as possible. Remember, you two are marrying for love, not obligation. That's something beautiful and not to be toyed with."

"Do you think he will try and stop the wedding?"

"Please, that boy does have to go home with me." Silas snappy comment made Chad chuckle. "You go get married to that beautiful woman and don't worry about Mallory. This is the last time he will be involved in your marriage, alright?"

Chad nodded.

"As a matter of fact, I was looking for him. There are a few of his exes here and I need to put in a threat to him for the record. He still has that pussy taste in his mouth and for some reason I can't fuck it out of him."

"Maybe because it's so good?" Chad eyes widened as Silas shot him an intimidating stare.

"Look, don't make me have to undo everything I said."

"Sorry." Chad bowed his head.

Silas released a grin that eased Chad's tension. "Good luck." He walked out of the room and Chad followed. As Silas exited out of the room, he made threatening eye contact with Bailey and then winked. "See you later, Bailey."

"What I do?" Bailey almost fell out of his seat.

"What did he say?" Marc asked.

"Not too much."

"You didn't sell your soul, did you?" Bailey asked.

"Silas doesn't collect individual souls. He has teams of attorneys and accountants for that." Marc answered that question.

"Hell, I didn't know that!" Bailey shouted out.

"He doesn't. What did he say? Whatever he said lifted your spirits," Uncle Myron added.

"He just told me not to worry about Mallory and his idle threats."

"I told you don't worry about that faggot."

"First of all, I would stop calling him faggot in his presence." Chad walked over and slapped Bailey on top of his head. "Something tells me that he has a bad temper and subzero understanding. Second, he has more control over Mallory than you do. I heard about the ass whooping Marek got."

Marc laughed.

"I heard about your ass whooping too, Mr. Devil's overcoat." Chad tagged Marc in the chest.

"Gentlemen, are you ready?"

"YES WE ARE!"

"There you are. I was looking for you." Silas rushed Mallory and planted the wettest kiss on him.

"This is bullshit, Silas."

"My patience is wearing thin with you. If you really want her, go in there and proclaim your love. Run in there and say, 'I love you and I want to be with you. I will give up my position and power at Haulm and The Abaddon. I will give up all my cars, houses, plane and all my money to be with you. I will subject myself to pain and death and maybe have my life reset for your love. I will divorce my wife, which will launch an execution. I will deny my true and honest sexual desires and love you and only you and be satisfied with that. We will be happy and poor and have alotta kids before my demise. I will love you all my life which will be short-lived because I don't know who will kill me first: my brothers, the board, my ex-lovers, or Heaven and Hell!' Run... Go tell her that."

"Now if I turn around and tell her that, you would be the first to kill me."

"I might or I might not. I would be heartbroken. You can have great heartbroken sex. There are a couple of guys that were flirting with me and I'm thinking about tapping Bailey's ass just for giggles."

"Then I would kill you. Leave Bailey alone. He's just extremely homophobic. He thinks being gay runs in the family like diabetes."

"Fine! You still want to go in there and tell her?"

"No. None of it's true. I don't love her like that, but I feel like I should."

"Maybe she feels the same way."

"I have to believe that...or else I will be selling my soul to her."

"Especially since your soul belongs to me." He grabbed Mallory by the waist.

"My soul is not yours...my ass is! Don't get that confused." He smiled and kissed his lips. Mallory exhaled as he tightly embraced Silas' body. "Besides, you just bought me a new plane. I can't leave you now."

"Yeah, you have alotta fucking to do, Mr. I-Need-My-Own-Plane." Silas held him closer. "Oh, my stars...you are beyond beautiful." Silas looked up and saw Brielle.

"Oh, sweetie..." Mallory said.

"Not you, nut! Brielle."

Mallory turned around and she was standing behind him in a platinum white A-line satin dress.

"Thank you. Silas, may I speak with you for a moment in private?" Brielle asked.

Mallory stepped away and Silas walked closer to her. He kissed her on the forehead as she lowered her head.

"Silas, I heard what you told him. I was going to call this wedding off until I heard his response."

"I didn't want you to hear that."

"I needed to hear it. I love Chad, but I was holding on to a small hope that Mallory would come to me."

"Oh yeah...that wasn't gonna happen." Silas answered cockily. "Not even if he wanted to!"

"He loves you. I don't know why, but he does. I'm entrusting you to love and protect him. He's my heart and if I must say so...and you can correct me if I'm wrong, but Hell hath no fury like a woman scorned."

"Are you threatening me?"

"You can take it however you need to as long as you're good to Mallory."

"Will you please go get married? Please!" He grabbed her hand and walked her over to Mallory.

"I'll see you later, baby." He gave her hand to Mallory, grabbed his face and gently kissed him.

"You're beautiful." Mallory said, caressing her hand.

"Thank you and thanks for doing this for me. I know it's hard for you."

"They are ready for you." The wedding coordinator whispered.

He smiled. "This is our last opportunity to escape." He raised his eyebrows.

"Stop Mallory, behave now."

Mallory wrapped her arm around his and they started to march down the aisle. With each step he took, Mallory felt his heart breaking. He tried to remember his wedding, but the only thing he remembered was being drunk and crowds of people flashing around him. He looked over at Brielle and she began to shine. "I guess this is the only way for us to walk down the aisle together."

She squeezed his arm. They reached the altar where the minister and Chad were anxiously waiting. Mallory had an overwhelming urge to kneel down, profess his love and beg her not to marry Chad.

As he turned toward her ready to bear his soul, he heard the minister ask, "Who gives this woman to be married to this man?"

Mallory's time passed and he lost his heart. Trying hard not to show any emotion, took a deep breath and said, "I do." Mallory stood back and watched his soul mate marry another man. He tried to mask his broken heart, but Silas saw right through his façade and slid to the front pew to sit by Mallory.

When minister asked the grave question, everyone looked in Mallory's direction - even the bride and groom. Mallory took a deep breath and bowed his head. Silas squeezed his hand and

Mallory looked at him with an endearing smile. Silas made the motion for the minister to continue quickly with the rest of the ceremony. Mallory's time truly passed and Brielle was a Haulm - but not his. He spent the rest of the ceremony in a daze.

CHAPTER FIVE

Mallory opened his eyes to find that he was completely naked and bed sheets were covering his head. As he tried to swallow, aches and pains echoed from his head to his toes. He attempted to turn over, but pains shot through his frail body. It was even painful for him to shed a tear. He felt a warm body sitting next to him and then he felt the covers being removed.

"You're going to be late for your meeting."

"I want to die, Silas."

"That's not on the agenda today, baby. You wanna try to squeeze it in after sex tonight?"

Mallory heard loud echoes of Silas' laughter. "Why are you shouting?"

"This is not shouting," he said in a low, loving tone. "THIS IS FUCKING SHOUTING!" He laughed harder.

"Why do you hurt me?"

"I didn't do this to you, you did. You were hammer-headed last night."

"Baby, speak English to me...quiet English."

"I'll put like this...the last thing you need is Viagra. I don't know what other shit was mixed with the ecstasy that you was smoking, but I do know the effects of Viagra. Your dick is hard now, isn't it? It's been hard ALL NIGHT. Believe me I was riding it...ALL NIGHT!"

"Silas, I hurt all over."

"And you should. You amaze me. You try to have this pristine reputation. You're a good guy, a quiet, conservative guy. But you really know how to get BUCK WILD!" Silas shouted.

"Why do you hate me?"

"I don't hate you. I'm angry, but I don't hate you. In fact, I will tell you how much I love you." He straddled Mallory and grabbed his head. "You know I don't share you, right? You know that I'm the only one to hit this piece of ass, right? And your dick belongs to be me only, right? You understand." Silas shook his head for him. "Well, last night after you fucked me in the restrooms, I let you make it."

"What restroom?"

"Every restroom between the reception hall and home. I don't know how many men you fucked. Well, I do know how many because I was watching you, but...I hate to say this, baby. You are BEYOND PSYCHOTIC!"

"Silas, please."

"After the second tattoo, I had to bring the fun home."

"Tattoos?"

"Oh, yes. You have two. I'm partial to the second one." He removed the cover and grabbed Mallory's body. "I don't want you to be late for this meeting. Marc wants you there. Some shit about HIC."

"I can't go."

"You play hard, you work hard. Get up...I'll make you some strong tea. A shower will make you feel better."

"Silas, I'm sorry."

"Don't be sorry to me. It's your reputation that's affected."

Mallory stumbled to the bathroom and sprawled out on the shower floor. The water did make him feel a little better, but he still ached all over. Silas walked in the bathroom and joined him in the shower. He grabbed his foot and started massaging it.

"Did I sleep with a lot of guys?"

"No, baby, just some...I would say more than a couple and less than twenty. We did go SANTA FE on this one dude and had a threesome with another and then you went off on your own. Watching somebody fuck is like watching sports to you, if you're not in the game, you want no part of it. I know for sure you were with some random named Quincy and the tattoo guy."

"Quincy? I don't know a Quincy."

"You acted like you did last night. You two were talking about finance and boring business bullshit, so I stepped away. When I came back, you were cumming. Quincy was a little unnerved when I told him that I don't share, but you handed him your business card, zipped your pants and walked away. I didn't get a chance to beat his ass down because I had to keep up with you. You propositioned some other guys at a table and bought them a round of drinks, but they bored you. Then you saw a tattoo parlor. You said you wanted a dragon like your daddy."

Mallory looked down and noticed a crucifix with letters inside printed on his lower right hip.

"No, that's not the dragon, but that's my favorite." Silas scooted closer to Mallory and bent down to lick it. "This one has *Xavier* going down and *lover* going across at the V. The dragon is on your ass."

Mallory slinked get out of the shower and walked toward the three-mirrored wall. He noticed a small dragon sitting on top of the word ESSAY. The tail encircled the word and the triangle tip ended at his tailbone. "You thought it was so cute and clever. I think it's confusing."

"Essay?"

"S. A." He threw a towel at Mallory.

"No, I didn't."

"Silas' ass. And you were a big ass last night." Silas smacked him on his butt.

"Oh, God."

"I wish I could have given you to God last night. You do some crazy shit. I figured you would want to remove the tattoo on your ass. But can you keep this one? I like this one." He kneeled and licked the tattoo again.

"I'll keep both of them if you forgive me." Mallory held his hand out, but barely supported Silas when he tried to lift him up off the ground.

"There is no need to forgive. You just remember what belongs to me. And if you are fucking anybody else, I have to be on either one of your ends." He bucked Mallory from behind. "Get dressed. I don't want you to be late."

Silas and Mallory finally made it to the restaurant, only to find Bailey there. Silas pulled Mallory's seat out and then sat with him. Mallory desperately tried to maintain a professional posture, but he failed when his head involuntarily hit the table. Silas ignored Mallory and ordered his usual meal.

"Is he okay?" Bailey whispered.

"I don't know." Silas leaned down and shouted. "IS YOU OK, BABY?"

Mallory lifted his head to deliver a look filled with daggers.

"Surprisingly he's living. He got hammer-headed last night." Silas instigated.

"I'm sorry, Silas."

"Look, I got a tattoo out of it, I'm fine. Are you hungry?"

"I can't eat."

"You need to eat something so it can soak up some of that alcohol."

"You were drinking, too?" Bailey shouted.

"Shut up, Bailey! We were all drinking. Hence the phrase, 'open bar'!" Mallory dropped his head back on the table.

A strange man approached the table and handed Silas a drink. "Would you like a screwdriver?" He smiled.

Silas smiled back. "I would love to." The man walked away and Silas kissed Mallory on the back of the neck. "I'll be right back, baby. I need to meet with this associate." He got up and rushed away, but left the drink on the table.

"Hey Mallory, can I ask you a question?"

"You just asked a question. The answer is no."

"Faggot, listen! Do you think that Silas cheats on you?"

"Silas would never cheat on me."

"He meets up with a lot of guys."

"So you're telling me that he engages in sex with every guy he is around?"

"Yeah."

"So when did you fuck him?"

"Not me, bitch."

"You have been around him. I'm just going along with your theory."

"Never mind."

"Silas knows a lot of people in his line of work. I can't imagine him sleeping with all those guys. That would be insane."

"Okay, I'm out of it."

"Out of what? Have you seen something?"

"It's just that he disappears with these associates a lot," Bailey mimicked Silas' reference by making quotation marks with his fingers. "He always comes back looking a little suspect. What's bricking?"

"Being aroused...hard on."

"That's fucking gross. Just watch your back, okay?"

"Fine. Where is Marc?"

"That's another one to watch. Something is up with him. You know, nineteen people have quit since you left."

"That's doesn't include the people who went with me?"

"Nawh. He's trying to dispute all of your contracts. I didn't see anything wrong with them. I mean you are a control faggot, but you take perfect notes. I can tell what you ate the day you signed the contract, but Marc's contracts are incomplete and vague and critical information is missing."

"Did you ask him about it?"

"Yeah and he bitched at me. You know he put me on administrative leave for a week! I have only been there for two months."

"What did you do?"

"Okay, to tell the truth, I was snooping and I found this account that is linked to one of his personal accounts. I asked him about it. He wrote me up, some bullshit about insubordination."

"That doesn't sound right."

"I know. The board restricted my access, so I can't get into anything."

"I'll give you my access, see what you can find. They can't restrict mine. But, use a little discretion."

"I'll have to or I will be out of a job and a home."

"Your home?"

"Yeah, some son of a bitch bought my co-op and is making us move. They said that they're building some cell tower for a generator. I have to move out by the end of this week."

"You know who bought it?"

"Some company. It's initials are TAE."

"The Abaddon Empire?"

"Yeah, you know that company? You think I can sue?"

"I don't think you want to sue Silas."

"I thought he was LTC."

"It's two-fold, like we are. The Abaddon is Hell. I heard him say that building was strategically centered in a nexus."

"I'm living at the gates of Hell?" Mallory nodded. "I ain't fighting that. I'm moving."

"You can stay at my house for a while. I'm not living there and my servants are restless. You will give them something to do."

"Why would you let me stay at your house?"

"Why not? Like I said, I'm not living there. I need somebody there to watch the place until MJ is ready. Why not you?"

"I don't know. Thanks, I guess."

"It's a great place to have parties. You have a lakeside view and you can use the boat. One of those Harleys is mine. I don't think that Silas would mind you using his bike. Harold is there to keep the cars up, so you don't have to worry about that. Just don't drive my Viper or my Aston Martin. Oh...and stay out of my bedroom, bathroom and closet."

"Anything else?"

"Yeah, don't fuck any of my servants. Especially the one that will climb on your dick from a chair. She's demented."

Bailey laughed, "Deal. Thanks. You're okay, faggot."

"One last thing...can you stop calling me that?" Mallory lowered his head

"It will be hard, but I will try." Bailey continued eating his food until his best friend showed up. "Que! How are you doing, frat?" Mallory's head shot up.

"Hey, BT. What's up?"

"Mallory, this is my line brother, Quincy Anderson."

"Hey, Mallory?" Quincy stood there smiling. He was a delicious chocolate chunk with a perfectly edged crew cut. His average smile was upgraded by his round-shaped glasses. His well manicure mustache and goatee framed his oval-shaped face. He had dark brown eyes that melted Mallory's headache away.

"Cheers, Quincy." Mallory said with a smile.

"How is Donna?" Bailey asked.

Quincy was so mesmerized by Mallory that he didn't answer right away. The awkward silence caught his attention and he quickly answered, "She's fine. She's getting fitted for her wedding dress."

"Another one bites the dust," Bailey laughed.

"So to speak," Mallory whispered.

"How are you feeling today?" Quincy asked Mallory as he safely sat by Bailey.

"I have real wicked hangover."

"Oh, just a hangover...no regrets?"

"I think I'll survey my regrets after I tend with this hangover."

"That was your boyfriend last night?"

"Yeah...he has a bad temper. I'm sorry if he frightened you."

"I was reeling so last night. I couldn't understand what he was shouting."

"What are you two talking about?" Bailey asked.

"Pool!" They said at the same time and then laughed.

"Well, Mallory is a pool shark," Bailey said.

"I know. I enjoyed him...playing with him last night. Maybe we can play again."

"Don't you think you need to teach your fiancée how to play pool?"

"I don't think she can handle the grip of the stick."

"Well, it does take skill to grip the stick." Bailey said, oblivious to the hidden conversation. They both frowned at Bailey.

A sharp pain shot across Mallory's face. "Oh Bloody Fuck! My head is exploding." Mallory bowed his head and squeezed his temples. He peeked up when he heard Quincy laughing.

"Famous last words," Quincy smiled broadly, exposing his sensual gap between his two front teeth. "Well, I got to go. I'm meeting Donna for lunch to pick colors for the reception. Stay single, Bailey." He shook his hand. "Stay in touch, Mallory." He patted him on the back. Mallory watched him closely as he walked out of the restaurant. He stopped short of the door, turned back and winked.

Although his face ached, Mallory flash a seductive smile. "So that's your frat?"

"Yeah, that's my boy. We were roommates and line brothers in college. We did everything together. I would cut for him. He's my best friend."

"Why do you hate gay people?"

"It's not natural."

"Have you ever had anal sex with a woman?"

"Hell yeah, all the time."

"That ain't natural. Neither is oral. I have a question, if your best friend was gay what would you do?"

"He ain't gay. He would never, in a million years, fuck a man."

"Hypothetically. What would you do?"

"That's my boy. I don't know what I would do. I guess I would be heartbroken."

"People get over heartbreaks. You were heartbroken when you found out that I was gay."

"That's because you didn't tell me. I had to find out the hard way. Shit, I was defending you against the family and I looked like a got damn fool."

"I'm sorry, but it's not like you made it easy for me. With all the name calling, what was I supposed to do?"

"You could have told me."

"Bailey," Mallory grabbed his hand and said in the most sincere tone, "I'm gay."

"No shit! Look, I'm trying to accept you." Bailey snatched his hand back so hard that it hit his chest. "It's hard, but I'm trying."

"Well, that is all I can ask for. You might be the only one who has my back here."

"Well, I will always have your back, but you need to watch your front with Silas."

CHAPTER SIX

Mallory made it a quiet evening at home. With Silas away on one of his three-day conferences, he enjoyed his time alone. He warmed up a big bowl of Silas' famous chili and grabbed a package of crackers and his bottle of TUMS. Since he had been with Silas, his diet had gone to the dogs. Before Silas, he couldn't remember the last time he ate junk food or even the last time he ate late at night. But now, it was an everyday occurrence. He knew that one day he would need to either get back to his dietary regimen or increase his exercise regimen to lose the extra ten pounds he gained since he and Silas became a couple. But there was something about comfort food - it was so irresistible.

As he flopped down on the buttery soft sofa, Mallory turned on the big screen television and set the source to the Abaddon channel to watch the raw footage of his Chroniclesations. This was one of the perks of dating Satan and there were many perks, including getting prohibited access to people's lives. Mallory wasn't concerned about snooping on others; he wanted to fill in the blanks about himself. The best thing about watching raw footage was just that - it was raw footage. There were no subjective thoughts that could sway an event, no misconstrued messages or one-sided stories. It was just raw footage... The Master Tape.

Against his better judgment, Silas gave Mallory all access to the channel. Mallory could be so convincing that Silas couldn't refuse him. After giving him access, he warned Mallory about extended viewing. Mallory shrugged him off when Silas advised him that he would waste his current life looking at the past and unresolved hurts could materialize into spirits if he didn't resolve the issues. Mallory lied and said that all of his issues were resolved. Silas knew it was a lie, but he gave him access anyway. Mallory could be so convincing.

As Mallory settled in, there was a knock on the door. He fought with himself about answering it, but the knocks got louder. Against his better judgment, he answered the door. It was Marc, who appeared to be a little tipsy and very disturbed.

"He's not here!" Mallory said and attempted to shut the door.

Marc shoved the door open, "I just need a beer."

"Well, take the elevator down to the ground floor, walk through the double glass doors and go to the bar across the street. I know they have beer there."

"There is also a beer in your fridge." Marc pushed Mallory aside and stumbled into the penthouse.

"Well, come on in." Mallory huffed sarcastically. He slammed the door and watched Marc stumble across the room, barely avoiding statues and end tables. He flopped down on the recliner and plopped his feet up on the coffee table. Mallory hated that. But Silas did it too, so he didn't say anything to stop Marc. Mallory returned to the sofa and picked up his bowl of chili.

"What are you eating?"

"One of Silas' masterpieces."

"Gumbo or chili?"

"Why don't you go into the kitchen and check?"

"Why don't you serve me? I'm a guest in your house."

Mallory laughed hysterically, folding his legs underneath him and settling down again. Marc sat there and watched him. After a while, he gave the fight up. Mallory was serious about not serving him.

Marc took a breath and willed himself up. He walked to the kitchen and fixed his bowl. He grabbed a beer from the fridge and sat at the island table in the kitchen. "What are you watching?"

Mallory didn't answer.

Marc grabbed his meal and sat very close to Mallory, which annoyed the Hell out him. "What are you watching?"

"I'm watching Daddy. Some of the times we spent together."

"From your Chroniclesations? These look different."

"This is a master tape. Unbiased and unedited."

"Silas gave you access? Why would he do that?"

"It's called a helicopter." Mallory answered. Knowing that it would gross Marc out, he continued. "He lays spread eagle on the bed. While in the swing, I sit in his lap, squeeze tight and twirl in circles until he can't stand it anymore." Mallory continued his hysterical laugh as he watched Marc grimace. "You asked."

Marc shook his head, trying to shake the image out his head, "You can watch anything?"

Mallory nodded his head yes.

"Cool...I wanna watch me and Mom."

"I suggest that you need to learn how to perform the helicopter."

"Mallory?"

"Ask properly, bitch!"

"Can I watch me and Mom?"

"I don't know what you can do." Mallory laughed again.

"See, that's why I can't stand your bitch ass."

"At this point, I don't give a damn. You're sitting here with me, you're watching Dad."

"When did he become Dad to you?"

"He's always been Dad. Do you know we used to live in Sweden and France?" Mallory inhaled a big spoon of chili. "And did you know that Dad had a jazz band and wrote songs? Many of them were top ten hits."

"No?"

"Did you know that Dad –"

"Started molesting you at four?" Marc interjected rudely.

"He was sick. He suffered from Sadistic Personality Disorder." Mallory inhaled another spoon of chili, trying not to let Marc's comments faze him. "Did you know that Dad spoke nineteen languages?"

"Did you know that you perfected your blow job at five?"

"He was very sick at the time and no one helped him." Mallory took a deep breath, "Did you know that Malcolm...I mean, Dad taught himself how to play thirteen instruments and taught me too?"

"Did you know that Dad taped you two fucking? He used to get off on it." Marc turned up the verbal abuse.

Mallory couldn't take it anymore. "I saw it. He used to so say, 'Damn! You're so much better than your sorry ass brother, Marc.' " He took a deep breath, "From what I saw you have a good gag reflex. Dad hated when I threw up on him. Pissed him off." He paused, "For someone who suffered the same fate as I, I would think that we'd be a lot closer and would support each other rather than be at odds."

"You would think that...and you would be so wrong. I'm not a faggot. I don't condone what Dad did! Neither did Mom!"

"Yeah, but your damn momma didn't do anything about it. She was so self-absorbed in her love affair with Uncle Mal that she didn't stop him."

"Yes, she did!" Marc shouted.

"Stop viewing. Switch to Marc's file. Childhood. Scan for Mother and assault."

The viewing started with Felicia cradling Marc, who had been crying all night. They went to Uncle Mal's house. She kneeled down, whispered something in Marc's ear, and then kissed his cheek. The door opened and Uncle Mal wrapped his arms around her and kissed her.

"Scandalous bitch," Mallory mumbled.

"She's not scandalous. Momma was sweet and supportive and protective." Marc tagged Mallory on the arm.

"I'll show you what she protected you from."

The viewing showed Felicia placing Marc on the bed and closing the door. She proceeded to get undressed and straddled Uncle Mal on the couch outside of the bedroom.

"Stop. Answer this question; did Felicia mention the abuse to Uncle Mal at any time?"

"NO!" A computer voice from the television answered back.

"Answer this question, who stopped the abuse?"

"Malcolm."

"Show."

Marc was sitting in the room crying. Malcolm was pacing back and forth in the room, appearing to be talking to himself. He finally kneeled down at Marc, grabbing both of his arms and Malcolm starting talking to him.

"What is he saying?" Marc asked.

"Audio."

"Daddy is SO sorry. Daddy is so sick. Daddy never meant to hurt you. Daddy will never hurt you again. Daddy's promises! NEVER!"

"Stop audio. Answer this question...after this day, was Marc ever touched or abused by Malcolm?"

"NO!"

"Thank you. Go back to Felicia and Uncle Mal fucking!" Mallory commanded, then he huffed, "Two poorly executed blowjobs and that was it!" Mallory sucked his teeth. "And you think it was your scandalous-ass mom who stopped it?"

"I told everyone that you probably enjoyed it when Dad fucked you. You two always had something special. Special language you two spoke in, special jokes you two used to tell, special way you two used to look at each other."

"If I were you, I would be jealous of me, too. Because at one point, that used to be you and Dad. But you couldn't handle the responsibility... the daunting task of satisfying Dad. Even after I left, you tried to take my place. Still couldn't handle it. Even tried to build a wedge between Dad and Marek, instead of protecting Marek from Dad's abuse. You offered up your own brother...and if he wasn't as strong-willed, he would have been abused too. Good thing for Marlon, he played handicap. Damn! What kinda brother were you?"

Marc got up and walked to the door.

"I guess the punch line is...no matter what you do, how you do it, or where you do it...I am still your baby brother. You are still my leader and I will follow you. You will have my allegiance. I love you always, Marc."

And with that, Marc stormed out of the penthouse, slamming the door behind him so hard that he caused two pictures to fall off the wall and shatter.

Mallory laughed, "Silas was right. Who says being nice isn't hurtful? Stupid bitch!" He went to the kitchen to get a broom and dustpan then walked over to the broken pictures. Mallory started picking up glass. As he picked up each piece, Marc's words started soaking in. Mallory tried his hardest not to relive the verbal attacks because he hadn't resolved that part of his life yet. The reason why he watched the master tape was to find a reason in his heart to forgive his Dad. But the words started to echo louder and soak into his conscience.

Mallory picked up the last large piece of glass when he saw Malcolm's reflection in it. He dropped the glass, took a deep breath and swept up the remaining pieces of glass. As he walked back to the kitchen, he saw his father on television, sitting on a high wingback chair. He quickly grabbed the remote, pressed the power button, but the television didn't shut off.

"Hello son," Malcolm said.

Mallory stood paralyzed.

"Are you okay? You're looking a little sick."

"You're dead! You're dead!"

"Not in your mind. Son, we are one. You will never be rid of me. You love me...we had such a special relationship."

"You're dead. I killed you."

"No, you merely rid me from my frail body. But you know, we can be one. I can be with you forever."

"NO! NO! NO! I killed you!"

"Son," Malcolm stood up and walked out of the television screen. "Don't fight it. I have been waiting patiently for you to receive me. Can we be one now? I can be with you forever." Malcolm grabbed Mallory's head with both hands. "We are one now." Malcolm dematerialized and Mallory was forced to inhale him. Mallory fell to the floor, seizing and fighting himself. After a while, he stopped. He finally stood up, cracking his neck. He walked to a mirror and instead of seeing a reflection of himself; he saw the reflection of Malcolm.

CHAPTER SEVEN

"Silas, do you have to leave tonight?"

"I'm not going to be away that long. Just a few days..."

"I know, Silas, but don't leave me, baby. This is a bad time for me."

"Mallory, chill. I'll be back. Why are you tripping about this?"

"I'm not, baby, it's just I have been having these bad dreams for months and they are getting worse. I can't sleep when you are not here."

"What do you think? Should I take my black Speedo styles or my silver competition Speedo styles? Shit, I'll pack them both. Baby, I'm just a phone call away. I'll talk you through it."

"Silas, I feel like my dad is in my head, haunting me. I can't stop the voices from screaming in my head."

"So, you're up to three valiums now? Take another one about two hours from now." He stopped and grabbed Mallory by the shoulders and fussed, "And when you take the shit, don't take them all at the same time like you did that last time. I had to redo the fucking shower after you fell through the glass door. Take a shower before you take them. And when you take them, go straight to bed and wait for them to work. Don't forget that you took them and go jogging and shit. Don't try to cook after you take them. Don't drive after you take them. Am I forgetting anything?"

"Don't fuck after I take them?"

"You bet' not fuck anybody while I'm gone...oh yeah and no more new tattoos." He twirled Mallory around and patted him on the butt. "Now will you be a dear and get my leather pants and ripped jeans?"

"Leather pants? In Miami? This time of year?"

"Too much? Too hot, you're right. Okay, get my mesh pants."

"Mesh? What kind of conference is this?"

"What? Get my shit and stop asking me so many fucking questions," he mumbled while he methodically packed his bag. "You'll be fine. I know this is the anniversary of your father's death, but you got through the death and the funeral. This will be a piece a cake. How many sheer shirts should I pack?"

"What's the name of this conference?"

"Umm...the...B-M-D-L Annual Conference in Miami," he stuttered out. "I'm scouting for new talent."

"Can I go?"

"No! It's a men's conference."

"I'm not a man?"

"Yes, you're all man, baby." He looked deeply into his eyes to maintain his sincerity. "I'm recruiting for new hires of the empire."

"Don't we have a department for that?"

"I like to recruit personally. Stop with the questions." He walked away and started pacing back and forth, reviewing his mental packing list. "I need my black leather belt and steel chunk belt. I guess I need to pack a box of my favorite condoms." He quickly flashed a smile toward Mallory. "Did I say that out loud?"

Mallory nodded.

"Marketing thought that it would be cute to pass out condoms...you know, Satan believes in safe sex."

"What kind of conference is this?"

"I told you. Look, if you can't sleep, spend some time with Bailey or with that insane niece you have or the foursome horsemen nephew clan. You'll be fine."

"What type of conference are you attending where you don't need a suit?"

"Thank you. I knew I forgot something!" Silas rushed into his closet and pulled out two suits. "What do you think the red suit with the black shirt and tie or the purple suit with the gold shirt and tie?"

"What wrong with a black suit with a white shirt and nice tie?"

"That's too...you. I got to be me. But you have a point; can I wear your poet shirt? I can wear that with my leather pants and a vest."

"So, what are you wearing with these mesh pants?" He held the pants in midair.

"Nothing!" He winked and snatched the pants.

"What's the name of this conference, Silas?"

"Done. I think I got everything." He wrestled the suitcase to close it. "So I'll call you when I get there. And Tuesday we'll talk all night, okay?" Silas pushed Mallory onto the bed and crawled on him, forcing him to lie back while planting a hard and wet kiss on him. "I love you, baby. I'll be back in two weeks."

"You said three days."

"I never said three days. Besides, it's a ten-day conference. I'll be back. If you need me, call me. I love you..." Silas fiercely grinded his pelvis on Mallory. "...so much. Daddy will be back to fuck the shit out of you, okay?" He jumped off the bed, grabbed his suitcases and rushed out of the door. "Call Bailey!"

Mallory lay lifeless in the bed. Once he heard the door slam, Malcolm's voice started shouting in his head. The voices grew louder and more painful. Mallory started feeling dizzy and confused. He tried to sit up, but he fell back. He crawled out of the bed and down the stairs.

He made it to the bar where Silas so lovingly left a note stating,

> You have only two bottles of Vodka in the house. Make this last for two weeks. Don't go buying any more. I have called all the liquor stores and distributors that carry your favorite brand. They will not sell to you. Don't try it and don't command anybody's soul because they won't sell to you either. Make the two bottles last. There are roughly seven glasses to a 1.75L bottle of Vodka. The two bottles should do. See how much I love you? I did the math.
>
> Bye lover.

Mallory grabbed the bottle and crawled on his knees to the couch. He swallowed five pills and washed them down with the entire bottle of Vodka. Tears fell from his closed eyes as he slowly waited for the voices to subside. He eventually passed out.

He woke up when the phone started ringing. He jumped up to answer it, but he fell back when sharp pains exploded in his head. He eventually crawled off the couch to the bar. He pulled the phone down to answer it.

"Silas?"

"No! It's Bailey. What are you doing? You missed a board meeting!"

Mallory held the phone away from his ear because Bailey was shouting so loudly. "I'm sorry," he whispered.

"I made some excuse for you. I had your typed agenda, so I conducted the meeting. Damn, you are so anal."

"Thank you."

"You okay?"

"No, I can't stop the voice." He said with a whimper.

"What?"

"Nothing."

"When did Silas leave?"

"Last night."

"Some guys are coming over to watch Monday night football. Why don't you come over tonight?"

"Okay..." Mallory faintly answered.

"Are you sure you're okay?"

"No." Mallory collapsed on the floor. Several hours later, he woke up to Tanic licking his face. He wanted to spring up to stop her from licking him, but he remembered the last time his head felt like it was exploding. He slowly sat up and grabbed the dog. "Why didn't he take you? He always takes you. You're not my guardian." He finally got up and opened the patio door to let the dog out. He walked upstairs and convinced himself that he needed a shower.

Afterwards, Mallory sat on the bed with his head between his knees. He mustered the strength to get up and walked into Silas' closet. He grabbed Silas' favorite pair of ripped jeans from the shelf. He snuck the jeans out of Silas' suitcase when he was rambling. Mallory believed that Silas was going to a conference, but he wasn't sure about the after-hour activities. He remembered Silas bragging that they were his 'Come Fuck Me Now' jeans and Mallory believed him. Hence, that was why they didn't make it to Miami. He slipped the jeans on then grabbed one of his Henley's. He slipped on Silas' mules, walked downstairs, gathered Tanic and her things, and left the penthouse.

Once he got to his old house, the voices grew louder again. The last thing he wanted was to have a psychotic episode in front of Bailey. He started the car and put in reverse, but Tanic jumped out of the car. He turned it off and got out. The dog was sitting at the front door, waiting for Mallory. When he got to the door, Bailey opened it.

"Hey!" Bailey said, slapping him hard on the back. Mallory flashed a fake smile. "You look like shit."

Mallory rolled his eyes.

"I mean, in regular guy terms, you look normal. But you ain't a regular guy. What's wrong?"

"Nothing, look, I don't know why I am here. I don't watch sports."

"Fine, come in anyway. You might like the cheerleaders." Bailey laughed. Mallory sat down in the back of the media room and tried to be invisible. A group of guys rushed in toward him as they tried to get a better view of the television.

"Hey guys, this is my cousin, Mallory." Bailey introduced him to the group.

"What's up?" The group answered.

"Want something to drink?" Bailey asked.

"Vodka is fine," Mallory replied.

"You brought Vodka? Shit, I can make some screwdrivers," one of the guys answered.

"No..." Mallory replied.

"What did you bring? No freeloaders, Bailey!" Howard, Bailey's useless friend, shouted.

"Chill out, man," Bailey shouted back.

"There's no Vodka over there?" He pointed to the bar cabinet.

"Nawh, we drank that last Monday." Bailey answered. "Tonight was supposed to be BYOB."

"BYOF, too. Are we ordering pizza?" Mallory looked up when he heard that familiar voice. It was Quincy. He perked up a bit.

"So, we have no liquor in the house?" Mallory stood up and smiled. Quincy smiled back. "Did you check the cellar?"

"What cellar?" Bailey asked.

"Let's take a tour." Mallory led the pack of men toward the back of the house. They walked down a staircase into a dark, long walk-in closet. Mallory opened the door and the light illuminated a miniature liquor store.

"Bailey! You have been holding out on us."

"I know I told you about this room." Mallory held the door open for the men, waiting for Quincy to pass through the door. "If you wish it, it's here. On your left are your dark liquors - such as your bourbon, brandy, whiskey and tequila. On your right are your light liquors - such as rum, Vodka and gin. The ready to drink Vodka is in the freezer down past the last shelf. Down this hall are your white wines and champagne. On the other side are your reds and merlot." Quincy finally made it through the door. He stopped and they exchanged lustful gazes.

"It's a pleasure seeing you here," Quincy grinned.

"The pleasure is all mine," Mallory answered, biting his lower lip.

"Why don't you go first?" Quincy asked, gesturing toward the entrance to the cellar. Mallory took several small steps directly in front of Quincy. He wanted to feel the heat of his warmth. He started blushing when he heard Quincy whisper, "You look delicious in those jeans." He smiled, but dared not to look back to catch the glimpse in his eyes. Mallory stopped short when he felt the burn of Quincy's breath and his huge bulge rubbing Mallory's upper leg.

"Where is your Hennessy?" Howard asked.

"Huh?" Mallory jerked and stepped forward quickly. "Oh, on the...um...on your left - on the middle shelf." He turned back and whispered, "You need to behave."

"How long should I behave?"

"Until the boys are gone."

"Let's leave them here. I really don't need to be in this room. I can't stand the vice."

"Everybody has a vice."

"Mine is Blue Bell Ice Cream."

"Hum...Bailey, can you pull out a case of Vodka for me to take home?" Mallory called out.

"I got you!"

While Quincy led him out of the cellar, Mallory stopped and shouted down in Bailey's direction, "Look in the kitchen freezer. There is always a roast or ham or something cooked."

"I take it you used to live here." Quincy grabbed his hand and led him up the stairway.

"Good deductive reasoning. How did you figure that out?"

"Well, you know where the hot spots are in the house and you still get mail here. You have a stack on the bar."

"You're so smart and nosey."

"And you're so beautiful." Quincy instinctively kissed him. Mallory grabbed his waist, bringing him in to his body as they leaned on the wall for balance. Quincy was strong, but not forceful. Although he initiated the kiss, he allowed Mallory to take control. Mallory slipped his hands underneath Quincy's shirt, caressing his muscular back. He felt himself sliding down against the wall, unbuttoning Quincy's pants. Quincy braced himself as Mallory fully accepted his dick. His breath grew labored with each suction Mallory delivered. They both heard the rumblings of the men downstairs, but Mallory didn't stop.

As Quincy released, Mallory took in every drop without hesitation. By the time, the guys made it back upstairs, Quincy gathered his strength and he assisted Mallory up from the floor. Bailey was the first to walk up the stairs. Mallory walked away to avoid eye contact with him. Quincy leaned against the wall and appeared to be waiting for the guys.

"What are you doing up here by yourself?" Bailey asked.

"I know I can't be around alcohol."

"I'm sorry, frat. I forgot just that quick. You're going to be okay?"

"Yeah, I think Mallory said that he was going to get me some ice cream." Quincy said, trying to fight back his smile.

"Okay. Let me know if you need anything."

They all returned to the theater room and settled down in front of the television. Quincy looked around for Mallory, but couldn't find him. He walked downstairs to find him rummaging around in the kitchen. As he walked behind him to touch his shoulder, Mallory turned around and jumped.

"Shit! You don't walk up on Death like that!"

"What?"

"Nothing. You're not watching the game?"

"I like this game better." He pushed him against the refrigerator.

"Quincy, the guys are upstairs. You're not worried about them catching us?"

"I'm a grown man. What do I have to worry about?" Quincy answered between kisses.

"Bailey, maybe?"

"You got a point." Quincy kissed him again.

"I take it you don't care about the point."

"So, is it my turn to slide down the wall or do you want to slip into something a little more obvious? I'm wishing for the obvious."

"I don't think I should be doing this." Mallory gently pushed him away. "I'm in a committed relationship with Silas. He won't understand."

"A committed relationship with a ho?" Quincy laughed, but Mallory didn't find any humor in the comment. "Okay, look, no one has to know until you're ready to have a committed relationship with a real man. Until then, I'll just be your secret supplement." Quincy bit Mallory's shoulder through his shirt. "Now, I asked a question. Is it my turn?"

"Do you like showers?"

Bailey and the guys were getting into the game when Mallory's cell phone rang. Bailey hesitated, but he eventually answered the phone. "Towneson cell phone."

"Clearly you're not Towneson." Silas commented.

"I'm your worst nightmare, bitch. What do you want?"

"Where's Mallory?"

"Not by his cell phone. He went to go get some food for the gang."

"Don't use my baby as an errand boy."

"What?" Bailey shouted. "The phone is breaking...up... I can't...hear you. I'm...hanging up now." Bailey shouted louder.

"Don't you hang up on me, bitch! You ain't on AT&T! This is an Abaddon signal, so I know you hear me clearly. So he's with you, good. Can you watch him for me? He's babbling about having nightmares and I was too busy trying to leave. I wasn't listening."

"What? So now I'm his babysitter?"

"No bitch - his family. He was trying to tell me that the anniversary of his father's death is tomorrow. Just keep an eye on him."

"Anything else?"

"Tell him I called and I love him."

"Where you at?"

"Miami...What! Hold on, Bailey." He heard Silas pull the phone away. "Don't let that motherfucker in! That's a fucking queen and his dick is too small." Bailey heard the entire conversation. Silas returned to the phone. "What did you ask me? Oh, yeah. I'm in Miami."

"You went to that Gay Republic Convention?"

"That one is next week. I'll be here for it. This is the Down Low Annual Celebration. I'm at a Back Door party." Silas heard Bailey choke on the other end. "You asked, bitch. Anyway, Mallory doesn't need to know that. I told him what he needed to know. No fill-ins. What! Hold on..." Silas failed to cover the phone again. "Oh Hell yeah, put that motherfucker in my room. I don't know if I should fuck him first or last. Oh and bring that queen back, we are SANTA FE'ing his ass tonight!" Silas howled. He returned to the phone. "Bailey, I gotta go. A man should not be packing all that dick. I think he's bigger than me. It can't be real. Oh damn. I gotta get off this phone."

"Fine faggot, bye!" Bailey hung up and threw the phone on the table.

"Who was that?"

"Mallory's faggot ass boyfriend. What did I miss?"

"He went out of bounds on the twenty. What do you mean Mallory's faggot boyfriend. Your cousin's squirrelly." Howard asked.

"No, my cousin is not a squirrel. He is..." Bailey took a deep breath. "...a homosexual."

"He's a faggot?"

"Please, let's not call him that, especially when he's around. He's prefers gay. Actually, he prefers no one knowing unless he's attracted to you."

"Shiiiit, he was looking at me when we were down in that cellar!" Howard shouted.

"No, he wasn't. He would never be attracted to you, Howard. You don't have a real job." They all laughed.

"You know that's how they are. They have all that money, fancy cars, big houses, stylish clothes and important titles. What does your cousin do?"

"Watch it, motherfucker. I have all those things and I'm not a faggot!" Bailey snarled. "And to answer your question, he's the VP over at Luxapher Technologies."

"Shit, what does his boyfriend do?"

"Who, Silas? Not a got damn thing. He's supposed to be the president, but he lets Mallory run it while he goes off fucking everything, everywhere."

"Your cousin is dating Silas Luxapher? Gay people stick together. That's what black people need to learn, how to stick together. See, Mallory got the hookup."

"Mallory was already hooked up before he got with Silas. He had his own financial company before he started working at Haulm Industries."

"Yeah, look at him now. I bet being with Silas, he got a lot more shit."

"The only thing he got from Silas was a fucking plane. Mallory has his own shit. This is his house; he just let me stay in it because he moved in with the faggot. Shit, Mallory has vineyards, real estate, cars and whatever the fuck he wants. Just think about it - he has it."

"What kind of plane?"

"One of those big planes..."

"Like a Southwest Airlines plane?" Howard asked.

"No, like a Royal Air double-deck plane. It's a pain to use because he has to catch it from Houston. He can't land the plane in Austin. Enough about Mallory, I'm missing the game."

"So he has to drive to Houston to catch his plane?" Howard asked.

"Fuck all what he had, why can't he be with a woman?" The other guy said.

"No, dipshit, he takes his jet to Houston. And he has been with women - beautiful women. You know Brie, my brother's wife?" Bailey made a goofy grin and nodded.

"She's a goddess. I always wondered how your brother got her," Howard ogled into space and shook his head.

"Right place at the right time. You know that sexy dip at Molina's. That supermodel, Elysse, with the clothing line? You know the fine-ass Texas Supreme Court Justice. That's his lawyer. He doesn't have her on retainer. He is the retainer. You know that beautiful pianist over in England. The one you were gawking at so hard that you bought her CD and you don't even listen to classical music. That's his wife. Now, she got his ass on retainer."

"He's married?"

Bailey nodded. "So is Silas and he has alotta kids. Can we stop talking about him? We have missed two touchdowns."

"So where's your boy Que at?" Howard asked.

"What?" Bailey sat back in his chair fuming, thinking about all the fine asses Mallory gave up to be with another man.

By the end of the fourth quarter, Quincy and Mallory appeared with bags in their hands. "Hey, what's the score?" Quincy asked.

"Eight heteros to two homos?" Howard said under his breath. The guys laughed, except for Bailey who shot up and hiked Quincy up against the wall.

"Where have you been?" Bailey screamed out.

"We went to get ice cream."

"It took that long?"

"We were talking."

"Bailey, stop." Mallory pushed him off Quincy.

"You need back up, brah?" Howard jumped up.

"Why does he need back up?" Mallory looked at the guys. Although they appeared to be angry, fear flashed in their eyes. "You told them. You invited me over here to alienate me."

"Mallory, it's not like that. Silas called and things went from there."

"Fine, I'll leave." Mallory announced.

"Yeah, leave. We don't need any fudge packers in this house!" Howard yelled out and Quincy went off.

"You're some stupid, ungrateful homophobes. You're watching this man's TV, eating and drinking his shit and then you have the audacity - that's nerve, Howard - to call him a faggot because you all are not comfortable with your own sexuality. How dare you? And you should be ashamed, Bailey, for allowing your mooching, asshole friends to insult your family. I hope you don't have my back like that."

"Quincy, you need to see how this looks," Bailey backed down.

"To me, it looks like you have new friends that are from the primate species. You know that I'm a recovering alcoholic and Mallory was just kind enough to take me away from the enticing element. Oh, what, are you scared of alcoholics too? You want to beat the fuck out of me and call me names?"

"Thanks, Quincy. There's no need. I'm used to this type of treatment from my family. You don't have to go through all of this," Mallory said quietly.

"Mallory...I'm sorry. I didn't mean to out you. This is hard for me and you know that. We talked about this." Bailey stepped back. "Guys, apologize to Mallory, please?"

"Fuck that! I ain't apologizing to no faggot!" Howard shouted.

"Obviously, when you told them I was gay, you failed to mention that I was Death, huh?" Mallory whispered to Bailey before walking toward the door. He stopped and turned toward Howard. "Your cholesterol level is 373 and you have 75% blockage in your arteries? I'll see you soon." He winked at Howard then walked out of the room.

"I'm going to walk him out. I can't stand the stench in here." Quincy followed behind him. "Hey Mallory, hold up." Quincy caught up to Mallory in the foyer.

"You don't have to walk me out. I don't need protection."

"I wasn't thinking protection. I was hoping for a good night kiss."

"Granted."

Mallory leaned against the banister and grabbed the nape of his neck, kissing him softly. Quincy maneuvered down one-step and positioned himself to control the kiss. He grabbed Mallory's arms and wrapped them around his waist. Mallory felt his warm hands slide in through the rips of his jeans and grab his back of his thigh, squeezing it tightly. He moved his arms up around Quincy's neck and enclosed himself in his rapture. The sound of men rambling above their heads stopped their kiss, but not their embrace. Quincy rested his head on Mallory's shoulder and nibbled his ear.

Mallory whispered, "That was a goodnight kiss? What does a good morning kiss feel like?"

"Well, I guess you have to be there in the morning," he smiled. The rumbling and loud voices grew from above. "Shit! I hate people like that with their small minds and stereotypes."

"Some of the stereotypes are true."

"I guess, but you're not a stereotype, you're a myth."

"A myth?"

"The myth of the perfect man."

Mallory gave him a quick peck on his lips and released him. He smiled and walked through the doorway. Bailey stormed down the stairs and interrupted his daydreaming. "Shit! Did he leave already? Did he seem mad?"

"No. He's fine." Quincy leaned back on the banister and reminisced over their stolen romantic evening. "Real fine."

"I'm supposed to keep an eye on him. His father died a couple of years ago and he is still hung up on it. Shit, I was supposed to watch him."

"He's a big boy. He'll be okay. I don't think he'll be back here if your loving friends are still around. It's not a comfortable environment."

"I know, I'm sorry."

"Don't apologize to me. You know I can't go back up there, right?"

"Booze and faggot-haters, I know, not your cup of tea. Maybe you and I can just hang out. Let's play some b-ball tomorrow."

"That, I'd like. I'm going home - I missed the game. Glad I Ti-Voed it."

CHAPTER EIGHT

"So you think you're better than me?" The phantom voice shouted out. Mallory tossed back and forth in his bed. A ghost appeared, standing on Mallory's bed.

"You killed me, you son of a bitch." The ghost pulled out a knife and started slashing Mallory's face and chest. Three knives stabbed Mallory's calves. He sat up, saw he was bleeding and tried to pull the knife out of his leg, but it was too painful. He removed the knife and blood started gushing everywhere. Mallory fell out of the bed and crawled toward the door. A man appeared and kneeled down, pulling his head back. "Where are you going, you little bastard?" The man was Malcolm. He pulled out another knife and stabbed him in the back.

Mallory screamed as he continued to crawl out of the bedroom. He opened the door, inched his way to the stairs and called out for Tanic. He looked around, but couldn't find her. He heard heavy footsteps coming closer, looked up and saw the Malcolm coming toward him with several knives. He tried to move, but couldn't feel his legs. He kept scooting back, fighting Malcolm off. He scooted back too far and fell down the stairway. As he landed at the bottom, he continued to hear the footsteps. He sat up and watched Malcolm walk down the steps with a dead, bloody dog in his hands. As he made it to the final step, he threw the dog at Mallory who lifted his arms to cover his face.

The room grew dark and quiet. Mallory couldn't see anything. The only thing that he heard was the sound of his own breathing. The door opened and an unbearable, bright light glared into the room. Mallory saw the silhouette of a man walking toward him. He tried crawling away, but the silhouette grew bigger as it came closer. His heart raced and he couldn't catch his breath. The silhouette kneeled down to grab Mallory's arms. He closed his eyes and began fighting again. The silhouette straddled him and held him down. Mallory screamed louder and continued squirming and fighting. He heard the silhouette calling his name. He bit the silhouette with so hard that it released him. He scurried away, but he didn't get far. The silhouette stopped him and turned him over. In mid-swing, he saw that the silhouette was Quincy. Quincy barely blocked the swing and grabbed his arms again.

"Calm down, baby. It's me. Are you okay?"

Mallory couldn't hear him. Sounds of ringing and shouting bombarded his head. Quincy helped him to his feet. Mallory looked down and noticed that he wasn't stabbed or bleeding. He looked around to see if he could find the dog. When he turned around, Malcolm appeared again. Mallory tried get away, knocking himself and Quincy down. Quincy fell backwards onto the coffee room table, pulverizing it and he lost consciousness. Mallory crawled on all fours to get away. With every movement, he felt that he was being stabbed. He crawled to a corner of the room and covered his head with his arms. He began rocking back and forth while the footsteps grew louder and stronger. The man stopped short, just in front of Mallory and kneeled down. It was Quincy again. Instead of physically handling Mallory, he decided to sit down next to him. Mallory uncovered his head and realized that is was Quincy sitting there alongside of him.

After an hour, Quincy convinced Mallory that it was okay to stand up. Mallory kept babbling about wanting to get out of the house, so Quincy attempted to guide him to the door. Mallory started shouting that he couldn't leave the house because he didn't have shoes. Quincy removed his shoes and placed them on Mallory's feet. They managed to get to the front door when Mallory stopped. He could not cross the threshold. Quincy pleaded and begged him to keep walking, but Mallory wouldn't move. Eventually, Mallory fell to his knees and cried. Quincy sat down next to him. He opened his arms and Mallory gratefully crawled within the safety of his arms. Quincy rocked and held him at the threshold of the door for the remainder of the night.

The sound of the elevator bell woke Mallory. He and Quincy slept at the front door. He went to move, but Quincy clenched him tighter.

"Don't hit me!" Quincy shouted out, holding Mallory's arms.

"I'm not going to hit you. What are you doing here?"

"You're talking normal now. How do you feel?"

"Strange. Why are you here?"

"Do you still want to get out of the house?"

"What? Quincy, what's going on?"

"Do you remember any of last night?" He released Mallory so that he could sit up. "Your head is bleeding. Let me get some towels." Quincy stood up and began to walk into the house. Mallory attempted to follow him, but he turned and shouted, "STOP! Don't go back in the house. You sit there...I'll find the towels."

Before Mallory knew it, he sat back down like an obedient dog. He was in a state of confusion. The light from the open door beamed through, hitting Mallory's leg. Mallory withdrew his leg quickly. Later, Quincy returned with some towels and a glass of water.

"I can't drink that. I need bottled water."

"What?" Quincy gently dabbed Mallory's head wound, cleaning the blood.

"I can't drink this water. It's has to be bottled water."

"Okay, it's not water, it's Vodka."

"Vodka?"

Quincy nodded.

Mallory took a huge gulp and barely kept it down. "This is not Vodka! This is refrigerated water."

"See, you drank it. You said that you couldn't. I'm going to grab some of your things and take you out of this house."

"Why are you here?"

"Once you left the house, the cravings started to hit me last night. So I was going to get a drink at the bar across the street. I came by to see if you wanted to join me and maybe even talk me out of it. When I got to the door, I heard you screaming. I knocked, but no one answered and you were still screaming. The door was open, so I came in. I saw you and you started to beat the shit of out me - calling me Malcolm. You knocked every craving I had for a drink out of my system. What were you tripping off last night?"

"Tripping?"

"Drugs, what drugs were you doing?"

"I don't do drugs."

"Come on, Mallory. That's how we met."

"I don't do drugs."

"Ss...ohhh...you're still in denial. Haven't hit that wall yet? You don't think you have a problem."

"Yes, I have a problem. I'm being haunted."

"That is called an addiction."

"Quincy, listen to me. I don't do drugs. Okay? I'm not a drug addict. Okay? See..." He lifted his arms. "No needle marks. I have my sinuses. Okay?"

"So...what pills did you take?"

"I take valium to help me sleep. That's it!"

"That's it? Why do you smell like gin?" Quincy took a big whiff. "Aged gin."

"I ran out of Vodka. I should have known not to drink gin. It makes me crazy. I should have just stuck with Vodka."

"You took valium and Gin together?"

"I needed to sleep."

"Come on. Let's go to an AA meeting. I think they have one this morning."

"I'm not a drug addict and I'm not an alcoholic." Mallory got up and walked back into the house. Broken furniture was strewn all over the first floor. He made his way upstairs and Quincy followed him. "I need to take a shower." Mallory walked into the bedroom and saw that it was also in disarray. He went to the bathroom. Quincy sat on the bed and quickly leaned over to remove the bottle that he was sitting on.

"Mallory...you drank this whole bottle?"

Mallory came out of the bathroom, vigorously brushing his teeth and nodding innocently.

"The AA meeting starts in 30 minutes. I'll even buy you breakfast."

"I have to go to work. I don't have time for that."

"Look, you can be fifteen to twenty minutes late for work. You're the boss. One meeting, I dare you." Quincy stood up and walked to the bathroom.

"I don't do dares. That's how I got Silas!" Mallory said, looking at Quincy through the mirror.

"I'll make it worth your while."

"I'm not an addict!" Mallory shouted.

Quincy walked over to the shower and turned it on. "Okay...then will you go with me? I need to go and I would like some company. Please? I'll wash your back...and your front."

"Fine...I'll go. You better wash my front really well."

"I can't believe you would drag me to some shit like that. This was demented." Mallory stormed out of the building. "I can check that off my list of fifty things to do before I die. I don't have those problems. My problems are bigger, different and much worse. I have handled a wife, kids and a job. I wish that was all I had to worry about. I'm running three entities. I have a family who hates me and I do not know why. My father tried to kill me and I have no idea what my destiny is."

Quincy quickly followed behind him. "We all have destinies. We're all put on this Earth for a reason."

"How would you feel if you were put on this Earth to destroy it?"

"Why would you say that?"

"Quincy, you don't know me. I have this...nevermind. You wouldn't understand."

"I'm trying to understand. Have you seen a therapist?"

Mallory stormed off.

"I don't understand why you're so angry."

"HUMANS! You all make me sick. You put things in little bitty boxes and think that everybody is supposed to fit in them."

"Humans? So what, are you an alien? Who are you to look down on people that are trying to better themselves?"

"I'm not looking down on you. You just don't know me."

"Then tell me. I'm a reasonably intelligent man. Tell me."

Mallory huffed and then answered. "I'm an angel."

"I think I'm going to hate this. What kind of angel are you?"

"I'm the angel of death. Actually, I'm the horseman, Death...of the Four Horsemen of the Apocalypse."

"Okay?" Quincy tried hard to appear sympathetic, but he was confused. "So...does anybody else know?"

"My whole family knows, Silas knows, you know."

"So the Valium you take, it's prescribed, isn't it?"

Mallory stormed off. Quincy wanted to chase after him, but he was interrupted by his cell phone ringing.

"Que Anderson."

"Hey, frat. Are we still on for basketball?"

"Uh yeah, I forgot. I went to an AA meeting this morning. My schedule is screwed."

"AA? I really hope I didn't set you off last night."

"Nawh brah, you didn't. I took someone who needs more than just a meeting. Hey, can I ask you a question? What's up with Mallory? Does he suffer from narcissistic disorder or some kind of traumatic stress?"

"The bitch is gay and dating Silas. That's stress enough. He's a little high strung, a control freak and I heard he has insomnia attacks, but he's okay."

"You think all that stuff is okay?"

"For what he does...yeah?"

"The angel of Death..."

Bailey paused. "He told you that?"

"Yeah, he said he's here to destroy the world. He says that the family knows. Why would you enable somebody like that?

Clearly, he's suffering from delusions but you're not doing anything about that. Why?"

"Look, Mallory is a genius and yeah, we use him. It's a complicated situation and you don't completely know the family dynamics."

"Maybe I don't, but I did experience one of his episodes. That wasn't pretty."

"When did you experience that?"

"Last night at his penthouse."

"Why were you at his penthouse last night? He wasn't the one you took to AA this morning, was he?" Bailey patiently waited for an answer, but Quincy was silent. "Quincy, answer me." Bailey begged, but he still didn't answer. "He's not your cause. You can't change him. Look, meet me at the basketball court, we need to talk."

"Nawh, frat. This one is calling me. He's needs someone."

"Yeah, that someone is in Miami. Let this go, frat. Mallory is a good guy, but if you keep dangling yourself, he's going to think that you're available. He'll do anything to get you. He might even go along with your program for a fuck. I know you don't want to be in that situation."

Quincy huffed.

"You'll lose the battle if you try. Come on, frat. Let it go...Quincy?" Bailey paused for several seconds, hoping that Quincy would be convinced. "Quincy, you can't save the world because someone saved you. I know this is killing you, but you don't understand him. He'll be fine as soon as Silas comes back."

"What if Silas doesn't come back?"

"This isn't your fight, Que. You're out of your league with this. Come on, Que. Meet me at the court. I'll be waiting for you, alright?" He paused again, hoping that Quincy was convinced. "Alright?"

CHAPTER NINE

Silas finally returned home. He slowly cracked the door, pushed it open forcefully with his foot. He dropped his bags and turned on the lights to find that the penthouse destroyed. The glass wall that separated the foyer from the living room was shattered. The painting of Mallory was torn down and ripped to shreds. As he walked, broken glass crackled under his feet.

There was broken furniture, blood smears and many empty bottles of Gin and Vodka scattered everywhere. He walked over to the phone and picked it up from the floor. He placed it back on the table and noticed that there were forty-two messages. He put the phone on speaker and turned up the volume. He walked toward the bar to find every bottle of liquor was empty. He started picking up bottles and placing his knickknacks back on the shelves. He didn't listen closely to the first message.

"Hey Mallory, this is Que. Give me a call."

BEEP

"Silas. Hi honey, it's your wife, V. I wanted to be the first to congratulate you. You said that you were going to be emperor. I should have had more faith in you. I guess you'll be coming home soon. I'll get ready."

He stopped to listen to that message. *Congratulations? What the hell is she congratulating me for?* Silas thought. That bitch bet' not be pregnant again.

BEEP

"Hi Silas. It's Emily. We missed you at Emmett's Memorial this weekend. I guess you're a busy man these days. Congratulations! Umm...I was wondering if you would give me a call. I would like to talk to you about something."

What the hell is going on? Silas walked into the kitchen to throw some bottles away and to grab a trash bag.

BEEP

"Mallory, this is Que. I know you told me not to use this number, but we need to talk. I need to see you. I know I said that you were driving me crazy, but it's like I'm addicted to you. I really need you. Please call me...if not I'm coming over."

BEEP

"Hey Saully, it's your mother. Congratulations, baby. I knew you could do it. Call your mother back."

BEEP

"Mallory...I'm sorry. Please don't shut me out." Quincy begged. "I really miss you. I need to talk to you. Please call me."

Silas walked out of the kitchen with two empty bags. "Was that mom?"

BEEP

"Saully! It's GRAM-ME! Call me, baby."

BEEP

"Saully, you received a unanimous vote? What did Mallory promise these guys? He's really been working hard for you. I guess you should be proud. Call your father back. We need to talk."

Silas was clearly confused by the messages, so he dropped the bag and started looking for Mallory. He walked up to the second level and into the bedroom. He opened the door to find the room in shambles. The drapes were torn and empty bottles of Vodka were scattered around. He placed the mattress back on the bed, straightened the sheets and sat on the edge. He wondered why Mallory would allow the house to be destroyed. Silas remembered he had complained about voices in his head, but he didn't think Mallory was on the brink of a nervous breakdown.

He sat quietly in the room for several minutes when he heard running water. He got up and walked into the bathroom. After a few steps, he noticed water was covering the floor. He rushed to the bathtub and it was overflowing. He shut the faucet off, but the sound of running water continued. Silas walked over to the shower and noticed that it was running as well.

When he opened the shower door, water rushed out and knocked him down. The water completely covered the already drenched floor. He crawled over and shut the water off. That's when he saw Mallory laying in fetal position in the corner of the shower. His arms and legs had slash marks and his nose was bleeding. Silas rushed over to see if he was still breathing.

"Baby, talk to me. Mallory, baby, what's wrong?"

"The voices...the voice...the voices..." Mallory whispered and his body shivered from the cold air. "The voices...the voices..."

"Okay? Let's get you out of here." Silas grabbed his arm and tried to pull him up.

"NO! YOU STAY IN HERE! I DIDN'T TELL YOU TO LEAVE!" Mallory shot up and screamed. He crawled to another corner and started rocking again. "The voice...the voices..."

Silas sat back and examined at Mallory closely. He could tell that Mallory hadn't slept. His sunken eyes showed the definition of pain and anger. "What are the voices saying?"

Mallory's tone changed completely when he answered. It sounded as if he was another person. "You useless bastard! You idiot! You're a stupid faggot. We will have no faggots in this house!" Mallory shouted in a dark tone. Silas was shocked. "You're stupid, you dimwit. You're not worthy to be alive."

Silas realized that Mallory was possessed. Mallory was so delusional that he didn't know that Silas was there. Silas walked over and asked him, "Mallory, where's Tanic?" Mallory eventually looked up and noticed Silas in the shower room. "Mallory, where's the dog?"

"She's dead. I killed her." His dark tone continued. "You're not worthy to have a living creature look up to you." All of a sudden, Mallory's body shook. He started panting and whimpered, "Silas...I want to die. Please help me die."

"I'll help you die, alright." Silas stormed out of the bathroom and rushed down the water-soaked stairs. He walked past the phone, not listening to the continuous flow of messages.

BEEP

"Mallory, please call me. I can't live without you." Quincy cried out. "I'm dying here. Please call me."

"He killed my dog! That's was an expensive dog. Do you know how many souls it cost for me to get that dog? He's not the only one that will die!" Silas stormed to kitchen, toward the utility drawer and grabbed the largest knife he could find, along with a roll of duct tape. "He's going to wish he was dead after I beat the shit out of him behind my dog. That's was my favorite dog!"

BEEP

"Mallory, this is Natasha. I tried to leave you a voicemail on your cell phone, but your mailbox is full. Make sure you delete this message after you hear it. You rushed out of here so fast that I didn't get a chance to talk with you. Here is the scoop. Silas is supposed to return on Wednesday."

Silas paused to listen to the message.

"We can schedule his surprise party on Friday. I called your brothers and they'll host the party. I had Silas' gift delivered directly to your house...so be on the lookout. Oh and I know when the surprise is out, no one will remember all your hard work, so congratulations, Mallory. You did an excellent job. He's going to be so happy that you got his ball approved with a unanimous vote. You know that hasn't happened in two hundred years. I guess the next step is to start planning for the ball. Bye!"

"My ball is approved? Unanimous vote? Full emperor status?" Silas was shocked and filled with so many emotions.

BEEP

"MAL-LOREE! OH Mallory!" Silas jumped when he heard Ethel screaming with a dog barking in the background. "When are you coming to get this man's dog? If you and Silas are fighting, I don't want to be in the middle of it. Don't hide this man's dog. I know that he's scared of me, but I'm a little scared of him too." The dog barked and she consoled her with a syrupy-sweet tone, "Oh...Chicago, your daddy misses you."

"HER NAME IS TANIC!" He shouted to the machine.

"Anyways, if you don't come and get this dog, Ima keep her and you're gonna hafta buy that man another one. Call me, baby."

"What is wrong with you, Mallory?" Silas placed the knife back in the drawer and grabbed a glass from the cabinet. He looked around and saw two bottles of Valium on the counter. One was an empty bottle and the other was an emergency prescription written two days ago. It was written for a month's supply but there were only eight pills left. He emptied the bottle and grabbed the meat tenderizer. As he placed the pills in a paper towel, the phone rang. "Luxapher." Silas concentrated on crushing the pills into a powdered substance.

"Hey, Saully. I have been calling you all week. What are you doing?"

"Hey, daddy. Beating a steak. What's up?"

"Congratulations!"

"For what?"

"Oh...we get approved and now we're too important for the ball? That's all you screamed about when I asked you to take over."

"You asked me to take over?"

"Son, are you okay?" Michael noticed that Silas sound a little agitated.

"No, Daddy! We're having problems at the house right now. I might have to call you back." Silas shouted.

"I won't hold you. I just want to know, when are you coming back to New York?"

"Why would I come back to New York?"

"Saully, you have to come back to New York. Now that you're approved for a ball, you have to get ready. You need to bind with your wife and introduce her as your empress."

"Bind with Vivian? Are you crazy?" Silas screamed at the top of his voice. "The last thing I want to do is bind with that bitch."

"I knew that you were going to say that. I was thinking...maybe you can ask Emily?"

"Emily...Emmett's wife, Emily? Why kind of crack are you smoking? Daddy, I can't deal with this right now. I have voices screaming at me and water everywhere and a missing dog. I don't have time for binding."

"Saully, you have to make time or you won't have a ball."

"Fine! I'll deal with it tomorrow. Tell Mom I'll call her later."

"Your mother called?"

"Yeah, to congratulate me. I think she wanted to talk to me."

"That's interesting. I don't think you want to bind with her."

"Bye, Daddy." Silas slammed the phone down. "Now, that was just utterly disgusting." He walked into the pantry and pulled out a bottle of Everclear, poured a tall glass of the grain alcohol and added the Valium powder to it. The phone rang again. "SHIT! WHAT DO YOU WANT?"

"Is that how you answer the phone now, your majesty?" A strange male voice was on the other line.

"Who is this?" Silas feverishly stirred the mixture.

"Your cousin, Trent."

"Hey, Trent, fancy you calling. How is the family, Joyce and the kids?"

"They're fine. What are you doing in Texas?"

"Fucking every guy I see. What can I do you for?"

Trent laughed. "Well, I wanted to see if you had chosen your empress. Everyone knows that you're not binding with Vivian, so I wanted to put my name in the hat."

Silas stopped stirring the mixture and started to cuss Trent out. "I CAN'T BIND WITH A GUY YOU –"

"That's where you're wrong. The ritual doesn't state a sex and it's been done before. You go back and read about Birsha, king of Gomorrah. Anyway, I'm interested. I know we've had our tiffs, but I'd like to think that we're over that."

Silas picked up the receiver. "What happen to you wanting to be the family man?"

"This is a great opportunity for both of us. We have each other's back, right?"

"Each other's back? Man, maybe you forgot. You outed me to the rest of the family. I had to marry Vivian to avoid being stoned by the elders." Silas shouted at the receiver.

"Minor setback. Anyway, you're resilient. You got past that. Come on baby, are you going to let that come between us?"

"I don't think it would work, I'm not a bottom!"

"We can switch off."

"I'm the fucker, I don't switch. I gotta go." He slammed the phone down again. The messages started flowing again, but Silas unplugged the phone, returned to the bedroom and walked into the bathroom. He noticed that Mallory had not moved from his spot. Silas grabbed several towels and covered him. He handed him the glass and instructed him to drink it.

"Is it poison?" Mallory whimpered out.

"Yeah." Silas forced out a smile.

Mallory gulped the drink and began convulsing. His voice turned dark again, "You stupid bastard. You should not have been born. Your mother should have aborted you!" Mallory shouted. "I should have ripped you out of your mom's womb. You're not worthy to be in my sight."

Mallory finally collapsed. His body lay lifeless, his eyes fluttered closed. Silas picked him up and put him in their bed, covered him gently and kissed his forehead. He walked out of the bedroom and down the stairs to the study. As he entered his office, he looked for his ancient book of Satanic Knowledge. He grabbed the book and started to search for Possession and Demon Takeovers, but he came across the subject of the king from Gomorrah. He glanced through the story. He slowly started walking toward his desk to sit down, but he remembered that his chair wasn't the most comfortable but Mallory's was. He walked over to Mallory's office and saw a huge, half-wrapped box on his desk with a card that Mallory scribbled a note.

Congrats, Silas. You'll be the greatest emperor ever - if not the best dressed. I love you and I'll follow you to the end of eternity.

My love, Mallory.

Silas sat at the desk and saw the box was halfway opened. He couldn't help himself and he gently ripped off the tape that barely secured the box. He removed the top of the box and pulled out a red and burgundy full-length chinchilla fur coat. His mouth hung open in surprise. He feverishly put it on and ran to the closest mirror to check himself out. As he ran his fingers through the fur on the collar, he felt the embroidered letters. He leaned in toward the mirror and saw three large black letters, *SXL*, on the collar.

"Oh shit! This is hot! Oh baby, this is hot." Silas pranced around and posed in the mirror. Eventually, he took the fur coat off and folded it back into the box. He glanced over and saw Mallory's ideas for invitations, location plans, board member gifts and the participants' giveaways.

"No, I'm not gonna do that." Silas pushed the chair back, left the room and returned to the bedroom to discover Mallory was not in the bed. He called out to him, but no one answered. He sat back on the bed and heard whimpering. He walked into his closet and saw Mallory covered in his shirts. He kneeled down and crawled over to him.

"I'm so sorry, Silas. I'm so sorry. I'm a waste...just a fucking waste. I just wanted to be perfect for you and I can't be. I'm just stupid."

"You're not stupid. You're just having a hard time right now. We need to find out how to help you. But you're not stupid. You're perfect for me."

"No, I'm not. I'm not good enough for you. You need a strong man. I'm just a stupid faggot. I'm an idiot. I just want to die."

"Is that what you want? Or do you want the voices to go away?" Silas asked softly.

"I can't make them go away." Mallory sobbed uncontrollably.

"I think I can help you. Will you let me help you?" Mallory nodded. "Come here. Come here, baby." Silas opened his arms and Mallory crawled into his embrace and laid his head down in his lap. "I love you, you know that? You're my perfect man. You're so perfect for me. And I know you would go to the end of Hell for me." Silas rubbed his head, fingering the curls in his hair. "I think

I know how to make the voices go away for good. Would you like that?"

"Yes...VERY MUCH." Mallory answered between sniffles.

"Do you want to bind with me?" Silas gently wiped his eyes. "It's a marriage ceremony where we combine our lives, powers and souls. We would share each other's' strengths and brilliance." Silas lifted Mallory's face higher. "We would be united forever, even after our deaths."

"But then, you would get the voices."

"Nothing can possess me and they'll go away."

"They will?"

Silas shook his head and then kissed Mallory's forehead.

CHAPTER TEN

It had been weeks since Silas asked Mallory to bind souls. Sitting in the dark, Mallory contemplated his next moves. His eyes were swollen due to his constant weeping. He had thirty-nine pills and a new bottle of Vodka sitting in front of him on the kitchen table. The voices in his head were screaming so loudly it made his nose bleed. Mallory picked up a hand full of pills and contemplated taking them all. He was so consumed with grief that he didn't hear Silas come in.

As he passed the kitchen, Silas noticed Mallory sitting in the dark. He went back to the door and turned on the foyer light so he wouldn't startle Mallory too much. The lights didn't faze him. Silas walked up to him and touched him on the shoulder.

"Why are you sitting in the dark?"

"I'm just sitting here thinking and I didn't get up to turn on the light," Mallory dropped the pills on the counter. "Sorry."

"I got something for you." He whisked over toward him. Mallory mustered a fake smile when Silas placed an oversized box in front of him. Mallory feverishly opened the box. He removed the tissue to find a purple robe. He pulled out the floor length garment. "I got it made for our ceremony. It came early."

Silas looked down and saw the pills on the counter. Although he was very concern, he didn't want to alarm Mallory. He casually swept them together and put them back in the bottle. He grabbed the Vodka and placed it on the other counter behind Mallory.

"It's beautiful, baby." Mallory smiled, but couldn't stop the tears from falling.

"It's going to be beautiful on you. Are you crying?"

"Blushing bride, right?" Mallory quickly wiped his face and bloody nose. The voices were still screaming in his head.

"That's some bullshit. Anyway! What are you doing tonight?"

"I don't know...I have that Death report to finish for Marc and the board."

"I'm getting you a Scribe for those damn reports and I don't wanna hear NO." Silas grabbed his hand. "Do you want to get married tonight?"

"Why do you want to bind with me? I'm not worth it."

"I think you're worth it. I wouldn't be here if you weren't. Besides, I'm the one who is supposed to get cold feet - not you, blushing bride." He grabbed Mallory's hand and guided him to the stairs. "I want you to go upstairs and take a long, relaxing bath then put that robe on with nothing underneath and meet me in poolroom in an hour and a half."

Mallory walked down the stairs to the poolroom. There were candelabras and large, black candles burning everywhere. A pathway of large candles led him to their private and heated pool. There were several people sitting in the pool area, but he saw no sign of Silas. A tall man stood in front of him and blocked his entrance to the poolroom.

Moments later, the man guided Mallory to the edge of the pool Silas walked to the other edge. The people stood up and started chanting. Silas beckoned Mallory to meet him in the middle of the pool. Mallory took a step of hesitation but when he stepped, he noticed that he was standing above the water's surface. As he stepped, he felt the ground move under his feet. As they met in the center, a spirit floated down toward them and began speaking. Mallory looked deeply into Silas' eyes and saw the vulnerability masked behind his normal everyday stern, hood demeanor. Silas clasped his hands, bowed to Mallory and declared asseverations in Latin. Mallory joined him, knelt and declared his asseverations in Latin as well.

The spirit continued chanting and opened a floating box from which he retrieved two identical rings. He blessed the rings and gave one to each of them. Mallory placed the ring on Silas' finger and Silas placed the ring on Mallory's. The spirit instructed them to turn their rings clockwise simultaneously. When Mallory turned his ring, he felt a sharp, piercing pain. Although he grimaced, he tried not to show any expression. A small, portentous ghost floated from Mallory's finger. He looked at his bleeding hand, but was unaware of the ghost. Silas grabbed his hand and placed his bleeding ring in his mouth. He nonverbally instructed Mallory to do the same by flashing his palm upwards. The ghost floated around the two. The spirit felt the ghost's threat and impelled it away.

After their blood oath exchange, the spirit continued chanting and the crowd stood up. The spirit floated higher and announced that the two may kiss and consummate the bond. Silas grabbed Mallory by the waist and kissed him hard. Mallory started to feel people tugging at him as they attempted to remove his robe. Two men grabbed his shoulders and gently guided him to lie down. Afterwards, they removed Silas' robe and prepared him to consummate the union.

As Silas was lowered down, his eyes flashed flaming red. His body was sweaty and infernally hot. His teeth grew sharp and edgy. Silas maneuvered deep inside him. Mallory felt like his body was being ripped apart and his flesh began to burn. This was not the feeling he experienced during their usual sexual acts. Silas' skin began turning beet red and his physique started changing. Mallory didn't recognize the being on top of him. As he clenched his teeth and endured the pain, the Silas stopped and whispered in his ear.

"Don't fight me. Get in touch with your true self and connect with me."

"I'll lose control."

"Not if you connect with me."

Mallory's closed his eyes and his breathing became labored. His skin turned clammy and cold. Every drop of sweat that fell from Silas' body turned into an ice when it touched Mallory. Silas gazed into Mallory's crystal blue eyes. As breath escaped his mouth, Silas saw the frost. Mallory's warm, French vanilla skin turned pastel shade of blue.

"Mmmm, now we can play and I don't have to be gentle with you." Silas viciously chomped into Mallory's shoulder. Mallory let out a blood-curdling scream as he ran his claws down Silas' back. Silas released his grip and screeched in unison. Mallory wrapped his monstrous claws around Silas' neck and began choking him violently. Silas lifted his body and began ferociously punching Mallory in the face, but it did not make Mallory release his grip. Silas finally grabbed his legs, lifting him up a bit and plummeted deeper inside him. When Mallory screamed, the windows from their penthouse blew out.

Mallory woke up to find himself in the refreshing, pristine, fluffy white bed. He was wearing white cotton pajamas, something that he would never choose for himself, but they were comfortable. He mentally checked himself to see if he was in pain, but he was fine. He closed his eyes to hear the voices in his head, but nothing was there. He could not remember how he got dressed – let alone how he got into bed. He lifted the covers to find Silas entangled in his lower body, sleeping hard and looking innocent. Mallory grabbed a few of his braids and began unraveling them. He still felt faint, piercing pains in his ring finger. He looked at the ring and attempted to tug at it, but he heard Silas' whimpering voice.

"You can't take the ring off. It will shred your finger and you will bleed to death. Then we will both die."

"So I'm stuck with you?"

Silas lifted up and smiled. "For eternity."

"Oh, damn. I was thinking about replacing you with someone else next millennium."

"You can think about it all you want. You just can't do it." Silas scooted up and kissed him. "Do you remember last night?"

"Not really."

"You have questions?"

"Kind of, I don't remember how we got here."

"Well, my subjects cleansed us and brought us back to Earth."

"Earth? I thought we were in the poolroom. Oh man, why do I not remember it?"

"When you turn into your true identity, you don't remember anything, do you?" Silas asked and Mallory shook his head no. "Why? Because it is too painful?" He nodded yes. "Last night shouldn't have been painful at all. It was beautiful and magical. Man that was the best fuck of my life."

"You're so silly." Mallory grabbed another one of Silas' braids and nervously unraveled it.

"I'm serious. I never could have done that with anybody else. That is the most sacred thing that I can ever share with you. We are essentially one now. I feel what you feel and vice versa."

"Then I feel sad. That's a memory that I want to have."

"Allow yourself to remember it. You'll be amazed. You're so beautiful in your true form. Maybe only I can see it, but you're so beautiful. Words can't describe it."

Mallory went to kiss him but Silas pulled back a little and looked in his eyes.

"So I have a confession. You may have probably figured it out but...I am..." Silas huffed.

"The real thing...you're a Coca-Cola Classic!" Mallory laughed. "I figured it out a long time ago."

"You knew I was the powerful Satan this whole time?"

"AH, yeah...the spider thing kept me thinking that you were human...but I got a couple of warnings from my ex-greatest love and there were some unexplainable things that you did...it wasn't difficult putting six and six and six together. Besides why would a human Satan be on a collision course with the Final?"

"I guess I was getting too comfortable around you." Silas let out a sigh of relief. "I thought you would be scared of me. That's why I stayed human so long."

"Is that the real reason? Some of the things you did didn't seem like you were acting or pretending to be human."

"We have the best of both worlds. We're angels, but we can see and worship God through human eyes. We're not supposed to do that, however after centuries of roughing it with the humans... how you not get attach to them. How do you not see His awesomeness? Your ex-greatest love doesn't get that. That's why he thinks he's equal to God."

Mallory grunted.

"When was the last time you spoke with your ex-greatest love?"

"Is there anything else you want to tell me before I answer that question?" Mallory was grasping at straws, hoping Silas would reveal other secrets and forget the Matthew question.

"Well, I do have something I need to ask you. Being that we're more than just a human couple now and we're basically combined to one and..." Silas sat up in the bed, looking more vulnerable than Satan should look.

"Why are you babbling? Ask me?" Mallory sat up with him.

"Do you want to share my throne with me?" Silas shouted it out. "You're practically an emperor since we are bound."

Mallory looked confused. He grabbed another one of Silas' braids and unraveled it. "What about your wife, Vivian?"

"I didn't bind with her. I chose you." Silas snatched the braid out of Mallory's hand. "I hate when you unbraid my hair. I have to go back to her and have it re-braided every time you do that."

"Oh, Silas. Why didn't you tell me?" Mallory lay back in the bed.

"Would you have not done it if I had told you?" Silas said, attempting to re-braid his hair.

"I don't know. Does she know about your choice?"

"She will when we announce it tonight at The Abaddon. Everyone will, even Daddy, if he doesn't know already."

"Oh, shit. He's going to kill me now."

"That's treason." Silas said, noticing that other braids were loose, so he gave up. "You can't kill an emperor. Wait, I thought you liked Daddy."

"I don't like your damn Daddy. He hates me. Wait, I'm an emperor now?" Mallory sat up in the bed again. "I thought you said we had to announce it."

"You're an emperor now, baby. We are bound. It is your choice to keep us a secret or not. I hope you don't."

"But you just said that your Daddy probably already knows."

"Them fuckers can't keep a secret. They tell Daddy every got damn thing I do."

"Oh, I guess I'll be suffering a fate worse than Death and Hell."

"There's not a motherfucking fate worse than Death and Hell. If there was, it would be somebody worse than me. I AM Satan! You can't get worse than me. I hate when people say that shit.

They make that shit up like... the stories about the boogeyman so that Daddy can fuck Mommy all night without interruption. Pisses me off. Did he say that to you?" Silas asked and Mallory nodded. "That old son of a bitch. He ain't fucking this relationship up." Mallory frowned at him. "What?"

"I have never seen you turn so red in human form." He gently caressed his face. "Give me some time to think about the emperor thing, okay?"

"Okay. Do you want breakfast?" Silas jumped out of bed and helped Mallory up as well. Before they began their decent into the living room, Mallory had an aerial view of the luxurious robe he wore the night before.

"Explain the robe." Mallory kissed him and walked down the stair.

As Silas walked down the stairs, he explained. "Well, if you choose to rule with me, this is a major part of your formal wear. You'll wear this at all the conferences and balls."

"It is such a huge robe."

"There is a detachment at the bottom so you can wear it like a coat. Put it on again."

Mallory slipped on the robe and sashayed around. "You looked good," Silas bowed to him.

"Thank you."

"What would you like to eat, your Highness?"

"Whatever your Majesty would like to cook." He bowed back in respect.

Silas grabbed his waist and pressed his body close to him. "Damn, I can fuck you in this robe."

"Are you supposed to do that?"

"I can do whatever the fuck I want," he said. Silas pulled Mallory down and they both fell on the couch. The robe covered them as Mallory enveloped Silas' body, kissing and softly caressing him. A violent knock on the door interrupted them. "Who in the hell is that knocking like that? I heard that knock all night," Silas said, obviously annoyed.

"I'll get it, you cook."

"You're quickly adapting to ordering me around, aren't you?"

"No one can order you around, my sweet." Mallory walked to the door and opened it. It was Uncle Mal. He was sitting on the ground, beating the door. He looked tired and stressed. Mallory quickly kneeled down and grabbed him. Uncle Myron ran out of the elevator toward the penthouse. He rushed to Uncle Mal's side and assisted Mallory in helping Uncle Mal to his feet. "Silas, bring me some water, please? Quickly?"

"I don't want to come in. Just tell me you didn't do it."

"How long have you been out here?" Uncle Myron asked.

"Two days. Mallory, tell me you didn't go through with it."

"Here! Uncle Mal, are you okay?" Silas handed Uncle Mal a glass of water. He frugally took sips of water to hydrate his throat. "You look like you need to eat something. Come in?"

"I don't want to come in, damn it! Mallory, answer my question. Tell me you didn't affiance with Silas. TELL ME."

Mallory eyes dropped. "Ah yes sir, I-I did."

Uncle Mal threw the water in Mallory's face. Silas stood back. "YOU STUPID FOOL! You stupid idiot! You're an idiotic, imbecilic rodent!"

"Stop Mal! Come on, let's go." Uncle Myron grabbed his arms and helped him to his feet.

"You go from one piece of poisonous cheese to the next. You don't care if it shocks you, cuts you and kills you dead. You just keep going, don't you? You're so stupid, Malcolm. You don't think at all! When are you going to learn?"

"Stop, Mallory Paul. Come on. You're tired!" Uncle Myron tried to pull him away. "You need to stop before you say something you'll regret."

"I'm not Malcolm." Mallory said.

"No, you're not. You're a stupid, narcissistic version of your dumb-ass father. No son of mine would have done something so vile and asinine."

"That's enough, Mallory-Paul! Let's go." Uncle Myron tugged him hard.

"I should have saved your mother instead of you. You're not welcome in the Haulm house."

"MALLORY-PAUL, SHUT UP!" Uncle Myron screamed out as he shoved him against the wall.

"I guess I'm announcing our union tonight." Mallory mumbled. He was broken and Silas was horrorstruck. Silas tried to grab his arm to comfort him, but Mallory pushed him away. He gathered his robe to go into the penthouse.

"So I guess that you're not staying for breakfast. You people are so wonderful. If I wanted to isolate him, I would not have to lift a finger. You do all the work. It's amazing and to think that he was going to keep it a secret and not take the throne." A wicked smile crept across Silas' face. "Thank you for the wedding present, Uncle Mal. Now I don't have to do all that work convincing him to join me. You sold him to me and I wasn't even buying." Silas slammed the door.

"DAMMIT, MALLORY! You have now completely alienated yourself from the entire present generation. Do you want to eat breakfast before or after you start on the future generation?"

"I didn't mean to say that. I was just..."

"So angry? You should know better by now. You're Pestilence, so your words become poison. SHIT! But I guess, eventually, he'll forgive you." They started walking toward the elevator. "That just makes my job harder. Why did you call him Malcolm?"

Uncle Mal's cell phone rang and it was Bailey. "Mallory Haulm."

"Uncle Mal, it's Bailey. Ummm...do you know Quincy Anderson?"

"No, son. Why?"

"Well, he was my best friend. He tried to commit suicide two nights ago. He just woke up and he's asking for you."

Shit, Malcolm! He thought. "What hospital?"

"H&H Mercy."

"I'll be there." He closed the phone. "Guess who I ran into two nights ago?"

"Who?"

"Malcolm's soul."

"Two nights ago? How did you know it was him?"

"I saw his transparent reflection in the mirror when I was driving over here. I almost had an accident - scared the shit out of me. At least I know where he is."

"Where?"

"In some guy name Quincy."

"Bailey's best friend? Why would he be in him?"

"Apparently the boy killed himself."

CHAPTER ELEVEN

"Hey Mallory," Marc approached his brother, who was sitting outside of Quincy's hospital room. "I heard about the fight between you and Uncle Mal."

"It wasn't a fight. He said his words." Mallory rolled his eyes.

"I guess he was pissed about the whole affiancing thing." Marc towered over Mallory. "So I guess since you're banned from the Haulm house, you're banned from the company too. Way to go, Uncle Mal. Don't worry, you still have to command souls. Make sure some of them get to Heaven," Marc patted him on the back and walked down the hallway.

"Hey, son." Uncle Myron approached Mallory and sat beside him.

"If one more person insults me, I swear..." Mallory snarled.

"I'm not going to do that. Uncle Mal was angry. He had a point, but he had no right to disgrace you. Obviously you love him." Uncle Myron words made Mallory frowned up at him. "You could have ordered him to be killed for treason. Mallory, all I'm going to say is, be careful. If you need to talk, I'm here. I know I'm not the best one to talk to because I tease you a lot, but I want you to know that I'm here for you. Don't alienate yourself from the family, please." He sat down.

"Alienate myself? From a family that doesn't want me? Are you serious?"

"You want the truth. You didn't hear it from me, but they fear you. You're so powerful and they know it. The only reason why they get away with insulting you is because you don't know it. They want to keep you down because that is the only way they can control you."

Mallory turned toward Uncle Mal and asked. "Do you fear me?"

"Yeah!"

"Why?"

"I don't know you. Maybe I never took the time to foster a relationship with you. I think you hate me."

"I don't hate you. I don't hate anybody - not even Dad."

"Then you're the better man. That alone makes you powerful."

Mallory wiped his face and took a deep breath.

"So you did affiance with Silas and announce it?" Mallory nodded. "How was it?"

"It was scary, but I got to release my inner self and I was free. It felt so good just to be who I am without hiding or being in fear. Silas said that I was beautiful. He was in awe of my true self."

"The Final self?" Uncle Myron slid that question in and Mallory nodded before realizing that he was telling his secret. "That's good."

"So you know. You're going to have me killed now?"

"You're protected. We can't kill you. That's treason. Silas knew what he was doing."

"You want me killed?"

"No. Not really...I think that you're viable to the existence of our family line. So far, you have done some bizarre things, but they have rhyme and reason to them. You haven't broken any rituals and you haven't killed anybody unnecessarily. I think you're needed." Mallory looked down as Uncle Myron continued. "Look, I want to leave you with two things. First of all, emperor or not, you are a Haulm. You may not like it, you may not want it. You may try to do anything to run from it, but that is just who you are and nobody can take that away from you or ban you. It is not a privilege; it's a responsibility. You stand up and take command of your position. Don't let anyone insult you. You're powerful."

"And two?"

"Finals lives are short and painful. Have fun. Have lots of fun. You're a special type of horseman. You have no rules. Live life to the fullest."

"Okay? Uncle Myron, if I need to talk to you..."

"My house and my door are always open. If you need sanctuary, you're always welcome." They both stood up. Uncle Myron bowed, which made Mallory nervous. He wanted to stop him, but he remembered his words and allowed him to pay respect. He turned to walk away. "One more thing..." He turned back and teasingly asked. "What does an uncle have to do to get a Jag?"

Mallory laughed. "Have Bailey tell Harold to get you one - on me!" Mallory sat down again and covered his face, taking deep breaths. He commanded himself to get up and look for Bailey. He knew that if he could find Bailey that he could find Quincy. As he turned around, Bailey was standing right in front of him.

"Bailey. How is he doing?"

"Fine, no thanks to you."

"I'm sorry. I would have gotten here sooner but..."

"You were off securing your future. So what do I have to do now, bow and kiss your ass?"

"No, Bailey, I'm sorry. I didn't know."

"You knew he was my best friend. You knew what he meant to me. If you were suffering so much, you should have come to me. You should not have subjected him to that shit."

"Do you honestly think I wanted him to see me have an episode?"

"I don't know, Mallory," he seethed in a condescending tone. "Do you think period? He's human. I could have handled the situation better."

"Yeah and you would have called me crazy?" He stood up to leave.

"Hold on, motherfucker." Bailey snatched Mallory's arm and swung him around. "I have never called you crazy. A faggot, yes and rightfully so, but I have never and would never call you crazy. Give me some credit."

"Well, give me some credit." Mallory snatched his arm away. "I didn't ask him to come over. He was there. Maybe I should have shown some restraint and pushed him away, but he was there and I needed someone. I was...scared."

"Well if you were scared, imagine what he was going through. I have nothing to say to you, Mallory."

"Bailey, please don't do this! You're the only person on my side."

"Why is that, Mallory? You keep fucking over your allies. I'm out. I want nothing to do with you and I have nothing to say to you." He walked through the double doors toward Quincy. Mallory stood in the hallway with his head bowed.

Just before the doors closed, Quincy poked his head through. "Mallory? You're not coming to see me?"

"Sure, yes! How are you doing?"

"Better, now that you're here."

"Maybe we should go, Que. You need to get some rest." Bailey said, pulling Mallory's arm to get him to leave.

"Hey, Quincy?" Silas strolled over to the pair, sucking on a lollipop.

"Silas?"

"I'm sorry, I missed your messages." Mallory said sadly, "I wasn't hiding from you. I was caught up..."

"We got married!" Silas announced proudly.

"Married? Wow! Congratulations," Quincy said in amazement.

"Thank you. Do you need anything?" Mallory asked.

"Yeah, an explanation as to why you would marry a bully," Quincy asked, looking at Silas.

Silas took the lollipop out of his mouth and moved toward Quincy. "Look, fruit loop, I'm not a fucking bully!"

"Stop, Silas," Mallory begged and gently pulled Silas back.

"Why should I stop? I mean, I don't know, how can anybody think this is your fault? You fucked this fruit loop for one night and I hardly think that was one of your best times. Shit, you did it under five minutes."

Quincy shifted his eyes from Silas to Mallory. It was clear that Mallory didn't inform Silas of his extracurricular affair. Mallory bowed his eyes in shame. "Seventeen. Besides, the length of time doesn't matter. It's the connection you make." Quincy said, staring at Mallory, daring him to look up.

"He made one fucking connection and it wasn't that long," Silas shouted back.

"Well, it appeared to linger...it's like it lasted for three weeks." Quincy was practically confessing Mallory's sin right in front of him. Mallory completely looked away. "I'm not angry. I'm just sad for you 'cause you settled."

"Shouldn't you be in a straight jacket?" Silas shouted.

"Shouldn't you be in someone's ass, Long Dick Dong?" Quincy snapped back.

"I got something I can put in your ass that is a little bit bigger than my dick, you fucking fruit loop."

"Silas, stop. I think we need to go." Mallory pulled Silas back again.

"Can I give you a congratulatory hug?" Quincy tapped Mallory on the shoulder. Mallory turned with his arms stretched, planning to give him a proper, safe-distance hug. However, Quincy wrapped his arms around Mallory's waist and pulled him extremely close. Mallory couldn't help but rest his head on Quincy's shoulder. "You smell so good...just as I remember. You're thinking about our time together, aren't you?"

Mallory nodded his head.

"When he forcefully shoves his tongue down your throat, don't choke. Just think of me and how I tasted in your mouth." He enveloped Mallory's earlobe with his mouth and started kissing him down his cheek until he got to his lips. He delivered a powerful kiss that Mallory couldn't resist.

"You gotta be shitting me!" Silas screamed out. Bailey walked out of the room just in time to blocked Silas' attack and pushed him away.

Mallory restrained himself and stopped the kiss. He turned and walked away without saying a word.

"You watch your back, you straight jacket fruit loop. I'll make this place Hell for you." Silas stormed out to catch Mallory.

"I'm sorry, Que. Mallory should've known better than to get involved with you. He's the reason why you're in here and he should pay," Bailey apologized.

"You think Mallory is the reason why I shot myself? He wasn't the cause, he was just the catalyst. You were the cause." Bailey was puzzled. "I have been in love with you since our freshman year in college and you're homophobic." Quincy walked away, leaving Bailey confused and bewildered.

CHAPTER TWELVE

Returning from a meeting, Mallory walked back to his office. He quickly grabbed Silas from behind and planted a sweet peck on the back of his neck before going to his desk. Silas was quickly distracted from practicing his putts, but it didn't upset him. An exploding smile graced his face before he quickly returned his attention to the golf ball and his target putt. After hours of silence, the two jumped when the intercom suddenly announced, "Emperor?"

"Yes?" They both answered and then looked at each other.

"There are four aggressive-looking men approaching the Emperor's elevator in search of the Emperor. Shall I let them in?"

Mallory shouted 'NO!' as Silas answered, 'Yes'.

"Confused." The intercom announced.

"Yes." Silas commanded.

"No, wait. Who are they?" Mallory asked the intercom.

"Haulm...Two from generation 1980 and two from generation 1950."

"Hell no!" Mallory shouted back.

"Yes, let them in." Silas commanded again. He quickly turned to Mallory and asked, "Did you piss them off?"

"YES! I woke up this morning." Mallory jumped up from the desk. "Why do you always favor Marc over me?"

"Mallory...come on, that's not true."

"If it's not true, show me. Turn him away." Mallory got up and walked out of the office.

"Emperor, they have reached their destination. Shall I open the elevator doors?" The intercom announced.

Silas paused for the longest time before screaming out. "SHIT! Yes, let them in."

"Where the hell is Mallory?" Marc asked, storming out of the elevator first.

"Good afternoon, Marc. How are you doing on this lovely day?" Silas pretended to hit his golf ball.

"PISSED! How could he do that? How could he just collect a major soul and not tell me?" Marc walked around, looking for him. The others found a seat and waited. "MALLORY! Bring your punk ass out here."

"Are you serious?" Silas pulled Marc aside. "Come on! You can't come in here and talk to him like that!"

"WHY THE HELL NOT!" Marc kept shouting.

"'Cause I can have your head on a stick at a moment's notice..." Mallory reentered the room. He turned to Silas as he continued, "And no one could stop me."

"How could you do that? How could you collect Michael's soul and not tell anyone?" Marc huffed.

"Michael who?"

"Michael Jackson, you bitch!"

"I DIDN'T COLLECT HIS SOUL! WHAT THE HELL ARE YOU TALKING ABOUT?" Mallory rushed to the desk and thumbed through his records.

"Emperor, there is a call from TMZ. Patching through," The intercom announced.

"Ah, sir?" A nervous voice said.

"Yeah," Silas answered coldly.

"Okay so... like what had happened was...an agent leaked out some news."

"Michael returning home?"

"Ah, yeah..."

"Got it...I'll call you back later on that. Disconnect." Silas stood between Marc and Mallory. "Mallory would not have known about that soul because he collects human souls. Michael is an angel. He's just returned home."

"He's dead?" They all murmured.

"He just returned home," Silas kept repeating. Marc walked to Mallory's desk and perched on the edge while Mallory sat in his chair. "Mallory, remember when I told you about angels coming down here? Well, Michael was a high-level angel who loved music and humanity. He thought he could change human thoughts and actions with his music, so God let him come down here for a while. But it was time for him to return home."

"He's really dead?" They kept asking.

"In his human form. Yeah!" Silas walked over to Mallory, kneeling before him and grabbing his hand. "But Mallory, he's back home with Our Father." He looked over to the rest of the group. "And his music hasn't died. It's still with us."

"I hear what you're saying, but it's not synthesizing with me right now." Mallory folded his arms and rocked back and forth, fighting back the tears forming in his eyes.

"What do you mean, he's not human?" Marc asked.

"Not to be funny in this delicate situation," Silas paused, trying to appear concerned but his arrogance exuded, "but do you honestly think a human can have that capacity of talent?" Silas stood up. "I'm saying this in the most sensitive manner possible, but seriously...there has been no one like him before and there will be no one like him after. Unless he comes back down here – which he won't. Humans are vicious."

"NOT all humans are vicious!" Marc tried to conceal his pain. "Not everyone believed that shit about him and them damn kids," Marc said passionately.

"That was only fabricated to throw some humans off his 'true identity' scent. That won't stick on him. Actually, give it some time and the truth will come out."

"He's dead. We've lost a great Black man." Marlon said, sulking.

"I guess he was a big pillar in the Black community," Silas paused, "Sss...ohh, this might not be good. Black people might wanna take the day off." Silas started pacing back and forth. "Hey...are ya'll so upset that you want to take the day off?"

Everyone shook their heads yes.

"OH DAMN! We planned for Black people to take the day off when Prez Obi won, but nobody did. Now this?" Silas started ringing his hands. "I need to schedule a meeting with Logistics."

"Silas?" Mallory looked up and asked, "Is President Obama an angel?"

"OH, HELL NAWH!" Silas grabbed his club and proudly announced, "But you gotta admit that's one of the best alliances Heaven and Hell created. American humans were going to fuck up the country again! We had to do something. And," Silas paused, "that's where Peter went. He became Obama's guardian angel."

"I lost my guardian angel to the president?" Mallory asked. It was obvious that he was a bit perturbed.

"And rightfully so! Come on...an educated Black man with swagger and a beautiful banging-ass wife. They have kids actually born into the marriage and they all work together to help him become president. You know we had to put their best people on that. Peter was a high-level angel."

"I think I'm taking the day off." Mallory stood up and walked to the elevator. The others got up and followed him.

"Hey, take the week. I need you next week for the inaugural ball and world summit." Silas shouted in Mallory's direction.

CHAPTER THIRTEEN

The following week was Silas' Inaugural Ball. Everyone celebrated and partied - except for Mallory. He was too busy crafting his sovereign speech – at least that was the reason he gave Silas. Actually, he felt awkward accompanying Silas to this huge event, not only his chosen partner to run the empire, but as his lover. He knew his wife would be attending. Mallory tried desperately to shy away from her scorned path.

Everyone was shocked, if not angry, at Silas' choice of emperors; however they had to accept his choice. Mallory tried tirelessly to show that being the emperor was a professional move, but Silas never hid their personal relationship. If fact, he made it a point to show that their personal and professional relationship was one. That created a lot of pressure for Mallory to perform. Never in a millions years did he believe that he would be ruling Earth and Hell – a tiny cry from Towneson Financial.

That night, Mallory agreed to meet his family for a late dinner. Marc and Marlon were sitting at the table when Mallory and Bailey walked into restaurant. Bailey left HIC to join Mallory and Silas at LTC. Against Mallory's strong opposition, Bailey felt it was a good choice. It was also a sneaky way for Marc to monitor Mallory.

They separated and Bailey went straight to the bar while Mallory saw the family and joined them at the table. "Hey, Marlon, Marc."

"You finally got my message. It would have been nice of you to return my calls." Marc fussed, nursing his drink.

"Hey, son, I guess I don't need to be here." Uncle Mal jumped up and hugged Mallory.

Mallory was shocked by his pleasant greeting. Things were still a little sketchy since the fight. "Hey, Uncle Mal. What messages?" Mallory quickly hugged him back.

"The messages that I left telling you that you needed to be here. We couldn't get in touch with you so we got Uncle Mal to come." Marc continued with his ranting.

"Good. I can go home. It's cold." Uncle Mal shivered off the chills.

"You can't go home, Uncle Mal. I'm not here as a horseman. Tomorrow's my big day. I'm giving the opening sovereign speech."

"You're here as the emperor?" Marc shouted at him with content.

"Yes! Silas gets the ball and party, I get the duties and work." Mallory replied. He saw the steam of anger gushing out of Marc's ears. "Why don't you come and stay with us at the castle? We have plenty of room, but you need to let me know."

"Hey, guys. Mallory! I thought you weren't coming." Uncle Myron sat down with his Irish coffee. "We have been calling you. Shit, I can go home. It is fucking cold here."

"Like I was telling Marc and Uncle Mal, I am not here as a horseman. I'm giving the sovereign speech tomorrow." Mallory coveted the strong brew that Uncle Myron was drinking. He quickly shrugged off the desire and continued. "We're staying at the castle. There is plenty of room there and it can be acclimatized to your preference. You're welcome too, Uncle Mal."

"Well, I'm staying with you." Uncle Myron said before sipping his drink.

"Uncle Myron...we need to project a united front. We all stay at one place." Marc snapped.

"Well, I guess we are ALL staying at the castle." Uncle Myron snapped back.

"I'll have Bailey make the arrangements." Mallory motioned to the server to get a drink.

"You think you control everything, don't you?" Marc leaned over and snatched Mallory's arm.

"No, I just control my world and unfortunately, you are in it." Mallory snatched his arm back. "Besides, you know how much you love being around your baby brother. You two can hang out."

Bailey walked up and sat at the table. "Hey, Daddy, Uncle Mal." He turned to Mallory and whispered. "Okay...the rumor is Haulm Industries started to fail after you left. We are in a weak position and several companies are thinking about joining together and taking us over."

"Really?"

"Yeah. Worst news, the audience attending this conference wants to see how strong you are. They say that Silas is weak and there's an assassination plot, but they need to know if you can be swayed to their side."

"I wouldn't betray Silas."

"Rumor is they are going to check you on that at the speech tomorrow."

"Bloody hell. Okay...we will talk about this at breakfast tomorrow."

"What are you two bitches heckling about?" Marc began slurring his words.

"Yo' stupid ass," they both answered. "Uncle Myron is staying at the castle." Mallory turned to Marc. "Are you staying?"

"Nope, we like the hotel." Marc commanded and then visually threatened at everyone else around the table.

He turned to Uncle Mal who bowed his head and nodded no. "Just make arrangements for one."

"I don't think we need to be in their room." Bailey squirmed around.

"Shh, I want to get Mallory's coat." Chad felt around in the dark looking for Mallory's suitcase.

"Why didn't pack your own coat?"

"I did, but his suede coat looks better with what I have on."

"Mallory's shit always looks better than your own clothes. I don't see why he lets you borrow his shit!"

"I only borrowed his sweater. This will go a lot faster if you help me. Turn on a light."

"I'm not turning on any lights. Do you hear those noises?" Bailey started to get jittery.

"No, do you think his coat is in this trunk?"

"No, look, you can wear my leather coat. Let's get out of here. I'm getting the willies."

"Okay, help me pull out this trunk. If it is not in here, I will wear your coat." Bailey and Chad grabbed one side of the trunk and attempted to move it. The handle broke and they both fell on the bed. Bailey felt someone's leg under him. He moved the covers and discovered that Silas and Mallory were in the bed having sex. Donovan walked in and turned on the light. Chad looked over at Donovan. He was wearing the suede coat that Chad was looking for. "That's the coat," Chad admitted.

"Oh shit! I'm going to be sick!" Bailey jumped off the bed and ran to the bathroom.

Mallory pulled out his earphones. "What are you doing in here?"

"I was looking for...oh my God!" Chad finally turned toward the couple. "You were...I'm sorry."

"Who moved the trunk?" Silas asked.

"I was looking for that coat. Please forgive me...oh God."

"Stop calling God unless you're cumming." Silas shouted, trying to kick Chad off the bed.

"Yes, he prefers Silas." Mallory bit him on the earlobe. "I was getting there, Daddy."

"Really? Okay, everyone out!" Silas pulled the covers back over their head and resumed their erotic pleasure.

"Let's go!" Bailey barely calmed himself and return to the bedroom.

"Oh...shit! Chad...wait...baby, wait...Chad, I wear the almond wool coat with that-that-that shit...sweater. It's in the...oh fuck...in the foyer closet. Oh Silas...Shit, daddy!"

"Let's get the fuck out of here before I throw up again." Bailey grabbed Chad and pushed him out of the room. Donovan watched intensely as he slowly backed out of the room. "Now, Donovan!" Bailey commanded again. Donovan turned off the lights and waited for Mallory's verbal release. Donovan mentally came when Silas and Mallory both released an animalistic screech.

"Mallory! Mallory, wake up." Bailey nudged Mallory until he woke up.

"Who died?"

"No one yet. Shit! It's cold in this fucking castle."

"Have you been drinking?"

"Yeah, I've been drinking, but I can't get warm. Scoot over."

"Why?"

"I can't find the damn heater! Your room is the only one that's warm."

"Do you realize that Silas will be back in bed soon?"

"The way he was partying tonight. I'll be gone before he gets here." Bailey kept pushing him over. "Besides, I'll have no ass for him to fuck if it freezes off. I told you, your room is the only room that is warm."

"You didn't ask for your room to be acclimatized?"

"I didn't know what that meant. I thought they were asking if I wanted pecan trees in my room."

"Stupid-ass Texan. You have to put on socks. I don't want to feel your crusty feet." Mallory reluctantly moved to the middle of the oversized king bed.

"Thank you." Bailey crawled into the high bed and fell fast asleep. Time passed and Chad shook Bailey to have him scoot over. He found a warm spot in the bed.

After several hours, Silas returned to the castle. He was in rare form and still high from the nights activities. He desperately tried to calm his animalist orgasmic craving by taking a searing hot shower before joining Mallory in bed. He knew Mallory took one of his V&V cocktails and would be out for the night, but he didn't know that the other two were sleeping on the other side. Lucky for them, he snuggled in close to Mallory and quickly fell asleep.

After a while, Donovan slid in on Silas' side of the bed. "Hey, Mallory? Can I talk to you?" He slurred out.

Silas groggily mumbled.

"Do you really love Silas? Do you think he is the guy for you?"

Silas grunted.

"I mean, he is a wonderful man, but is he right for you?" Donovan continued his drunken babbling.

"Mallory is perfect for me." Silas turned over back and growled.

"Silas?"

"In the flesh."

"I'm sorry."

Silas turned over to his left side and propped his head up with his arm. "What's up?"

"Nothing. I was just thinking about your proposition you made tonight." Donovan whispered. "I like you, but I don't want to be another one of your delights. I want us to have something special."

"You wanna take Mallory's spot?" Silas began fingering his lips.

"Am I wrong for feeling that way?"

"No. Feelings are not wrong. Actions sometimes can be. Do you really want to betray your cousin like that?" Silas pulled him closer.

"I don't see it as betrayal. You know that you're too much man for one guy. Besides, Mallory is always busy and you need someone just for you."

"He makes me happy."

"So can I...maybe more. I want to be your number one."

"My number one spot is taken. Unless you pull some hellacious tricks out of your hat, it will stay taken. Mallory is a great man. Why don't you settle for number two?"

"I don't settle. It's number one or that's it." Donovan pulled away.

Silas was too tired to fight off the urge. "Okay...well, I'm cold right now and I am suffering from a touch of insomnia. How would you handle that?"

"I would kiss you from head to toe. I would make love to you until you pass out."

"How bad do you want me?" Donovan grabbed Silas' hand and pushed it down his pajama pants. "Would you fuck me in the bed right now?"

"Mallory is on the other side of us sleeping."

"Would you?" Silas repeated, he is lustful labored breaths grew harder.

Donovan reached for Silas' body. In one motion, Silas was on top and deep inside of him. It happened so fast, Donovan couldn't catch his breath. He looked over to see Mallory tossing a bit. He bit down on his lip to stop from screaming. Silas moved toward his lips and kissed him hard. Donovan bit Silas' tongue, which aroused Silas more. He decided to let go and fully accept Silas' passion and with that, he let go of the idea of being discreet.

Chad heard noises and felt vibrations in the bed. He covered Bailey's mouth and then pinched his nose to wake him up. "Hey, I think they are having sex again." Bailey looked over to see Mallory still asleep. He shook his head no. "Well, one of them is." Bailey removed his hand.

"Mallory is sleep."

"Do you hear that?"

"Who is that?" Bailey whispered.

"Don't cause a scene. If Mallory wakes up and Silas is fucking somebody else right next to him, he will command all of our souls." Chad waited for Bailey's nod. "I think it's Donovan."

Bailey eyes bucked wide and Chad covered his mouth again to stop him from screaming. "I'm too drunk to deal with this right now and it is too cold to move," Bailey groaned softly. They both jumped when Donovan let out a soft cry, then they looked over at Mallory, who was still sound asleep. A few moments later, Silas screeched quietly and the vibrations stopped. Bailey mouthed, "Go back to sleep. We'll deal with this in the morning." Then he closed his eyes.

Silas woke up and realized that he had been cuddling Donovan all night. He shot up and looked over toward Mallory, who was still sleeping. Then he noticed Bailey and Chad on the other side of him. "What the fuck? Three monkeys in the bed?" He shook his head. He leaned over and kissed Mallory on the cheek. "Wake up baby. I don't want you to be late."

"Five minutes, please." Mallory mumbled.

"Five minutes." Silas crawled out of the bed and left the bedroom. Later, he returned with a hot cup of tea. "Five minutes. Baby, get up." Silas nudged him and handed him a hot cup. "I got something hot for you and I started your shower. I need you up. You don't want to be late for breakfast with the leaders." Silas walked to the bathroom. "Come on, baby."

Mallory grabbed the tea and laid it on the bed. "I'm getting up. The shower is hot?" Mallory sat up slowly and craving his hot cup of tea.

"Yes, I will wash your back." Silas guided him out of the bed and they retreated to the bathroom. Silas returned to the room to find that Donovan was the only one left in bed. Mallory left the bathroom and stumbled toward the closet. As he collected his clothes and laid them on the bed, he noticed that Donovan was on Silas' side of the bed.

"What is he doing here?"

"There was no room on your side." Silas quickly answered.

"Oh. We need to call and have all their rooms acclimatized. I can't deal with sleeping with them another night. Too much tossing and turning and moving and shaking."

"I'll handle that. You need to get dressed, Emperor. Big day!"

Mallory slowly dressed and recited his speech. He walked out of the room toward the kitchen area where Bailey and Chad were engaged in a heated discussion. Although he tiptoed into the room, Bailey shut down the argument and tended to Mallory. "Good morning!" Mallory sung out.

"Hey, cuz?" Bailey said nervously.

"Cuz? O-kay? How was your sleep?"

"Eventful." Chad said and Bailey nudged him hard.

"What?"

"Nothing. Are you ready to go?" Bailey spoke up.

"Yes, I just need to grab my overcoat."

Uncle Myron joined the group and they exited the castle. The three boys climbed into the back of the crème Rolls Royce Phantom, allowing Uncle Myron to sit in the front. Mallory fumbled with his things and realized that he forgot his speech. He attempted to get out, but Bailey grabbed his hand and questioned where he was going.

"I forgot my speech on the bar."

"I'll get it!" Chad and Bailey shouted in unison.

"Okay...I know that I'm the Emperor today, but guys, I'm not that spoiled. I'll get it. Anyway, I want to give my baby a kiss."

"I'll kiss him for you." Bailey interjected, grabbing his hand.

"You're demented. This cold weather is getting to you." Mallory snatched his hand and climbed out of the car. "Let me go." Mallory hopped out of the car.

"Shit! Was Don awake when we left?"

"We shouldn't have left him in the bed. What is his fucking problem?"

"What going on?" Uncle Myron asked.

"Silas and Donovan were..." Chad couldn't bring himself to complete his statement.

"Hell, I'll say it. They were fucking last night, Daddy...in the same bed with Mallory. He was sleep. How do you sleep through something like that?" Bailey paused. "Okay, we have two choices. We can go in and defend Mallory or defend Donovan."

"Why don't we wait to see how Mallory reacts? If he doesn't say anything, we know nothing." Chad tried to reason with Bailey.

"I like your reasoning, but I can't leave Mallory hanging like that. We need to tell him."

"Well, at least wait until after the speech."

Mallory strolled back into the castle and jogged toward the kitchen. He grabbed his speech from the bar, folding it and stuffing it in his overcoat while walking toward the bedroom to look for Silas. As he walked closer to the master bedroom, he heard noises. He grabbed the knob in a rush to open the door, but he couldn't bring himself to twist the knob. He finally took a deep breath and opened the door. Donovan was on top of Silas, rocking his cares away.

"I will be your number one. Say it, Silas...say, 'You are my number one'."

"Oh...shit! You can be any number you want. Oh fuck, I'm cumming!"

Mallory backed away from the door and collided with the wall behind him. His cell phone rang and he quickly retrieved and silenced it. His eyes flooded with tears and he barely caught his breath. He wanted to scream.

"What's that noise? I heard ringing," Donovan froze.

"This place echoes," Silas breathed out.

Mallory flew down the stairs and toward the door. His cell phone rang again, but he waited until he got outside to answer it.

He flipped the phone open and saw that it was a message from Silas.

> Hey baby... Or shall I say Emperor? I love you. You mean everything to me. I wanted to wish you happiness - you don't need luck. You're gonna blow them away with your speech. I know that you are. You are my one and only love. I love you...I think said that already. But oh well, I love you, my baby. Look for me...I will be sitting with your brothers."

Mallory was flabbergasted. He rushed back into the castle to confront Silas, but he paused when he saw him strolling down the stairs. "What are you doing here?"

"I...um...forgot my spe..." Mallory couldn't speak nor could make eye contact with Silas.

"Your speech? Didn't I tell you to put it in your overcoat?" He grabbed Mallory by the lapels and gently opened the coat. He pulled out the folded paper. "See, here it is." He placed the paper back in the pocket. "You're not going to throw up, are you?" Mallory nodded. "Stay here and I will get you a hot towel to wipe your face."

Silas walked away and Mallory stood - paralyzed and dazed. He couldn't believe that Silas tainted the bed that they shared with his cousin. At that moment, he jumped when he felt a hot towel cover his face. Silas gently wiped his eyes and nose. He adjusted and buttoned Mallory's coat. "Did you get my message?"

Mallory nodded. By this time, he barely managed to look into Silas' eyes.

"I love you so much. You're my number one. You mean everything to me. Good luck out there. I'll be there before you know it." He embraced Mallory strongly and then released him a bit to kiss him. Mallory never closed his eyes. In fact, he focused on the stairs and saw Donovan standing there. Mallory began commanding his soul. Donovan tried to fight it, but Mallory's anger was too strong. Eventually, Donovan collapsed and Silas broke the kiss. He looked back to see Donovan lying unconsciously on the stairs. He turned around and saw Mallory walking out of the door. "He knows. SHIT!"

Mallory walked back to the car. He quietly got inside, not making eye contact with anyone. He motioned for the driver to leave. Moments later, Mallory opened the door and vomited. Everyone sat motionless in the car and patiently waited for Mallory to regain his composure. He motioned for the driver to resume and then opened his door and vomited again.

Uncle Myron nervously smiled at the driver and said, "Don't worry; he always throws up before a big speech."

Several stops later, they finally made it to the hotel. Marc was impatiently waiting for them to arrive. Once the car stopped, Mallory flew out of the car and whizzed past Marc.

"Wait! We all need to walk in together – whether you are an emperor or not!" Marc shouted, but Mallory didn't stop. He flew past the door attendant and security. Unbeknownst to him, everyone bowed as he sped through the corridor. He flashed passed Michael who lowered his head in respect. He finally located a restroom and barricaded himself inside a stall. Moments later, Michael walked in. He surveyed the stalls to find Mallory at the end, sitting on the floor, rocking and holding himself.

"Is everything okay, your majesty?" he asked through the stall door.

"Yes, thank you."

"Do you need anything?"

"Peace and quiet, please."

"Mmm...isn't that what we are battling? Peace."

"Leave me, please!"

"My apologies if I offended you. I only come to offer my humble services, Mallory."

Mallory opened the stall door and Michael stood tall before him. He kicked the stall door disrespectfully with his foot.

"How rude...even for an Emperor."

"I'm not an Emperor. I'm the forth horseman, Death."

"Now that you know your rightful place, get out there and make my son proud. He gloats on you. How strong and resilient you are. How understanding and patience you are. How caring and sharing you are."

"Please, just leave me alone."

"I can't do that in your time of need."

"I need you to leave me alone, please. I'm gathering my thoughts for the speech and that's it." Mallory stood up and opened the stall door, forcing Michael out of the way without touching him. He rinsed his face and took a deep breath.

"So why do you look as though someone has cheated on you? Mallory, I knew a man just like you."

"And the moral to this story is?" Mallory folded his arms.

"He was a sensitive man as well. He couldn't accept certain things, such as the concept of sharing. I knew you were the same way. When I asked you to leave my son, it was for your own good."

"Bullshit, you didn't want him to be with a bottom feeder."

"Humans are bottom feeders. You're a little higher up."

"Thank you for your humble services, Allen. I will take it from here." Mallory rinsed his mouth again.

"As you wish..." Michael walked toward the exit door.

"Wait, you're Allen?" Michael smiled and winked as he left the restroom. "This is bullshit! I'm fucking my dead father's boyfriend's son. Oh, this is demented. Being with Matthew was nothing."

Just then, Bailey and Chad walked in. "Are you okay?"

"Yes, I'm ready." Mallory straightened his clothes.

"Mallory, you know that I have your back, right? I would never do anything to hurt you." Bailey began pleading.

"Why are you telling me this?"

The door slammed open and Marc shouted. "Mallory, you missed the breakfast. The summit is about to start."

CHAPTER FOURTEEN

Mallory walked on stage and looked out into the crowd. He poised himself and cleared his throat. As he began to speak, he noticed Silas sneaking into the room. Mallory's throat became hollow and dry. Tears dropped uncontrollably. He forced himself to look down at his speech, but his teardrops smeared the words. He was crashing and burning right before the summit's eyes. He closed his eyes and began reciting the speech that was burned into his memory. He cleared his throat again and eloquently spoke to the audience. As he spoke his last words, the crowd was silent. He exited the stage with his head bowed. As Silas stood up to catch him, the master of ceremonies announced his departure and requested a recess. The crowd stood up in respect, which slowed his exit.

"Mallory, wait!" Silas shouted. Mallory rushed down the stairway and through the double doors. He turned left, but saw his brothers approaching, so he darted right and headed toward another set of doors. "Mallory, wait!" Silas trailed closely behind. Mallory finally reached the outside doors, but Silas waved his hands and had the door shut down. He finally caught up to Mallory. "Wait, let me explain."

"There is nothing to explain. Just let me go, Silas," Mallory pleaded, trying to hold down his emotions.

"I need to explain."

"LET ME GO!" Mallory's voice echoed and his anger bellowed into the room.

"Oh damn," Marlon flew down the hallway and stopped short of Silas. "There are people falling out in the auditorium. I think they're dying!"

"Let me go, Silas. Just let me go." Mallory pleaded. His eyes began turning blue.

"No, we need to talk about this."

Just then, Michael rushed into the hallway and shouted, "People are dying left and right. What is going on?" He looked at Silas, then to Mallory. He saw that Mallory was transforming before his eyes.

"Sir, two-thirds of the audience is dead." Silas' guards reported.

"Mallory, stop! Let me explain."

"Let me go!" Mallory shouted again and this time his voice echoed like thunder.

"There are 37 people alive." MJ reported, sensing the souls in the room.

"Shit! People are dying, Silas. Let him go!" Bailey shouted.

"Stop, Mallory. We need to talk, baby. Control yourself." Silas walked closer to him. "I'm not letting you go until we talk about this."

"Silas!" his dad commanded. "There are fifteen people still living in this room. If he is killing these people, let him go!"

Bailey jumped down from the stairs and pulled the emergency release to open the doors. Mallory quickly flew out of the auditorium and disappeared into the cold, gloomy air.

"He doesn't have his coat." Silas sat at the bottom of the steps. "He's gonna freeze."

"I'll get him his coat! You just stay away from him." Bailey shouted and rushed out to find Mallory.

Mallory hoisted himself next to the bar and nursed a drink. He couldn't believe that Silas slept with his cousin and even worse, he couldn't believe that Silas did it right behind his back. Literally! As Mallory sipped his eighth Vodka tonic, he felt someone standing behind him. To Mallory, it looked like Quincy. He flashed a fake half smile and pulled up a chair. Quincy ordered a Scotch and water, which was peculiar to Mallory since Quincy was a recovering alcoholic. They sat in silence for several moments, before Quincy broke the silence. "What are we drinking to?"

"Stupidity."

"Isn't stupidity a choice?"

Mallory looked at him harshly. Quincy's statement sounded very similar to a comment that Malcolm made. "I heard Bailey say that one time. How does it go? You're born dumb, you choose to be stupid and you die an idiot."

Mallory huffed, "Malcolm incarnate."

Quincy sat silently for a moment. That was something Malcolm said. "Sorry, I guess I listen to Bailey and your uncles too much. They're characters."

Mallory nodded.

"Are you okay?"

"No, Quincy. My brothers hate me. I'm not respected in my family and I'm running an empire that I don't want. My boyfriend, that I love dearly, is fucking my cousin. Everyone keeps taking things from me and I'm bloody pissed about it."

"Suck it up. It can be worse."

"Is that what they teach you in AA or are you just taking this opportunity to enhance my pain for your revenge?"

"I wouldn't do that to you, son."

Mallory downed the drink and ordered another one. "Maybe I'm not satisfying him. Maybe he is getting bored with me. Maybe I'm just too much of a high-maintenance emotional wreck."

"Maybe he is just an ass wipe that fucks what he sees. He just has an insatiable appetite."

"I have an insatiable appetite, but I'm faithful." Mallory pointed out.

"You do, son?"

"Yes, you don't remember?"

"That one night that we spent together was a blur to me. I vaguely remember." Malcolm took over so much of Quincy that he'd forgotten most of Quincy's memories.

"Vaguely remember? We spent three weeks together. You don't remember any of that?"

"Yeah, I do. We had a great time." Quincy stuttered. "We were at your penthouse. We had a great time in the pool and we romped around all night."

Mallory downed his drink and stood up. "You don't remember. I see how Marek feels about my blackouts."

"Yes, I do." Quincy stood up. "The first night that we were together you had that sexy tattoo of the dragon on your washboard abs that journeyed down...." He smiled and then realized that was not a good memory for Mallory. "Why are you getting so angry?"

"You're not describing us; you're describing my fucking boyfriend. I didn't have the tattoo the night I fucked on the pool table in public!" He grabbed Quincy's drink and downed it. "Close my tab. He's paying for his own drink." He stormed out of the bar.

As Mallory walked in circles around the small town, he felt so angry and hurt. He passed people on the street and nonchalantly watched men fall to the ground, clenching their chests and dying. After a while, Mallory turned around and noticed that he left a trail of dead men in the wake behind him. He tried to calm down, but every time he passed a man, it was a death sentence. Mallory fell to the ground and screamed. Bailey finally found Mallory lying in the snow outside the bar. He kneeled down to see if Mallory was breathing.

"Why don't you just kill me now?" Mallory mumbled. "I know you want to."

Bailey replied, "Look, there are two questions I am not going to ask you. One, are you okay and two, do you want to kill a motherfucker because you will piss me off if the answer to either one is no."

"Then kill me now." Mallory ordered.

Suddenly, a dark shadow covered his body and made him shiver. "I'll take it from here." Michael said, reaching out his hand for Mallory.

"Fate worse than death and Hell is Satan's dad stalking me."

"You can lay there and sulk or you can do something about it. Either way, I'm not going anywhere."

"Oh, bloody hell!" As Mallory grabbed his hand, a bolt of lightning hit the ground and the dead men began to stir. They came to life and slowly sat up. Mallory lifted himself up and looked around at the newly risen dead. "You did that?" Mallory asked.

"No, you did that. I just redirected your power."

They returned to the bar and Mallory ordered a bottle of Vodka just for himself. "I know you're a happy man now!" he exclaimed sarcastically.

"I warned you, but you didn't listen. You were the arrogant one, thinking that you could hurt my son. A fate worse than death and Hell is an eternal broken heart with no forgiveness.

You can never hurt my son, 'cause he has no heart." He then mumbled, "Thanks to your father."

"What did my father do to him?"

"He stole my son's innocence." He paused. "Your father was a serial male predator. He preyed on the weakness of men for his pleasure. He used their shame for his enjoyment. He targeted men who were vulnerable - men who didn't want people to know what their secrets were. He used it for control. He thought I was his prey once. I let him play the game. I liked it - the power he thought he had was intoxicating. Then when he tried to blackmail me, it backfired. I didn't care what secrets he had about me, they weren't my secrets. He was pissed." He paused, "So he took it out on Silas. He knew that Silas had a big crush on him and he twisted my little boy and made him into a mini Malcolm. Sad to say, I was too love-blind to see what was going on."

"You were in love with my dad?" Mallory huffed. "I remember the flowers and wine that you sent him."

"That was the one thing your father couldn't stand...someone loving him. That's why he hated you so. If you would've just hated him, he would still be here."

"You blame me for that?" Mallory asked in anger.

Michael bowed his head in shame, "I know I shouldn't, but yes. However, that's behind us now." Michael leaned back in his chair. "You have done something that no one has been able to do in hundreds of years. Gain complete loyalty in the empire. And that stunt you pulled at the conference showed your strength. You killed off all of the naysayers and you proved that the empire was still strong. The spirits love you. They think you're irreplaceable."

"I didn't do it for me, I did it for Silas."

"Understandably, but they see you two as one. They won't accept him without you. You're powerful."

Mallory frowned, "Do you know what powerful means to me? FUCKED! I am so bloody fucked. And do you know why I am so fucked? Because I don't know how bloody fucked I am!"

"I never saw it that way. Regardless, you can't walk away from the empire."

"Why not?"

Michael paused before he confessed, "It would collapse."

"How is that my problem?"

"I guess it's not. But I would greatly appreciate it if you stayed. Maybe I can make you an offer. Stay for a year. Just long enough to complete your vision and I'll try to get you out of it and forgive you for killing my lover."

Mallory laughed, "I don't give a rat's ass about your bloody lover," He paused, "You have a year...from today. And if I'm not out, I'll walk away, then turn around and watch it collapse with a smile plastered on my face."

"Thank you, Mallory."

"Don't thank me." Mallory took a deep breath, "I'm going on holiday."

CHAPTER FIFTEEN

Mallory sat at the café table reading the paper and drinking tea. He looked up when a shadow fell over him. It was Matthew. He wanted to jump up in his arms and embrace him, but instead he flashed a sweet smile. He never parted his lips.

"Hello, Emerald." Mallory nodded. "I was just in the neighborhood and I saw you sitting here. I thought I would stop by and say hi." Mallory's smiled melted. "I was dropping in to cheer you up?" Mallory eyes dropped. "Okay, I have been watching you for weeks and I didn't know how to approach you. I thought this would be a good time to see you, since this is the third day that you haven't sobbed." He peered up at him. "He doesn't deserve you. You know that, aye?"

Mallory returned to reading his paper. "I deserve you?"

"Yes, you do! I have always been the best man for you... Even better than that Chuckie character." Matthew claimed proudly. He wanted sit down, but he waited until Mallory was ready.

"You know, I have been trying to reorganize my life and I don't get something. You forced me to be with you on many occasions. Our first time wasn't in Amsterdam. Was Amsterdam a farce?"

"It was the first time that we were together as humans." He paused. "Emerald, I'm sorry. I guess love to me means something different than it does to you. You can accept rejection. I can't."

"If I could accept rejection, why I am sitting here pissed because Silas rejected me?"

"Because you don't know how to reset his life yet." Matthew laughed, but Mallory didn't find the humor in his comment. "I'm sorry." Matthew searched for any comment that would cheer him up. "You're unforgettable. I remember every time we were together."

"Really?" Mallory perked up a bit. "Every time?"

Matthew nodded.

"How many times were we together?"

"During college or after college?"

"Both."

"College...37 times. After college, 517."

Mallory smiled. "You remember every time?"

"Pick a time."

"78th..."

"Amsterdam."

"You're going to say Amsterdam for every time." Mallory lowered his head.

"No, I won't. Our 98th time, we were in Sydney for New Year's. You came four times. Our 162nd time, we were in Hong Kong for some conference. You came a number of times. You kept sneaking out of the conference, remember? And, our 218th time, we were in that hot air balloon. Neither one of us came."

"Don't remind me of that." Mallory lightened up a bit. "Have a seat. What about the 300th time?"

"We made love on the roof. That was the turning point in our relationship. I enjoyed it every time, except for two. The first time...I'm sorry for that."

"And the last time?"

"I'm really sorry for that. I was so angry...but I didn't know how to express it. Please forgive me."

Mallory lowered his eyes. He folded his paper and grabbed his cup of tea. "Do you want some cheesecake?"

"I shouldn't." Matthew profusely nodded his head.

"What are you doing, watching that Heavenly figure? You know that you want a slice of cheesecake. Is it turtle or...oh...regular with Oreo crust with lots of whipped cream."

"Stop it. You're sinful."

Mallory waved for the waitress. "Can I get a slice of your Oreo cheesecake and a cappuccino? Thank you."

Matthew smiled. "You're wrong."

"And you're still beautiful." Mallory smiled.

"I wanted to comfort you a long time ago, but I didn't know how you would take seeing me. Our last meeting didn't go so well."

"So you came down just for me?"

"You're the only reason I come to Earth, Emerald." The waitress brought a beautifully decorated plate of Oreo cheesecake with a mountain of whipped cream on the side. Mallory grabbed a fork and cut a small piece. When he fed him, Matthew's eyes rolled to the back of his head as he slowly allowed the cheesecake to melt in his mouth. "Maybe you're the second reason why I come to Earth." They laughed.

"Want to bump me to three?" Mallory prepared his cappuccino with six sugars and more cream.

Matthew took long sips of his delightful drink. "This tastes so good. It is so hot, creamy and sweet and velvety smooth."

"Like you." Mallory smiled and fed him another piece.

"I miss us," Matthew confessed between bites.

"I do too sometimes. It was simpler with us."

"It was just about us, no one else. It only got complicated when others were around."

"True. Matty, I'm so tired. I'm tired of fighting and screaming and living. I'm tired."

Matthew heard the frustration in his voice. "Oh, baby, it's okay." He grabbed his hand, "I'm here now. Your angel is here." He kissed Mallory's falling tears. "Do you want to see Heaven?"

"And get a headache again?" Mallory frowned and quickly retorted. "I don't think so."

"Come on...I think I have something for the 'After Heaven' headache." Matthew wolfed down the last bite before leaving.

Mallory woke up in Matthew's arms. Matthew was rubbing his chest. He slowly opened his eyes, anticipating the pain in his head. "I don't have the headache."

"I'm allowing you to remember. You deserve a little piece of Heaven."

"You were my little piece of Heaven. It's amazing how you feel when you're up there. How people love you and worship you."

"Like they worship you in Hell? Do they bow to you in Hell?" Matthew started interrogating him, knowing very well that he knew the answers.

Mallory sat up. "It's not the same. It's quiet and peaceful and serene in Heaven."

"Like you can't command that when you're down there. I've seen you do it, Mallory."

Mallory wanted to change the subject. "So, when are you leaving?"

"Baby, let's not worry about that." Matthew grabbed his arms and pulled him down.

"When, Matthew?"

"Why are you worried? Just enjoy the time we have."

"I can't just enjoy the time. I have a bad habit of getting accustomed." Mallory sat up again.

"I don't know. Let's just enjoy this time for now please."

CHAPTER SIXTEEN

"So you're excited about The Open?" Marc practiced his golf swing.

"Hell, yeah! Mallory worked so hard to get me an invitation. I wonder does he remember that it's this weekend."

"He worked hard? You've been playing golf since you were in diapers. If you didn't have to take over, you would've been pro and Tiger would be nothing to people." Marc shouted his praises, but made sure that he didn't mention Silas' brother's death. "You're the one who maintained a 65 shooting average. What'd he do?"

"He handled the politics behind it. He pulled strings so I could get the invitation but make it look like I wasn't pulling any favors. He's better at that than I am." Silas tried hard not to show that he was missing Mallory. "Don, baby, don't forget to get my clubs out the trunk." He winked at him. "This is my last shot. After this, I'm going to the empire full-time. I think Mallory is getting tired. Is he, Bailey?"

"I don't know... I'd say that he is fine."

"Silas, why did you buy his company back?" Marc asked.

"At the time we were still together and he asked. Nicely, I might add." Silas recalled Mallory walking into their bedroom, fully covered in whipped cream. "Shit, I couldn't say no. I can never say no to that boy." Silas looked down at his ring and mumbled to himself, "I miss him so much."

"What if he wants to buy HIC?" Marc inquired. "You gotta protect us."

"Protect you from what? That's stupid. What do you need protection from, Mallory? He belongs there! He was just helping me out until I was ready to run the company. What's to buy?"

"Mallory doesn't think straight all the time. He walked away from the company."

"No, he didn't, Marc! I remember you pushed him out." Silas barked, "Marc, now you're overreacting. Besides, we have an agreement. Don't give him a reason to come after you. I'm handling him from my end. He has plenty to worry about than going after you."

"Oh, he won't come after me. I have a contract out on his ass. All I need to do is say GO!" Marc positioned his club for a swing.

"WHOA! What is this contract?" Silas snatched the club from Marc's grip.

"Mallory has enemies. You can't protect him from everything."

"We have an agreement!" Silas tapped the club on Marc's chest hard.

"I will hold you to your agreement. But you're not my only option." Marc huffed, snatching the club. "Speaking of which, where is your lover boy?"

"I don't know." Silas sulked. "Where is my plane?" The attendant rushed out to meet with Silas and the group. "Where is my plane?" he asked again.

"Your father took your plane and there was an unscheduled flight for the other plane. But, it is due back as we speak."

"I have to wait?" Silas shouted out.

"Only moments, sir," The attendant looked up, "Actually, there it is now."

The group of men watched as the plane landed and taxied in their direction. Once it stopped, the workers scurried around to get the plane ready for the next flight. The door opened and Mallory exited the plane with his arm wrapped around Matthew's waist. As they descended from the plane, everyone was shock.

Marc's moth flew open, "Oh my –"

"FUCK!" Silas shouted.

"Who is that?" Bailey asked.

Once Mallory reached the bottom of the stairs, he kissed Matthew on the lips then walked toward the crowd.

"How in the fuck can you use my plane for this shit?" Silas shouted out.

"Your plane?" Mallory snapped. "Bailey, what does that word say on the belly of that plane?"

"I don't want to be a part of this faggoty bullshit, Mallory." Bailey recoiled.

"Answer my bloody question!" Mallory shouted.

"Tenacious." Bailey regrettably answered.

"Isn't X-stacy your plane?" Mallory snapped in Silas' direction.

"Both of them are mine!" Silas snapped back. "I gave you that plane as a company perk."

"You did? Oh, my...I'm sorry I misunderstood. Let me see...my penthouses in Austin, Denver and San Francisco are company perks. My flat in London, my villa in Thailand and choice of exotic cars that I drive in any city that I travel to are company perks. My time off when I want it, my 19.2-million part-time salary, the ownership portion of the company and my global memberships to gyms and spas are company perks." Mallory paused and swallowed hard, then shouted, "But that bloody plane that you see here, I EARNED THAT BITCH by doing

BLOODY handstands while you fucked the shit out of me. That is NOT a company perk. Don't get it twisted, there is a reason Donovan doesn't have one." He turned to Donovan. "And if you get any wild ideas, it takes him 22 minutes to cum...that is if you're lucky enough and he fucks you before he has a shot of Hennessey. My record is three times a night, in case you're interested."

"You're a son of a bitch!" Silas shouted, grabbing Mallory's arm.

"No motherfucker I'm flexible. You're the son of a bitch who thinks he can find something better than me."

"I never said that he was better than you." Silas whispered softly.

"He's something because you're with him now. But, he will never be me." Mallory said and wrestled his arm from Silas' grasp.

"Mallory..." Silas grabbed for his arm again, but Mallory snatched it back. "Are you going be happy with Mr. 43-strokes?" Silas said. "I have the liberty to get more strokes in golf and will still win the game more than you will in the bedroom."

"Humph," Mallory popped Silas collar, "Well, take all the strokes you can get on the golf course, because that's the only quality stroking you gonna get. Has he even gotten to the level of a Dodge Neon, let alone a paper airplane?"

"Fuck you, Mallory!" Donovan shouted.

"Position taken. My brother is back. Say hello, Matthew."

"Hello, Matthew." Matthew mimicked Mallory's sarcasm and then waved to Marc and winked at Marlon.

"Matthew, I take it everything is well!" Marc said darkly. "And in order!

"Very well and in order," Matthew answered back and then smiled when he saw Marlon shot him the finger. "Where is my friend, Marek?"

"Don't tease if he's not here. Shall we go?" Mallory grabbed Matthew's arm and escorted him to the Bentley. "You want to drive, baby?" He handed the keys to Matthew and opened the door for him.

"Mallory, that's a company perk and he NOT an employee." Silas angrily reminded him.

"No, this is your personal car. I would never let him drive any of my cars. Angels can't drive; you know that, Road Rage Ho!" Mallory countered before slamming the car door. Matthew started the car and peeled off.

"Handstand? How can you do a..." Bailey began picturing the scene in his mind and he grossed himself out. "I guess we are not going."

"We're going. I'm not missing my Open for some bullshit," He watched as Matthew sped off. "That motherfucker took my car and gave it to a son of a bitch who can't drive. My clubs!" He turned and delivered an Earth-shattering shout. "MALLORY STOP!"

Matthew slammed on the brakes and threw the car in reverse. He stopped just short of hitting Silas. Mallory jumped out just as the trunk popped open. He grabbed Silas' golf bag from the trunk and threw it on the ground. All of Silas' custom-made clubs flew out of the bag.

"Good luck. I hope you shoot a million." He got back in the car and Matthew scratched the gears before peeling off again.

Marc watched them both drive away. "I hope Mallory don't fuck my contract to kill out of place." he sighed.

CHAPTER SEVENTEEN

The next morning, Matthew woke up to find Mallory out of bed. The aroma of bacon floated through the air. He slowly crawled out of bed and inadvertently walked into Silas' closet. Although it pissed him off that they stayed at the penthouse and not Mallory's house, he loved Silas' taste in clothing. He grabbed one of Silas' t-shirts with 'EVIL' plastered across the chest and a pair of his jeans. He walked out of the bedroom and down the stairs where Tanic, the dog, met him at the bottom. He picked her up and walked into the kitchen.

"Why didn't we have a dog?" Matthew asked Mallory, who was so enthralled watching the U.S. Open that he didn't answer. "Mallory!"

"Yeah, baby. Breakfast is ready."

"Why didn't we have a dog?"

"I'm dog-phobic," Mallory snapped back. "Besides, we had a son. Phillip, remember?"

Matthew grunted and then walked into the kitchen. He grabbed a strip of bacon, placed it in his mouth, and allowed the dog to take a bite.

"Did you just kiss that dog?" Mallory walked up behind him and startled him.

"No!" Matthew lied. "But a dog's mouth is cleaner than humans."

"How about angels?" Mallory asked sarcastically. "Don't kiss that dog. I made you a southwestern omelet."

"An omelet? No waffles?"

"Oh, I forgot you like waffles. The omelet is good." Mallory said, making his plate and then bee-lining back to the television.

"When did you start liking golf?" Matthew asked, but Mallory didn't answer. Matthew sat down and caught a glimpse of the game. Silas was tied for first place on hole fifteen, ready to tee off. "Are you really watching this?" Matthew asked. Mallory still didn't answer as he moved from the couch to the floor to get closer to the television.

Silas swung his driver and hit the ball 313 yards into the fairway. "YES!" Mallory shouted to himself, realizing that Matthew was getting frustrated. "You don't know how much effort I put into this man."

"Probably more effort than you put into me." Matthew said as he picked at the omelet. "You know I don't like eggs and peppers, right?"

"I forgot. You want something else?" Mallory asked without taking his eyes off the television.

"I want you to pay some attention to me." Matthew said.

"Okay, I'll make it in a minute," Mallory answered impassively. After a few moments, Matthew slammed his plate on the table and stormed into the bedroom. Mallory never flinched. He was glued to the game. "You better win, you son of a bitch. As much as you put me through, you better win." He shouted at television.

After a while, Mallory asked without turning around, "So do you want to eat—" not realizing that Matthew had left the room. He huffed and sulked back to the couch when he realized Matthew wasn't there. "This is going to be a bitch of a day." He got up to search for Matthew. As he returned to the bedroom, he heard the shower turn off and he sat on the bed waiting for Matthew to come out.

Matthew walked out of the bathroom into the bedroom. He saw Mallory lying on the bed, rolled his eyes, and walked into Silas' closet. A few moments later, he walked out with a fresh pair of Silas' khakis and one of Silas' favorite golf shirts. Mallory was still lying on the bed, watching him.

"Let's get out the house," Mallory suggested.

Matthew finally flopped on the bed, still rolling his eyes. "Where are we going, to a driving range?"

"I'm not arguing with you." Mallory pushed Matthew down on the bed and rolled over on him. "Let's go visit the Creamery."

"Do you not love me anymore?"

"I'm not going to fight with you." Mallory nuzzled his nose against Matthew's ear. "Let's fuck."

"I'm not worth the fight?"

"Can you tell my dick is getting hard?" Mallory pressed his pelvis against Matthew.

Matthew pushed him back and asked. "Is that how Silas speaks to you when you're angry?"

"Look, if you're angry, then take it out on me." Mallory wrapped his arms around Matthew's body and bit his ear, "I'll be your whipping boy."

"Where is my Emerald?" Matthew whispered in his ear.

Mallory sat up for a moment and then jumped out of the bed. "Fine, you have five minutes to bitch."

"Are you serious?"

Mallory beelined for the bathroom. "We're going to the creamery."

Meanwhile, Silas was getting ready for the sudden death hole. He had been tied for first place with Tiger Woods for the entire tournament. Tiger brought his A-game, but Silas stayed on his heels. They stood at the designated hole and waited for the coin toss. Heads won which meant Silas went second. The two walked toward each other and shook hands.

"Good luck," Tiger said coldly.

"It is an honor," Silas answered with a smile.

As Tiger turned to walk away, he started limping. The weather had suddenly turned cold, which made his knee throb. This was the very thing that Silas had been waiting for - weakness. Tiger studied the hole before placing his tee in the ground. He hit the ball 165 yards. To the crowd, he appeared confident with his stroke, but Silas read fear in his eyes.

As Silas surveyed the hole, he felt a sudden dull pain. It felt as if he'd been running fast and suddenly hit a brick wall. He instantly shook it off and placed the tee just left of the center. As he wound back to hit the ball, a sharp pain pierced his side. Silas hit the ball so awkwardly that it bounced off two trees and landed in the fairway, making it a perfect tee off. He dropped to his knees, clutching his side. Michael and Marc ran to his aid. Marc snatched a towel from Silas' caddy and cupped Silas' face. He wiped sweat from his brow and asked, "Hey! What's up?"

"Where's my ball?"

They both looked up and then Michael answered. "It's in the fairway, son. What's wrong?"

"How many yards do I need?"

"About thirty..."

"How many does he need?" Silas huffed out.

"Twenty-five? Are you okay?"

"Walk me to my ball."

Marc grabbed Silas' bag from the caddy. He grabbed his arm and they walked down the fairway. Marc looked over and noticed blood on Silas' shirt. He stopped and leaned on Marc, watching Tiger hit the ball. The ball landed on the green, one foot short of the flag. Everyone sighed.

"Thirty yards?" Silas asked between labored breaths. Marc noticed that blood was escaping his mouth. "Give me my pitching wedge." Silas grabbed the club and walked to his ball, using the club as a cane. Everyone clearly noticed that Silas didn't look at the green to determine where or how hard to hit the ball. He closed his eyes and with a loud grunt, he swung. Everyone watched the ball closely. Silas hit the ball so high in the air that when it finally came down, it hit the flag and fell into the hole. The crowd went wild. Marc ran to the fairway - not to congratulate Silas, but to catch him in mid-fall. Marc reached him too late and Silas hit the ground hard.

Marc landed on his knees, screaming Silas' name, but he didn't respond. The EMT ran to the fairway and put him on a stretcher. Blood ran out of his mouth and his shirt was drenched with it, combined with sweat. Michael guided the EMT to the ambulance. He, along with Marc and Bailey, jumped into the vehicle and they were rushed to the closest hospital. The hospital staff cut Silas' shirt open to locate the wound, but were unable to find it. Silas was bleeding through his skin. As they tried to resuscitate him, the monitor went off and his heart stopped beating.

Silas found himself standing on top of a small hill. He looked down and saw tire tracks burned into the ground. His eyes followed the tire tracks until he saw the Bentley that was crashed into a big tree. It was the car that Mallory and Matthew took from him couple days ago. Silas ran to the car to find Mallory passed-out in the passenger seat. He tried to open the door, but he couldn't because as a spirit his form wasn't solid. He screamed through the broken window to Mallory who finally woke up. Mallory tried to gather enough energy to open the door, but realized he couldn't. Silas kept yelling, begging him to get out.

When he finally moved, Mallory screamed and clutched his left side. Silas noticed blood oozing between Mallory's fingers. He looked in the backseat and saw that his sword had pushed through the passenger seat and impaled Mallory. Silas couldn't grab the sword nor could he move him. He screamed out again to Mallory, who kept floating in and out of consciousness.

Silas started paced back and forth, wondering what to do. He realized that smoke was emanating from the back of the car and ran back to Mallory, screaming and begging him to get out of the car. Mallory tried again and succeeded in pulling the sword out of his side, but that took all of his strength. His head hit the dashboard as he passed-out again. Silas kept screaming for him to wake up. Exhausted, Silas collapsed onto the ground. Mallory was out cold and Silas couldn't do anything about it. He couldn't think of a way to save Mallory. As Silas watched the blood blanket the passenger seat, he bowed his head.

"Please, don't die. Please, don't die." Silas raised his head when he heard small explosions. He screamed out again, "Don't let him die, God, please. PLEASE, God, don't let him die."

A man appeared in the driver's seat and replied, "Silas, if I save him...you will have to fulfill my promise."

"ANYTHING! PLEASE!"

"I will need you to choose Humanity."

"I'LL DO ANYTHING! PLEASE SAVE HIM!"

The man disappeared and the car exploded.

CHAPTER EIGHTEEN

Mallory found himself sitting on the ground by the side of the road. He looked both ways to see where he was but the area was unfamiliar to him. Even though the sun was bright, there was a dense fog of the ground. Although his body ached, he stood up and took a few steps. He looked both ways again, but there were no cars or trucks around. He was on a strange-looking deserted road. He started to walk down the road, but he stopped because he didn't know which direction to go. He looked down, but he couldn't see his feet. The road was covered in fog. He took a deep breath and then chose to walk to his left.

Mallory heard music from afar and looked back, but there was no car or truck in sight. As he limped along, the music grew louder. All of a sudden, a metallic orange Lamborghini appeared and its door opened. Mallory leaned down to see who was inside the car and recognized the short, pudgy man holding a Starbucks coffee cup.

"Going my way?" The man smiled.

Mallory returned the sentiment with a sarcastic flair. "Should I be going your way?"

"I can make the journey easier."

"Or harder. It depends on what humorous, sadistic mood you're in." As Mallory slid into the car, his pain made him grunt.

"Are we in pain?"

"Isn't that the only time we ever meet? When I'm in pain - figurative or otherwise?"

"I see we are out of sorts today?"

Mallory huffed and then asked with a crack in his voice, "Am I dead?"

"Not yet..." The man commanded the door closed. "Do you want to be?"

Mallory didn't answer. As the man sped off, he turned the volume up on the radio and started singing.

"They're going to sue you for copyright infringement," Mallory said.

The man smiled and continued singing, "So go ahead and come home and leave that booze and drugs alone. Oops, I betcha thought that I didn't know - what do you think I'm picking you up for? Because you were untrue, rolling around in a life that I gave you. Boy, dropped them keys, you're only a co-pilot, please. Standing at the crossroad holding a bottle of Vodka or two, telling it, I'll never ever find a God like you. You got me twisted."

The chorus of the song sounded like Beyoncé's, but the lyrics were different. "You must not know 'bout Him, You must not know 'bout Him."

The man sung in a commanding tone, "So don't you ever for a second get to thinking that I AM REPLACEABLE!"

Mallory smiled, "Wow, I needed that reminder."

"You need a lot of things.

"Do you give anybody else this much attention?" Mallory asked through clenched teeth as he fought the pain.

"Only my favorite sinners." He answered.

"I bet you tell that to all the sinners."

The man laughed, then sang, "To the left, to the left. To the left, to the left." He leaned over, waiting for Mallory to sing.

Mallory indulged him and sung softly, "Hmmm...to the left, to the left. Place your burdens in a box to the left."

The man sang loudly, "So don't you ever for a second get to thinking that I AM REPLACEABLE!"

Mallory smiled, which relieved some of his pain.

"I don't know why you fight me so. You know I love you."

"I guess because You are a reminder that I'm supposed to love myself and I don't do that some days. And when I see you, you make me feel guilty."

"My love doesn't hurt, Mallory. It shouldn't be a burden or guilt. Maybe there are some other issues."

"You know my issues, why don't you tell me?" Mallory snapped.

"Mallory, you know I'm not going to fight with you." The man grabbed his hand firmly. Mallory felt the anxiety release from his body. "You need to forgive yourself. The choices that you make are only as good as the tools you have in your life. I know you love your father and you feel bad because you think you shouldn't have. But you were a child and children are supposed to love their parents."

Tears fell from Mallory eyes.

"Forgive yourself for your choices. Love yourself for who you are. And if you can't do that, then love yourself because I love you."

Mallory nodded his head like an obedient child.

"Now, do you want to die?"

"No...no," he answered between sniffs.

"I thought so. Your time hasn't come yet." The car stopped and the door opened. "Look, you have an hour before you bleed out. MJ is at that restaurant next to the church." He pointed to Frenchy's Chicken Shack. "Tell him to take you to Ben Taub Hospital after you leave the church."

"Wait! I can't go back to Ben Taub. They will lock me up again." Mallory opened the door then thought. "You want me to pray now?"

"Yes, I want you to pray for forgiveness, not from me, but from yourself."

"Okay," Mallory crawled out of the car. "I guess I should say thank you."

"I will accept it, but this rescue came in a form of a prayer from Silas. Sometimes I feel that he loves me more than humans."

"I think he does."

"That was why he gets so upset with me. But he made me a promise and by God I AM, meaning me, I'm gonna hold him to it."

"What was the promise?"

The man laughed, "You have an hour, Mallory." The door closed and the car sped off, leaving Mallory alone. He limped inside the church.

When he came to, Mallory was lying in a hospital bed. He felt groggy and his body ached with pain. He tried to move his hands, but tubes and wires were in his way and his feet were bound. He wanted to scream, but his throat was too dry and ached profusely.

MJ quickly jumped from his chair and ran to Mallory's aid, grabbing a cup of water. Mallory tried to drink it, but when he touched the cup, the water turned to ice. MJ heated the cup with his hands and tried again. Mallory fought with the cup.

"Uncle Town, I need to you to focus." MJ ordered.

"I hurt," his voice scratched out. He lifted his head a bit, looking for the button to dispense his medication, but it was not there. "I hurt!"

"I know." MJ took the cup from Mallory. "They found some records from the last time you were here and you were tagged as a pain killer abuser."

"What?"

"Yeah, Uncle Marc put the fuck on you! No pain meds - not even during surgery."

Tears fell from Mallory's eyes, "I hurt, MJ!"

"You know I got you!" MJ shook a pill bottle. "But I need you focus. You can't swallow ice."

Mallory took a deep, painful breath and grabbed the hot water again, but it still turned to ice. "I don't need water."

"Yeah, you do. If it wasn't for me, you would still have a tube down your throat. If you woke up with that tube, everybody in this hospital would be dead. Now focus!"

Mallory popped the pills in his mouth and grabbed for the water.

"Stop fighting me, MALLORY!" MJ shouted, "Allow me to help you."

Mallory clasped his hands together.

MJ grabbed his head and served him the water. "Good boy, you should feel better soon." MJ pulled his chair closer to the bed. He sat down and grabbed Mallory's hand. "We almost lost you. You lost so much blood. We didn't know what happened, so I looked in your Chroniclesation. I hope you're not mad."

"No, that's why I taught you how to view the Master Tape and I gave you Silas' access."

"Matthew crashed the car on purpose, but we don't know why. After he crashed the car, he dematerialized in thin air."

Mallory grunted.

"I was scared. I don't want to lose you."

He took a deep breath. "You're my favorite."

"I know," MJ smiled, "Sometimes I wish you were my dad."

"Really, even with the embarrassing gay thing?"

"It's easier to get over an embarrassing father than to fill the vacancy of an absentee one." MJ's words broke his own heart, but he was not going to let a tear fall. "Besides, who else would sleep with my Trig teacher so I could pass the class?"

"Which one was that, the Asian woman?"

"No, that was Monty's Trig teacher."

"I thought Monty's was the big black woman."

"No, that was Mauryn's Trig teacher." MJ laughed, "Well, it's a good thing that Maxwell is good in Trig."

"But not in English...uhh, that was a hairy man." They both laughed until Mallory started coughing. "Sometimes, I wish you were my son."

"Well, momma would have LOVED that opportunity. I think she is still willing."

"Marc will kill me!" Mallory cleared his throat. "I owe that son of bitch...painkiller abuser! Motherfucker!"

"Look, I need you to calm down. If you don't, your body temperature won't go up and they'll keep you in ICS and label you terminally ill. Then you would be on suicide watch."

"Is that why my feet are bound?"

"Uncle Marc. He told them that you were homo-suicidal." MJ snickered at the comment.

"Why are my hands not bound?"

"'Cause, I didn't want you waking up killing people when you couldn't scratch your nose."

"Have I killed anybody in hospital?"

MJ paused then answered, "Eighteen, but Silas showed me how to reverse it." MJ explained, "You were in pain and you were acting out. It's resolved now. We are just worried about you. You need to get better."

"Speaking of the devil, is he around?"

"He's never left your side." MJ leaned in, "I think he is scared that you might kill him."

Mallory whispered, "I've tried. If I could, he would have been dead a long time ago!"

MJ laughed, "I gotta go, Uncle T. Are you gonna be alright?"

"Are you going to leave that bottle?"

"EVERY FOUR HOURS UNCLE T, not a minute sooner!" MJ held the bottle for a moment before letting it go. Mallory tucked the coveted bottle underneath his pillow. MJ leaned in again and whispered, "I love you," and then kissed him on his forehead.

Mallory watched him walk out and saw Silas. He wanted to rush to Mallory's side, but he stood at the door, watching. Mallory finally broke the awkward silence and said, "If you really loved me, I would have a morphine drip right now."

"Who says that you don't?" Silas leaned on the door.

"I don't feel it."

"It's not on. Besides, you gotta wait four hours... until you can something else."

"I didn't take those pills!"

"Mallory, I saw you take them!" Silas shouted.

Mallory pouted, "My back is itching." Silas rushed over and removed the covers. Mallory couldn't turn over because his feet were still bound. "You couldn't stop Marc from putting the fuck on me? I told you that you never stand up for me against Marc."

Silas didn't respond. He removed the restraints and rolled Mallory over. He massaged his back while gently running his fingers over the stitched wound where they had to remove his kidney.

"I'm so tired and terribly cold."

Silas covered Mallory with a blanket and crawled next to him. He touched the IV bag and it turned into a morphine drip. He tucked the pillow underneath his head and wrapped his arm around Mallory. He kissed the back of his neck and said, "Let's get your mind off this coldness and anger. Let's consume something. Close your eyes and let's collect lost souls in Hell and I'll keep you warm."

"I'm not angry, but I do want to talk."

"Not a good idea right now. Come on, this exercise will be easy," Silas kissed the back of his neck. "Just focus..."

"This exercise is a waste of time. Let's talk about us. That will keep me warm." Mallory paused, "How did we get here?"

Silas huffed. "I don't know...but I do know that I don't want to lose you. You're everything to me."

CHAPTER TWENTY

Kirby sat on the couch, patiently waiting for Silas to come downstairs. Silas was hosting a mega Back Door Event that was the king of all events. People were flying in from everywhere - it was to the point that this event was like the Superbowl, or something close to it. He was so excited that Silas s asked him to be his personal escort, but he was a little put-off because of the reason he'd been asked. Silas still hadn't told Mallory about his million-man campaign. Silas believed that it wasn't a good idea to let Mallory know, especially since he didn't accept the situation with Donovan. Kirby thought that was stupid, because everyone knew about all the affairs that Silas had. Kirby believed Mallory was naive to think that he could possess a man of Silas' caliber and have him all to himself.

Kirby was growing impatient. He knew that Silas was upstairs waiting on Mallory hand and foot. He didn't understand why Mallory had to come home two days after the accident. The hospital begged him to stay in order to have his wound heal properly. Even his family ruled against him leaving. But Mallory put up a huge fuss and Silas' guilt forced him to cave in.

Kirby hated Mallory...or at least he hated Mallory's position in Silas' life. Silas never doted on anyone like he doted on Mallory. If Mallory desired it, Silas would jump over the moon to make sure he got it and that angered Kirby. Furthermore, their relationship put Kirby on the back burner and that angered him more. The only times they could be together was during Silas' Events and even then Kirby would have to share him with thousands of men.

Flipping the extravagant invitation between his fingers, Kirby tried to think of ways to get rid of Mallory. He knew he couldn't kill him. Not only would he not be successful at it, but Silas would have his head on a platter. Kirby couldn't have an affair with him because Mallory wasn't attracted to him. He couldn't just come out and tell the truth about Silas either because that could prove to be fatal in so many ways. As he searched for a scheme, he stopped flipping the invitation.

I can't tell him...but he can find out on his own, Kirby thought and laughed aloud. He quickly jumped off the couch, looking for a location where he could inconspicuously place the invitation for Mallory to find. As he walked in circles, he said to himself, "In the kitchen, nut!" He placed the invitation on the island bar and put his medication on top of it. As he walked back to the living room to sit on the couch, he was satisfied with his scheme until he thought about how Mallory would respond when he arrived at the event.

He pictured it...Mallory would walk in and see all of the men kissing, cuddling and practically fucking everywhere. He would search around to find Silas, who would be occupied by three to four men at one time. He would get angry and...

Kirby popped out of his daydream and jumped when he felt Silas tap his shoulder.

"Ready to go, babe?"

I can't do it. I need to get my invitation, Kirby thought. *They are marked...personalized. Silas would know it was me.*

"Are you nervous?"

"No...I just need to get—"

Silas grabbed his hand and pulled him up from the couch. He planted a reassuring kisses on Kirby's lips. Silas knew that those kisses melted Kirby every time. "I'm the one who should be nervous...I'm the one who's trying to break a record tonight."

"I know, Daddy, but..."

"SILAS!" Mallory screamed from upstairs.

"Coming!" Silas rolled his eyes and quickly escorted Kirby to the door. "Wait for me, baby, okay? Pick any car that you want to drive tonight."

"The green Jag?" Kirby asked with an irresistible smile, knowing that it was Mallory's special car. He saw Silas squirming, trying hard to say 'HELL NAWH', but Kirby knew two things about Silas – that he would never accept no for an answer and that he couldn't give no as an answer either.

"SILAS!" Mallory shouted again.

"If you really want to baby," Silas said softly, but his eyes gave Kirby an 'I DON'T WANT NO SHIT' message. "Now go!"

"Silas," Mallory finally made it to the bottom of the stairs.

Silas quickly rushed to his aid. "Boo! You're not supposed to be walking."

"I'm tired of lying in the bed."

"Mallory, you're still bleeding."

"I cannot stay in that bloody bed. Please! I'll lounge on the couch."

"I don't want you bleeding on my couch."

"SILAS! DAMN IT!" Mallory's head started spinning. "I'll go back to bed. Just leave, have a good time."

"Look, I will stay here if you want me to."

"All week you have been talking about this event. How special it is...how exciting it is...the BIG MMC!" Mallory sprawled out on the couch, which was exactly what Silas didn't want him to do. "What does MMC mean?"

"It means I don't want you bleeding on my damn couch. And I know what you're about to say now. 'I can't move... I'm tired.' Get up, Mallory and go back to bed."

"Okay! LEAVE. Enjoy your bloody event."

"Are you getting up?" Silas shouted as he hesitantly walked toward the door. "Look, I trust you. NO DRINKING, NO CHRONICLESATION WATCHING, NO UNSUPERVISED SHOWERS, NO TALKING TO MARC AND GETTING UPSET! NO VISITORS - NOT EVEN THE MEMBERS OF YOUR FAMILY THAT YOU LIKE!" He grabbed his keys. "Am I forgetting anything?"

"No new tattoos?" Mallory said with a smile. "Good night, Sile. I'll be careful and I promise to go straight back to bed."

Silas blew him a kiss and hastily rushed out the door.

Mallory finally took a deep breath. He had no intentions of going back to bed. Mentally, he was restless and full of energy, but physically, he was spent. He looked over at the wet bar and wished, *but even if I wanted to, I couldn't lift the bottle. And the ice is the fridge.* He huffed again. He finally gathered enough strength to get off the couch to crawl to the kitchen. As he made his way to the island, he pulled himself up.

Mallory screamed like a kid in a candy store, "DRUGS!" He mentally went over Silas' 'NOT TO' checklist. "He didn't mention drugs!" Mallory chirped aloud. When he grabbed the bottle, he noticed a black and red inflexible cloth invitation. He pulled the wax seal, carefully unfolded the invitation and pulled out the announcement card. After Mallory read it, the invitation disintegrated in his hands and a gold key materialized in its place.

"Million Man Campaign...that don't sound right. Oh, listen to me... That don't!" Mallory went through Silas' 'NOT TO' list again. "Well, he didn't say anything about me leaving or driving. I can't take a shower, but I can get dressed." He wanted to run up the stairs because mentally, he saw himself with bouts of energy. However, his body quickly leaned on the chair and refused to make any sudden moves. "This might take a minute. I guess if I'm leaving the house, I can't do drugs. But then again, one little pill won't hurt."

It was two hours later when Mallory arrived at the MMC event. He was pissed that Silas took his Jag and the other cars were being routinely serviced. He was forced to pull out his vintage Aston Martin. He hadn't driven it since his walk on water debut. With all that shifting, Mallory was too tired to get out of the car, but he was determined to find out what Silas was doing.

He stepped out of the car and the valet quickly grabbed his keys and climbed into the car. There were spotlights highlighting people as they partied. It was orderly, but the crowd appeared to be waiting for something. As Mallory began to head toward the event, the valet blew the horn to get his attention.

"Sir," the valet called out. "You forgot your key. You can't get into the party without it."

"Thank you."

"You must be really VIP. There were only ten gold keys given out."

Mallory smiled and walked away. "Really VIP? That's a new one." Once he reached the door, he handed the key to the doorman.

"You will need it later. Follow me." The doorman grabbed Mallory's arm and guided him through the party, escorting him to a private elevator. Mallory walked into the all glass elevator car and the doors closed. He turned around and looked down to watch the party recede as he ascended to the top floor.

The elevator stopped and the doors opened, but there was one problem. He encountered a locked door directly in front of the elevator that was blocking the entrance. Mallory couldn't get off the elevator. Then he remembered the key. He quickly retrieved it from his pocket and placed it in the lock. As he turned the key, he felt cold shivers run down his back.

When he opened the door, his mouth flew open. The only illumination came from a black light. There was a sea of men: short, tall, fat, skinny, cute and some were beyond gorgeous. Mallory took several steps inside the room before he was greeted by two God-awfully endowed, naked men.

They must be twins. Mallory thought. He was so intrigued and disgusted by their lack of uniform that he became overwhelmed with their sea of questions.

"You're late."

"Where is your key, honey?"

"Oh my...he does belong here."

"Have you been touched by the dragon?"

Mallory never spoke a word, but his facial expression spoke volumes. Above Mallory's head was a huge neon sign that flashed, Welcome to Banned in Vegas. He looked around and there were sights that both aroused and disgusted him at the same time.

There were two men sitting on the Craps Table. A one man was getting off by watching the other two men sit on tall glasses relieving themselves. On another table, there were two groups of three or foursomes, on a table having sex. Mallory couldn't quite figure it out. The object of the game at that table was to get as close to 21 inches before you got BUSTED. Mallory gasped when he saw Roulette table – Spin the Bottom. In the midst of Vegas night, there were random groups of men on the floor, getting off while several men urinated on them. There were men being spanked and spanking other men with whips. There were Jacuzzis, hot wax showers and baby oil.

The twins prattled on with their questions.

"Is this your first time here?"

"It can't be," The other guy answered. "He has a VIP key."

Mallory finally cleared his throat and spoke, "Pardon me, can you indulge me for just a moment? I have strange request. Where can I find some unopened bottled water, Purell and clean napkins?"

The two men smiled, "LOL! We'll get that kit for you." One twin whispered to the other, "He's one of those, LOL."

One twin quickly walked away while the other twin completed Mallory's registration. "I'm assuming that you haven't been touch by the dragon." He placed a flexi-metal bracelet on his wrist and then continued, "Once you get your kit, I will need you to proceed upstairs to your right. Are you a bottom or top?"

"I'm flexible."

"Yes, we all are, dear. But what do you prefer?"

"I prefer to watch."

The guy huffed, "I don't think the dragon will approve that tonight. He's attempting to break a record."

"What's his record?"

"In one night, six thousand men." The guy smiled. "He averages around fifty-five hundred, but that's until he got this boyfriend, then his numbers dropped. Rumor is the boyfriend is sick and can't put out, so he's trying to catch up."

Mallory tried to mask his contempt. "Do you think his boyfriend knows about this?"

"O, M, G...his boyfriend would have a fucking cow if he found out. That's why we have the super security now - special keys and the personalized invitations. We couldn't go the normal route of The MMC virus email. We were told that his older brother is a snooping pest. Anyhoo, we can pick him out a mile away. If he shows up, we will know."

"What happens if he shows up and gets to this point?"

"He couldn't possibly get to this point. We know how he looks – clean cut, shaven and extremely conservative. He wears a suit everywhere he goes. He would stick out here. We know the make and models of all his cars. They all have the license plates of 'D-I- BLO.' He only has one flashy one and Kirby drove that one tonight. Kirby is such a lucky man to know the identity of the dragon. Rumor has it that he can fuck the dragon anytime he wants. Not even the boyfriend can do that. Oh, I'm rambling. What was I saying? Oh...nothing flashy, he has the standard, conservative Benz and BMWs. He would never possess a key and the bracelet would glow."

Mallory tucked the bracelet under his sleeve and was relieved that he decided to wear one of Silas' loud-colored, long-sleeve polo shirts and acid-washed low-rise jeans with tears in all the right places. He was also glad that he didn't take the time to shave his newly and unusually gruff face.

"Ah, here is your kit. Top or bottom?"

"Top."

"Well...once you get upstairs, you will need to remove your clothes and prepare to be touched by the dragon." Much to Mallory's surprise, the twin grabbed Mallory's dick and stroked it hard. "Well, it looks like you don't need a fluffer."

Mallory was speechless. He finally mumbled, "I took something before I got here. I didn't want to waste time."

"Hmm...nice size, too. Maybe later you can meet me at the Black Jack Table. You can be my Ace of Hearts." He stroked Mallory several times and smiled before letting him go.

"Thanks Jack."

Mallory slowly walked up the stairs as he watched a plethora of sexual acts, which he thought could only be performed by cartoon characters. He started feeling weak, but he dared not to touch the handrail. Once he reached the top of the stairs, the thick aroma of musk incense overwhelmed him and he became faint. He leaned against the wall and opened his kit. It was filled with condoms, Purell, Clorox wipes, a pair of gloves, breath fresheners, a cock ring and long cellophane strip. Mallory searched for the bottled water, but it wasn't there. He slid down the wall to attempt to get some fresh air when he heard several strange noises flowing from his left. He wanted to crawl toward the noises, but when he looked at the floor, white, semi-dried splotches seemed to glow and highlighted by the black light. He wanted to leap off the floor and scream. Instead, he started hyperventilating and panicking.

"This is not the time for an OCD attack. NO OCD attacks, MALLORY," he said aloud to himself. He quickly grabbed his Clorox wipes and ripped the package open. But instead of wiping the floor, he covered his nose and mouth, hoping the disinfectant smell would calm him. The noise became louder and distracted his obsession with the filthy floor. Mallory stood up and headed in the direction of the noise. There were several men talking, shouting or screaming and there was one deep, animalistic noise. The sound was quite frightening, yet he found himself drawn to its source. He arrived at a curtain and pushed it aside. Behind it was a security guard waiting in the wings with an earpiece.

"You here to relieve me?"

"What? Oh...uh-huh," Mallory answered vaguely.

"Cool. Okay, he's almost done with these guys. Just open the curtain and let them go. They have instructions on what to do, but just in case, they need to shower and get detoxified. They can't be allowed to remember his appearance. HUMANS, they talk, you know?"

"Yeah...okay."

"Any questions?"

"Uh...no."

The security guard turned and walked away.

Mallory stood, petrified, his body pained with fear. His eyes became fixated on a fifteen-foot tall, dragon-like monster. The monster had horns down its back. Its hands and feet were bound to stakes to keep them spread apart. He was being whipped with chains and the men were riding his horns while others attacked the dragon. Mallory was so engrossed in watching the dragon that he didn't hear the guard come back into the room. The guard tapped Mallory on the shoulder and he jumped.

"Sorry. I forgot the tazer. Hopefully you won't need it."

"Huh?" Mallory realize that the guard was handing him the tazer gun. He reached out to grab it, but his bracelet slipped from under his sleeve and illuminated a bright, piercing blue. Everyone froze and their eyes floated toward Mallory. With a nervous smile, Mallory started backing away, tugging on the bracelet. He heard a rumble and then people began screaming.

Once Mallory reached the stairs, he started to turn around, but the dragon exploded through the wall and roared, "WHAT ARE YOU DOING HERE?"

Mallory was so frightened that he lost his footing and fell down the length of the stairway.

The dragon roared again, "WHAT IS HE DOING HERE?"

"We will handle it, Sir!" The guard shouted. "But you can't be seen. Please go back!"

At the bottom of the stairs, everyone watched Mallory lie on the floor, bleeding and unconscious. One man, dressed like the security guard, walked through the crowd, pushing everyone aside. "I'll dispose of him."

Mallory finally opened his eyes and saw the crowd around him. A man approached him and kneeled down with a blindfold and a gun. Before the man covered Mallory's eyes, he realized that the man was Quincy. Before he could speak, Quincy shot him.

CHAPTER TWENTY ONE

Malcolm, using Quincy's body as a medium, stood by Mallory's bedside and waited for him to wake up. Silas arrived shortly thereafter, but God prohibited him from going into Mallory's room. "What in the Hell is he doing here?" Silas questioned.

"Making amends with his son?" God responded.

"That's Malcolm? Oh, he can't be in there! He'll succeed in killing Mallory."

"No, he won't. It's not in his conscience to act out like that."

"Malcolm has no conscience!" Silas shouted. "He's a sadistic sick dick!"

"Don't worry about Mallory. He is safe right now. Let them be." God changed the subject, "You know we haven't spoken in a while."

"I haven't been in trouble. Well, not trouble that I can't get out of on my own." Silas smiled. "You miss me?"

"You know I do. You're my favorite."

"That's your running punch line. We all are your favorite!" Silas' thoughts turned serious, "Is he going to be okay, God?"

"He'll survive this. No worries. Why don't you give them some space? Go home and we'll talk."

"Every time I talk to you, I get homework assignments. Nawh, that's okay. We'll talk later! I'll give them some space...but that Quin-colm is on a SHORT LEASH with me! I don't trust him."

"Do you trust Me?"

"You setting me up for something - I ain't answering that. We'll chat later...Amen!" Silas departed in a hurry.

Mallory faded in and out of consciousness. When he did wake up, he saw Marlon and Janet grooming and talking to him. His four nephews fussed over his medication, bag drips and bandages. He thought he saw Marc several times, but Marc's behavior was evasive. He never checked on Mallory, he just hovered over the medication bags. Mallory also noticed that when Marc left, he floated into a cold, darkened state.

In the coldness of the night, Mallory felt the needles being removed from his arms. He tried to wake himself up, but couldn't catch his breath. He felt someone moving his bed and heard people talking over him. A wool blanket tightly covered his face and body, smothering him. He then felt rumbling and the movement accelerated. Mallory heard the blade rotation of a helicopter and fought hard to wake himself up. As he began to win the fight, pain crept into his body. He fought through the pain and the restraints so that he could remove the wool blanket from his face. Before the pain took over, he looked over and saw Michael, who grabbed his hand and said, "You're gonna be fine. Marc can't hurt you anymore. You're safe."

The pain was so overwhelming, Mallory passed out again.

"So, how do you feel?" Michael asked, pouring Mallory a glass of water.

"Exhausted, but good. I crave exhaustion. It doesn't allow my mind to wander."

"Hmm, I was warned about that mind. Your mind is becoming a battlefield. It's not good." Michael answered.

"I think my battlefield is the least of your worries," Mallory paused, "Why am I here?"

"You're an investment to me. I need to keep you alive. Your brother and your lover have plotted to kill you."

"I believe the first half of that. My lover is only capable of breaking my heart."

"Not that lover," Michael mumbled. "I warned you to leave Silas," Michael stood up. "What hold does he have on you?"

"What hold did my Dad have on you?" Mallory retorted.

Michael looked away.

"It's indescribable the hold they can possess," Mallory snickered. "And the bad part about it is... that I miss him so much. I miss his burning-hot body holding me so close, so tight. He used to joke that I was his ice cube, I kept him cool through the night." Mallory turned over and settled in the bed, cradling a king-sized, down-stuffed pillow. "He would snuggle up behind me and squeeze me...and even limp he felt hard and long. In the middle of the night, we would end up fucking...I tried hard not to wake up...but it never failed... When we came, we woke up. Either I would turn and snuggle on his chest or he would nestle under mine." Mallory smiled as he remembered the good old days. "I used to bitch at him about messing with my alarm clock." He took a deep breath, "but that sleep was better than any V&V cocktail I took. I miss him so."

Michael turned to walk away, leaving Mallory with his fantasy.

"Hey, Allen, do you miss my Dad like that?"

Michael never spoke a word as he closed the door.

CHAPTER TWENTY TWO

Silas walked up to the door of his father's Texas estate. Before he could knock on the door, Michael opened it and blocked the doorway.

"Hey, Dad?" Silas was confused.

"What are you going here, son? Your mom's not here."

"Actually, I'm here to see Mallory."

"Umm...he's still sleep."

Silas looked at his watch for a moment and saw that it was 11:13 A.M. Silas knew that even if Mallory were deathly ill, he would not be asleep at this time. "Okay? Um...are you going to let me in?"

Michael didn't want to answer that question. "Mallory will be fine. He just needs his rest."

"ARE YOU LETTING ME IN?" Silas raised his voice.

"Why don't you go home...and enjoy your time away from Mallory?"

Silas stepped closer to the door and said, "Dad, I want to see Mallory. We need to talk about some things before it's too late."

"That's not a good idea, son. He needs his rest so that he can stay productive."

"Productive? He's not a machine, Dad. He's human and he's..." Silas tried to force his way into the house. "I'm not standing for this."

Michael pushed him away. "Son, go home. Mallory will be taken care of by us now."

"US? Who is us?"

"Us! The Abaddon Empire. He's a part of the empire," Michael's announcement shocked Silas. "I didn't do it - you did. You made him a part of the empire when you slated him to be you."

Silas started toward the doorway again and Michael held his arm out to stop him from entering the house.

"There was a reason why I didn't bring Malcolm into the empire and he was just as smart, if not smarter than Mallory."

"Malcolm was NEVER smarter than Mallory!" Silas shouted out.

"You lost him, he's a part of the empire now," Michael stated as he pushed Silas back down the steps. "Why don't you go back home and have one of your parties?" Michael suggested. Silas turned to walk away, but not before he heard his father say, "Malcolm was smarter."

Silas turned back and shouted, "No, he wasn't! He chose you! That was the dumbest thing he ever did!" Silas stormed back to his helicopter.

"Was that Silas?" Mallory asked, walking down the stairs.

"No, just a messenger." Michael quickly closed the door. "Want some breakfast? It's going to be a busy day."

"This is bloody Hell," Mallory sulked. He really wanted to see Silas. Even in the midst of their anger, Silas always came home and they always had breakfast together. Even though he never had to ask Mallory if or what he wanted for breakfast. It was just ready.

Michael walked up and met him on the stairs. "You know, Silas is probably lying on his back, six foot under with men. Working his way through a crowd as large as Minute Maid Park.

He's gonna run out of gay men to fuck before he turns forty. That boy can scr—"

"Thanks, Michael. I got the gist of his behavior." Mallory faked a nonchalant smile. "I need to change my suit, so I will meet you at the board meeting."

"Want me to go with you?" Michael gingerly suggested.

"No, thank you! I'm a big boy - I can change myself." Mallory departed from the house before Michael could give a rebuttal. Mallory headed straight for the car, feeling the need to get some distance between himself and Michael's overbearing, fatherly concern. In addition, he needed to discover the truth behind the poisoning rumor involving Marc and Silas. As he started the car, he dialed Marc's house number.

"Haulm residence," Claire answered the phone.

"Happy birthday, love! Where is your husband?"

"That cheap-ass son of a bitch is in the garage fixing the coffee table. His sorry ass is too cheap to buy new furniture. Oh, but Lil' Ms. Putout can get anything she wants." Claire replied sourly. Claire was referring to Marc's long-term affair with Amanda; who just so happened to be one of Mallory's old girlfriends. "I have been with that bastard for over twenty years. I bore his seven kids and put up with his shit and I can't get any new furniture? And he thinks I'm fucking him today as a birthday gift! FUCK HIM! He ain't getting any ass from me and he won't be getting it up for her ass either."

Mallory stayed silent. He knew that Claire was a mild-mannered woman, so when she went off on a tirade, she was dangerous. Over the years, they were fair warning that she was about to explode, but Marc often missed the clues. She was a force that he didn't want to deal with.

"Mallory?" Claire asked.

"Yes, love?"

"I'm sorry. I didn't mean to unload on you. Thank you for listening, though! Did you need him?"

"Actually, I was on my way over there."

"Umm...do you think that is a good idea?"

"What do you mean?"

"I mean...you just got out of the hospital and you're still weak...I didn't mean weak...I mean..."

"Claire, I'm fine. I just want to chat to him."

"Yeah, but your chats end up in fights and I'm not in the mood to protect –" Claire stopped mid-sentence. "I didn't mean that. I'm just so angry right now."

"Claire...I'm fine."

"I know you are, baby. Hey, why don't you bring Silas? He can defuse—"

"Claire, I'm not a wimp."

"Of course you're not, dear. Just bring Silas." She hung up.

The conversation left Mallory feeling sour. He just wanted to talk to Marc, but Claire was right. Their chats often ended in a fight, but Mallory was ready for anything. He resented the fact that Claire insinuated that he wasn't able to protect himself. Even after the hospital stay, he felt strong enough to handle anything. The more he thought about their conversation, the angrier he got. That wasn't the first time she insinuated that he needed protection. And she wasn't the only one who made those insinuations. But he wasn't weak, so he felt that it was time to show them.

Mallory felt a familiar, yet sharp pain in his chest again. The last thing he needed was a visit from his Ego. It had been years since they had exchanged conversation and Mallory didn't need his distraction. He wanted to show everyone, especially his Ego, that he wasn't weak. He just needed the perfect opportunity.

Before he knew it, he found himself pulling into his parking spot at the penthouse.

Mallory whisked out of the elevator and made a beeline for the front door. A cold chill ran up his spine when he grabbed the doorknob. The last time he saw Silas was when he left to go to his big MMC event. Mallory vaguely remembered the two naked men interrogating him before letting him into the Sodom and Gomorrah affair. Mallory didn't remember anything after that, but he had a bad feeling that things didn't go right for him that night.

When he opened the door, a familiar fear struck in his heart. There were men in the living room, dining room and kitchen; groping one another. Flashes of that night bombarded his mind. That night, there had been a sea of men committing acts that were beyond Mallory's allowed imagination. Slightly disgusted then, now, he was pissed. It was one thing to commit these acts, but it was another to bring the acts home.

Before Mallory could reach his office, one of the men grabbed him and slammed him against the wall. "I like you...and I want that." He said as he forcefully grabbed Mallory's ass.

"Seriously, that's the romantic line that you're using?"

The guy flipped Mallory around and pushed his face against the wall. "If I like what I want, I take it. I want you."

Mallory huffed in pure anger. "Okay...I need to take care of some business with the dragon first and then I'll come back to you."

"I want you before the dragon!" The man shouted in Mallory's ear while trying to rip his pants off.

Mallory had to use all the strength he had not to snatch the rude man's soul from his body. He quickly answered back, "Look the dragon is waiting for me and I'm late. Do you want to take my spot with the dragon? I'll let you tag me all day."

"You're late?" He stepped back. "Nawh...I'll wait."

Mallory rushed to the office and grabbed Silas' favorite golf driver. He quickly snuck up to the bedroom and pushed the door open. What Mallory saw made him nauseous. From what he could detect, there were seven men in the bed and Silas was in the middle of the testosterone pile - stroking away. Before Mallory knew it, he swung the club and hit Silas across the back while he was in mid-stroke. As Mallory swung the club, men were jumping out of the bed, trying to escape. Mallory jumped on the bed and kept swinging - not hearing Silas crying out to him.

In a moment's flash, Mallory was tackled and he landed on the bed. Silas pinned him to the bed, screaming at him. Mallory couldn't hear anything he said. He just closed his eyes and kneed him in the groin as hard as he could. Silas painfully rolled over. Mallory tried to crawl out of the bed, but Silas grabbed his legs and held him down. Mallory reached back and elbowed Silas in the nose. He knew that really hurt him. Mallory jumped off the bed and retrieved the club, but before he could swing it, Silas was standing in front of him.

"What in the Hell is wrong with you?" Silas wiped his bloody nose.

"This is what you've been doing while I've been slaving in that Hell pit."

"Mallory, you don't understand."

"Make me understand."

"Mallory," Silas took several steps forward, but stopped when Mallory raised the club to swing. "Can we talk about this?"

"What is there to talk about? I'm fighting the board and your dad and you're fucking around? Is this what the Million Man Campaign is about? This is how you spend your time? Every day you promise me that you'll come and take your spot and I've been waiting for you. I'm a bloody fool."

"Mallory...you don't understand."

"You don't love me anymore?"

"YES! I LOVE YOU BABY! It...It's j-j-just..." Silas started stuttering, which Mallory had no patience for today. He swung the club, barely missing Silas. "You don't belong to me anymore!" He paused in pain, "You belong to the empire."

"I thought YOU were the empire." Mallory swung the club and tagged Silas, knocking him out. He walked out of the bedroom and went down the stairs with the club in his hand. The men were standing around, looking to react to Mallory's aggressive actions. He rushed up to the man who threw him against the wall. He angrily shouted, "You ready? I'll let you tag me first if I get to tag you back."

The man shook his head and flopped on the couch.

Mallory was fuming as he stormed out of the penthouse. He knew that Silas would come after him once he came to. Mallory wanted him good and angry. So instead of going to the garage and taking his car, Mallory ran to the helipad and took Silas' helicopter. He knew that would piss Silas off beyond normal circumstances because he would have to drive and that meant a severe case of road rage and accidents. Mallory wanted a fight and Silas gave him the perfect opportunity. Mallory's next stop was Marc's house.

Before Mallory knew it, he was pounding on Marc's door. When Marc opened the door, Mallory bum-rushed his way into the house. He was acting nervous and jittery.

Marc shouted, "What the hell?" He completed his thought internally. *You're not dead!*

Mallory grabbed his shirt, "I need you to protect me from him! He's beyond angry!" Mallory shouted, just inches from Marc's face.

Claire stormed in the living room, "What is going on?"

"Mallory got himself in some shit," he answered Claire. "Who is angry?"

Before Mallory could answer, Silas was banging on the door. He arrived a bit quicker than Mallory had anticipated. Marc pried Mallory's hands off his shirt and answered the door. Claire watched as Mallory's expression changed from fearful to deviant. She quietly backed into a corner. Before Marc could open the door, Silas kicked it open.

"Hey, Dude! I don't want no shit! Let's talk about this!" Marc tried to reason with Silas gingerly, but he was beyond the state of reasoning.

"Mallory! We need to talk. Let's go home," Silas stormed inside the house, heading directly for Mallory, who was shuffling around, trying to dodge him.

"Fuck you! I don't give a bloody fuck want you want to say to me," Mallory picked up a chair and threw it at him.

"Mallory, I'm not gonna fight you," Silas dodged the chair. "I just want to talk." Silas kicked a coffee table out of his way.

Marc tried to catch the table, but it flew up and crashed to the floor. "Oh...stop! Hey, what are you fighting about?" he continued to try to diffuse the situation.

"NOTHING!" Silas dismissed Marc's question.

"NOTHING? SO, I'M NOTHING TO YOU!" Mallory grabbed a vase and threw it at Silas, who knocked it away, smashing it into the wall.

"STOP!" Marc screamed.

"Mallory," Silas stopped trying to chase him, "Let's take this home."

"HOME? You defiled our home with those...those..." Mallory jumped on top of the bureau. He started throwing Marc's wedding china at Silas, who was using his arm as a bat as he knocked each plate, cup and bowl into the wall. Mallory threw a dish with each word he uttered, WITH! ALL! THOSE! GRIMY! ASS! MEN!

"Grimy?" Silas detected a change in Mallory's accent. "The Ego rears its ugly head!"

Bloody fucker! Mallory ran to the corner and grabbed one of Marc's golf clubs.

"Oh, we're playing golf again?" Silas tried to push past Marc to get to Mallory, but Marc desperately and barely kept them separated.

Mallory started swinging. Silas grabbed Marc and pushed him on the couch so that he wouldn't get hit and then charged after Mallory. He kept swinging the club. At one point, Silas grabbed Mallory and threw him against the wall. Marc finally got up and grabbed Silas, pulling them apart. Mallory got his bearings, swung the club and hit Silas in the back. The hit didn't faze him, but it angered him to the point that when Mallory swung the club again, he caught it and broke it in half.

Marc desperately tried again to keep them separated, but he was losing the battle. Mallory started throwing anything he could get his hands on, but Silas always managed to dodge the objects.

Silas finally roared, "BRING YO' ASS HOME NOW!"

Mallory flashed a wicked smirk and taunted, MAKE ME.

With that, Silas exploded as his eyes flashed a fiery red. He charged Mallory with Marc between them. The force drove them all from the living room to the piano room. Mallory tripped on the hall rug and they all fell on Marc's antique wingback chair, shattering it into splinters. With Marc in the middle of the battling twosome, Silas grabbed Mallory's throat and began choking him. Mallory tried to fight him off. Silas felt Mallory's skin temperature dropping, but he didn't release his chokehold.

Moments later, furious Mallory pushed both men off him and they flew into the air, hitting the wall. Marc landed on top of Silas, but Silas pushed Marc off him and jumped up to attack. When Marc saw Mallory's eyes flash blue, he decided to let them fight. Silas eventually caught Mallory and thrashed him against the wall. With his hands around Mallory's throat again, he slid Mallory down the length of the wall into a bookcase. He commenced to banging Mallory's head against the case, but Mallory fought back. At one point, Mallory grabbed a carved wooden elephant and smashed it against Silas' head. That stunned Silas long enough for Mallory to free himself from Silas' grip, but it wasn't long enough for him to get away. Silas grabbed Mallory by the collar and tail of his suit and threw him up to the second floor.

Marc and Claire stood still for a moment because they felt that Mallory was hurt. Intending to check on him, they waited for an opening. As they looked around and surveyed their home, they realized it was trashed beyond repair. By the time he could utter a word, he heard Claire gasp. Mallory got up and climbed on top of the banister, getting ready to jump down for round two.

Marc shouted, "NO, DADDY! PLEASE DON'T JUMP AGAIN! I'll do whatever you want, Daddy. Please don't jump again."

Silas and Mallory stood in shock. Mallory held his palms in front of him in a non-threatening gesture and jumped down from the banister. Silas looked over at Marc, who was clearly suffering from some mental breakdown or posttraumatic stress.

When Marc finally looked at Silas, his expression changed from deeply distressed, to pure embarrassment and finally, to anger. Mallory walked down the stairway to the first level. He was ready for round two. Silas was never the target. Marc was, but Mallory need to get him riled up.

Silas finally saw through the plan to attack Marc, but he was not going to let Mallory be successful. Not today. After all, he still had a score to settle. When Mallory marched his way toward Marc, Silas stood in his path. Before Mallory could attack, there was a knock at the door. Claire ran to the door and opened it, not bothering to ask who it was. There were four men from the Abaddon Empire, dressed in dark grey suits. They were waiting to escort Mallory to the board meeting. Since Mallory had never arrived at the meeting, Michael sent a crew to escort him back.

"This is not over," Silas informed Mallory in an angry tone.

"It was over when I learned that you sold me to the empire."

"I never sold you! How could you think that?"

"How can you stand there and tell me that you're not the empire? You made me a part of it and I leaped after it, thinking it was you...that I belong to you. I was a fool!"

"Mallory! You don't understand. We need to talk about this."

"Too late. If you're not the empire, then I'm nothing to you. I don't belong there and I'm taking care of it today." Because the four men observed that Silas and Mallory were in a heated discussion, they quickly rushed into the house and surrounded Mallory. One man grabbed Mallory's arm and began pulling him away.

"See! They're taking me away and you're not even stopping them. I'm nothing to you." Before Mallory was whisked away, he looked at Marc. "I'll be back for you." Once he reached the door, he whispered to Claire, "I know you have my black card. Go buy whatever furniture you like. Happy Birthday."

CHAPTER TWENTY THREE

Silas strolled into the restaurant. "Hey, Marc, Marlon, what's up?" He greeted the boys and sat down.

"Hey, Silas. I guess we need to be more specific when we ask for Death." Marc said sarcastically.

"Har, har, har. You called me not him. What do you want?" Silas retorted. Marek walked up to the table and, in doing so, startled Silas. "Oh, shit!" He frowned. "Look what the war dragged in."

"Hi to you too, bitch," Marek answered back.

"I guess you really did want Mallory." Silas stood up. "What do you want, a fucking hug or something?" He forced himself to pat Marek on the back.

"Or something named Mallory." Marek forced himself to return the pat. "Where is he? Why are you here?"

"Cuz your dumb ass brother said that Death needed to come to dinner." Silas said as he sat down again. He purposely pushed his chair away from Marek.

"Death? When did the devil become death?" Marek pulled Silas up from his chair and sat in it.

"Tell him Silas...I really want to hear this," Marc instigated.

"And I thought Marlon was the bitch," Silas snapped back.

"Hey!" Marlon frowned, waiting for Silas to sit down so he could kick him under the table.

"Mallory and I have been coupling...and one thing led to another and we binded, combined our life forces. He is I and I am him!" Silas tried to explain.

"Not him, He dumb ass!" Marlon interjected, correcting Silas like Mallory would normally do.

"I caught wind of the coupling thing, but binding?" Marek leaned back in his chair. "You finally trapped him."

"I didn't trap him. He was fully aware of his choices. We love each other." Silas took a big sip of water. "What the fuck are you smiling at, Marc?"

"I'm just happy that my brother is home. Nothing else. How is Mallory? Or an even better question is, when was the last time you saw Mallory?" Marc snickered. "Was it since the fight? Oh and hey thanks for redecorating my house."

"You're a funny looking man, Marc!" Silas took another gulp of water. He looked around the table and noticed that they were still waiting for an answer. "Last week or a month or six months ago...or so. We're having our downtime right now. Besides, he's busy working on some presidential campaign to complete another level to Hell."

"Should you be working on that? Aren't you the empire?" Marek asked.

"I will when I need to. I don't need to be there right now. Mallory is handling it all. He'll call me when he needs me."

"Explain to me how you got him to work for you!" Marek shouted.

"Silas sold him to the empire," Marc started laughing, "Isn't that what the fight was about?"

"No, it wasn't. Marc has those details about how he came to work for me." Silas turned to Marc. "You wanna fill him in on how you were pushing him out of the company? He had nowhere to go." Silas jumped up to hug Uncle Mal, who arrived at the table. "Uncle Mal, how are you doing?"

"Hey, son, where is Mallory?" Uncle Mal asked. Silas frowned at him and moved over without answering. "Marek! My boy! You made it home."

"Yes, sir, home safe." Marek stood up and hugged him.

"Welcome home, Marek!" Quincy grabbed Marek and gave him a hearty, fatherly hug.

"I don't know you, but thanks!" Marek answered, returning the hug.

"I'm..." Quincy wanted to explain, but thought it was too soon.

"Quincy...this is Quincy. He's your daddy!" Silas instigated.

"Funny, bitch. I'm Bailey's friend!" Quincy quickly added.

"Who just so happened to start hanging out with Uncle Mal... Like your Daddy used to," Silas continued his instigation with a cocky grin.

"Go fuck a duck!" Quincy shouted. "Where is Mallory?"

Silas rolled his eyes. He motioned for Marlon to move so that he could sit next to Marc. "You're a bitch. You know that, right? You could have told me that Marek was here."

"I specifically said, Mallory you need to come to dinner. Marek wanted it to be a surprise. I guess I forgot that Mallory doesn't live there anymore. You still let Marek ruffle your feathers?" Marc inquired.

"You know I can't stand his ass. He makes me sick," Silas fussed.

"Could you possibly be scared that because Marek is home now that he might make Mallory end this relationship? It's not going to be that hard since your relationship is on the rocks."

"I wouldn't say it is on the rocks. We still love each other. We just need breathing room."

Marek sat up intently, listening to Marc and Silas' conversation. Marc continued with his teasing. "Yeah, but Marek has power over Mallory...power that even I can't break."

"Yeah, he bends over backwards for Marek," Quincy teased.

"He bends over forward for me!" Silas shouted in defense.

"And when was the last time you had him in that position? Was it before or after Matthew's presence?" Quincy continued his teasing at Silas' expense.

"Oh, Quincy! With your identity theft issues, do you want me to permanently put you in a straight jacket?" Silas threatened him.

"Now if you could have done that, wouldn't you have done it after I fucked Mallory?"

"What time would that be, when he was seven or when he stabbed you, Malcolm?" Silas snapped back.

"STOP IT, YOU TWO!" Uncle Mal was wringing his hands. "SILAS! Where is Mallory?" Uncle Mal wasn't ready for everyone to know that Malcolm was still alive, but Silas was throwing insulting hints.

"What do you mean Matthew's presence? He's been hanging with Matthew again?" Marek asked.

"In Mallory's defense, since I was told that a horseman can't degrade another horseman –" Marc sarcastically retorted.

"OH! You recognize him as a horseman now?" Silas screeched.

"LIKE I SAID, you can't degrade another horseman when he is not present. He only did that to piss Silas off. Silas has a man-fucking addiction and Mallory wanted to get him back."

"It's not an addiction, it's a campaign. I have a campaign to fuck every man I see." Silas corrected Marc in anger. "Except you,

Marc, although you were close with the email viruses." Silas huffed. "...or Marlon... although you're a bitch..." Marek looked at him. "Now YOU? I want to fuck you, Marek! But I'm adding 'up' and that takes a different meaning!" Silas seethed through his teeth. "I want to fuck you up real bad!"

Marc laughed, "Needless to say, Mallory didn't fall for any of his tricks and Matthew was a little pissed about it."

"He almost died behind it, didn't he?" Quincy added. "Silas?" he looked over in Silas' direction for clarification.

"LET'S CLEAR THE AIR WITH SOME THINGS...I'M JUST THE CLEANUP GUY. I DIDN'T KICK MALLORY OUT OF THE COMPANY, I DIDN'T ATTEMPT TO POISON HIM AT THE HOSPITAL AND I DID NOT SIC MATTHEW ON HIM - MARC DID!" Silas screamed out from the top of his lungs. Everyone in the restaurant stopped and turned in his direction.

"WHAT!" They all shouted in unison.

"I think you need to go fuck a duck, Silas! Feathers and all!" Marc shouted.

"You would do that to your own brother, Marc?" Quincy raised his voice this time. "Why would you do that?"

"I don't understand something, Quincy," Marc lashed back. "Why are you here? You're not a horseman."

"Oh, you're wrong there, buddy! He's just as much of a horseman as I am!" Silas continued his insults.

"Fuck you, Silas."

"Oh please...I'm bricking out of this world. I would love to show you all my wonders. I'm a grown ass man now...with new tricks."

"You can't handle me. You couldn't handle me when you were eighteen."

"You don't remember? I can handle anything my daddy has fucked. Believe me, I'm the latest version of the best ride you ever had."

"Fuck this shit. Where is Mallory?" Marek started getting angrier and more flustered.

"Oh my God! Is that Mallory with your dad?" Marlon asked Silas. They looked on as Michael stood up, waiting for Mallory to leave the table. As they were walking out, Michael grabbed Mallory's arm and it appeared that they were engaged in an intimate conversation.

"I don't know Allen. I can't betray him like that." Mallory tried to reason with Michael. "I thought I could, but you're asking me to overthrow him completely. That's harsh. I really have to think about it."

"Take as much time as you need to think about it. I believe it's for his own good. He doesn't belong there. You're the better man, you built the loyalty and you possess the leadership and the vision. I mean, Mallory, who would have thought of creating another level of Hell? Corporate America! That was brilliant. You can't stop now." Michael attempted to stroke Mallory's ego.

"I don't know. I need to check his gauge, but I'm not ready to see him. He already thinks that something is up. I don't want him to think that we are tag teaming against him. I can't stand lying to him and I can only avoid him for so long."

"You want him off your back? I think I can handle that."

"I don't think I like how that sounds." Mallory took a step forward and noticed his family swiftly approaching, following behind Silas, who was noticeably angry. "Oh, bloody hell! It's Silas."

"What are you doing with my Dad?" Silas yelled, plowing through the crowd.

Michael pushed Mallory back as he approached Silas. "Hey, son. Mal and I were just having dinner before a show." He leaned in closer to Mallory.

"MALLORY, YOU GOTTA EXPLAIN THIS!" Silas roared.

"What kind of explanation do you want, son? A verbal one or physical one?" Michael leaned down and kissed Mallory.

"SO YOU ARE FUCKING MY DAD NOW?" Silas lunged at his father, but Marc and Marlon held him back. "Is that what this bullshit's about? So you're trying to get back at me for the Million Man Campaign by fucking my Dad?"

Michael released Mallory's lips and Mallory stood frozen and speechless. This bad scene seemed to repeat before his eyes and he couldn't find his mental remote to fast-forward to the safe parts. Michael kissed him in front of Silas, his son Satan... the real one. Mallory couldn't decipher if he actually saw Marek or not and he thought his brain was playing tricks on him. He mentally checked out and calmly walked out of the restaurant.

"How dare you kiss my fucking son, you son of a bitch?" Malcolm shrieked. He used Quincy's body to plow through the group, practically pushing everyone over. The brothers were confused. Silas was the only person not shocked enough to stop Quincy from attacking his father.

"Your son? Aren't you a little young to have a son that old?" Michael asked while wiping his lips.

"No, you bastard. That's my son, Allen. You keep your fucking hands off him." Malcolm then used Quincy's body to push past Silas and lunge after Michael. Michael's guards caught him, pushed him back, and then whisked Michael away.

"Malcolm?" Marek asked, clenching his chest.

"Yes, I'm Malcolm. What's your point?"

"Guys...I don't think I'm feeling well," Marek whispered and then collapsed.

"Damn it! Marek..." Marc kneeled down to see if he was breathing. "We need an ambulance."

"He's just having a Mallory-induced heart attack." Quincy teased. "Silas, this is a perfect time for you to take out the competition for Mallory's affections."

"You take him out. You're Death, bitch." Silas stormed off after his father.

CHAPTER TWENTY FOUR

Mallory stood at the doorway to Marek's hospital room. After forty-five insulting and threatening messages from Marc, Marlon, Uncle Mal and Silas, he got the news that Marek was home. He had mixed feelings about seeing his brother. On one hand, he was ecstatic. With Marek back, things could get back to normal. He could return to the company and they could resume fighting the battle as before. But with so many things changed, how could it get back to normal? He was no longer the lone horseman begging for respect and love. He was the emperor of The Abaddon and his presence alone commanded respect. Mallory had no idea how Marek would take his newfound power. Furthermore, he wanted a confession from Marek about his affair with Stacy.

As he walked into Marek's hospital room, it saddened him to see tubes and needles pinned in his brother's body like a voodoo doll. He wasn't ready to let him go and commanding his soul was out of the question.

"Hey, you. When did you start lurking around hospitals at 2:30 in the morning?" Marek asked with a weak voice.

"This is death's hour. I'm just making my rounds."

"Well, round yo' ass over here and see about me." Mallory took a few steps closer to the bed. "Pardon me; I can't stand up to bow right now."

"Just dip your eyes in respect," Mallory said coldly.

"How about this?" Marek shot him the middle finger. Mallory looked away. "Sit me up."

Mallory grabbed the remote for the bed and elevated the headboard. He took pillows and stuffed them behind Marek's back and head. "Are you comfortable?" He asked and Marek nodded. He looked around to find a chair and Marek grabbed his hand to capture his attention. Mallory looked back at him and Marek bowed his head in respect. "It could have waited until you could stand." Mallory informed him.

"Hopefully, by the time I'm standing, you will just be a horseman and not an emperor."

"I take it that you're going to be here for a while. I'm not planning on relinquishing my position anytime soon."

"But I'm back," Marek announced. Mallory lowered his head. "You know what? I'm getting dizzy. Lower me back down?" He grabbed the remote to lower the bed, and then he scooted a chair closer to the bed, holding Marek's hand. "You're an emperor now and you have been busy fucking the devil, his daddy and a suicidal alcoholic who strangely hangs around Uncle Mal." Marek didn't know if Mallory stayed around long enough to realize that Malcolm was still alive.

"Every story has two sides."

"Tell me your side."

"Yes, Silas and I were together, but I didn't sleep with Allen. Yes, I had a tryst with Quincy, but that was back during a time when Malcolm's voices, or should I say soul, was haunting me. Silas inadvertently released Malcolm's soul from my body when we affianced, thus making me emperor. Quincy was a casualty in all of this when he committed suicide. It is speculative that I drove him crazy, but he was an alcoholic before I met him. He was already suffering."

"So you found your Allen. Who would have known?"

"Who would have known that when I stopped looking for him, he would appear?" Mallory took a deep breath and continued, "He wants me to overthrow Silas and take over the empire. I don't think I can do that. After all his bullshit, I still love him so much. And even after everything he did to me, I could never hurt him like that. He's still everything to me."

"What did he do?"

"Let him tell it, not hitting the million man mark. He says that he did not profess his fidelity to me. He's not human... he doesn't feel like he should play by human rules. That the empire should have been enough for me to see that he loved me. He doesn't see why I'm so angry. That was a blatant act of betrayal. I just like people to tell me the truth. I don't like finding out things."

"He doesn't deserve you. You deserve somebody better."

"Like who? I drive humans crazy. Matty wants me to be up in Heaven with him and he won't have it any other way. He tried to kill me a couple of times."

"Stupid fucker. You don't deserve him either. You don't need a man who is going to isolate you from your family."

"Hmm, you're right. Family, I guess family is important." Mallory bowed his head. He took a deep breath and asked, "So do you have anything to tell me?" Mallory wanted Marek to confess about the relationship with Stacy.

"I'm back. I'll be in the office on Monday. Am I going to see you in the office on Monday?"

"No, you won't." He got up and walked toward the door. "You will still be in here on Monday. The heart attacks I cause leave a man incapacitated for at least four days. Remember Malcolm?"

"I'm in better health than Malcolm and I have fewer secrets to hide. I'll be out of here sooner than you know."

"There should be no secrets between us, Marek. We're brothers, aye?" Mallory didn't wait for a response. He just walked back to the door and turned to say, "I'll meet you in the office when you get back. Get some rest, you'll need it. Oh and welcome home."

CHAPTER TWENTY FIVE

Mallory strolled into the penthouse. As he walked past the kitchen, Silas was standing in front of the refrigerator. He was freshly dressed in a black, double-breasted suit, which was odd for him to be wearing at four o'clock in the morning. Mallory slowly walked toward him, looking at him strangely. Silas had cut his braids. Those long, curly, flowing locks were now a mere conservative tailored cut. The only thing Mallory barely recognized was Silas' honey brown eyes, which possessed a strange look – a strange look of fear.

Silas looked up and closed the refrigerator door. Much time had passed since they both felt each other's touch and both men fought the urge to ravish each other. But with much restraint, they stood still, waiting for the other to make a move.

"Coming or going?" Mallory asked.

"Going, I have a...meeting at 5."

"Meeting or a date?"

Silas looked away in guilt.

Mallory didn't care what he had scheduled. He could schedule a war, but Mallory knew that if he wanted Silas, Silas would cancel Armageddon and tee times to stay home with him. The only thing standing in Mallory's way was himself and the betrayed feelings he had toward Donovan and the Million Man Campaign.

"I won't keep you long. I just want to talk," Mallory barely uttered.

"Sure, make it quick." Silas huffed.

Mallory turned away and walked upstairs.

Silas sat on the couch impatiently waiting for Mallory to return. Several minutes passed and he started fidgeting. "Mallory, I have to go. You wanted to talk," he yelled in the direction of the bedroom. A few more minutes passed and Silas jumped up and stormed into the bedroom. He looked around to find Mallory, but he wasn't there. "Mallory! Can we do this later? I really have to go."

Mallory walked out of the bathroom, completely nude.

"You have my undivided attention," Silas informed him in a completely different tone.

Mallory hesitated a bit, but then rushed into Silas' arms, practically knocking him over into the bed. He kissed Silas hard. Silas didn't resist. He wanted to flip Mallory over and release the passion that had built up only for him, but he felt Mallory's actions were a little suspect. He slowed his conquest and lifted Mallory's body so that he could satisfy his curiosity.

"Who got you all worked up?" Silas looked in Mallory's eyes and saw pain. He knew that he caused the pain that was building in the wells of Mallory's eyes. He wanted to retract his question, but it was too late. Mallory lost his fire. He started to get up, but Silas held him down. "No, I just want to know who I need to send the 'thank you' card to," Silas cracked a smile and Mallory softened up a bit. "If I said I was sorry, would that make you feel better?"

"I don't know, would you mean it?"

"If it made you feel better...yes. Mallory, so much shit has happened. I never meant to hurt you. That was the last thing on my mind. Now I don't know where we stand...I mean you and my dad—"

"I would never hurt you like that. I'd rather sit and make you miserable forever before I sleep with your father."

"Oh, I got over that. You ain't that crazy and he ain't that stupid. After I calmed down, I pictured your face. It went from guilt to disgust. You know how you look when you're about to give a big speech. That was you. You looked like you were about to hurl."

"I did...several times. That was just utterly disgusting. All I could see was the anger on your face. Silas, I don't want your empire and I would never deceive you by overthrowing you."

"Yeah, once again I had to calm down. I figured that you didn't want it. After what I put you through, if you hadn't taken over already, you weren't going to do it if my daddy coaxed you." Silas paused and grabbed Mallory's face. "Baby, I gotta believe when I say that I didn't sell you to the empire. I know I promised you that I was coming back...but I don't feel like I belong there. I just don't belong there. I don't want to be there."

"But I was only there because of you."

"I know you did baby. You were becoming a phenomenon, an AWESOME Satan. Better than I would've been... even better than my brother. I just thought that I could become you; Death and you would be happy being me, Satan. But, I lost control of the whole situation. I missed you. I missed us. We were so great together."

"Were? I guess we were."

"Saying 'we were" hurts me too," Silas wanted to change the subject. "Being Death is not easy. I mean your got damn family started treating me like I was you, for real. Even Uncle Mal was taking cheap shots at me," Mallory smiled. "Them sons of bitches are brutal. Shit! I can't tell you how many times Marc and I were about to go to blows, especially when I heard about the poisoning thing. I was not behind that and I will make that right."

"It doesn't matter now."

"So Marek is home. How do you feel about that?"

"Torn, I wanna go back but I wanna stay here."

"You can go back, I'm not gonna stand in the way. Besides, you being at the empire a little less will force me to take more control."

"I like being emperor. I love being with you. I know that I'm overwhelming to you sometimes, but I can be myself with you. You're the only one I can say that about. You're not afraid of me."

"But I'm not faithful." Silas pulled him closer and kissed him softly. "I'm not built that way."

"You're going to be late for your date."

"Oh, the board can wait. I'd rather be with you." Silas finally rolled over and found his favorite place - on top of Mallory. "I'll just tell them that I was working you...making you take back that 60-month resignation."

"I guess you thought that was brilliant - putting that 'resignation clause' in the smallest print of the contract, thinking I wouldn't catch it."

"And I guess you thought it was cute - resigning one day after you signed the contract...like I wouldn't find out. Oh...and just so you know resigning from LTC is not the same as leaving the Abaddon."

Mallory hid his guilty expression by snickering as he fingered the waves in Silas' tailored haircut. "Silas, can I ask you a question?"

"Yes? I'll stay with you forever. We can start over," Silas smiled.

"No, silly. Why didn't you tell me about the dragon thing?"

"My true form?"

"That's your true form?"

"Yeah...I didn't think you'd like it. I mean, we did it once and you never mentioned it again."

"I didn't remember it. Why didn't you tell me about the Million Man thing?"

Silas slid over to the side of the bed. "That campaign was something that I created out of anger and lust when I was young. Like you, I kept hiding my true self and...I needed a way to let loose." He pulled Mallory close. "But being with you gave me a clean side and a redeemable side. Since you gave me that, I wanted to give you that back. I mean, I worked really hard to get you back to where you were when you first moved here...when you didn't drink or do drugs. You were perfectly clean... not tainted. I wanted you to stay that way."

"So this Kirby...is he tainted?"

"Yeah, I was his first real love and he would follow me to the end - including the MM thing. He just wanted to be close to me, so he would accept me any kinda way. I didn't want you to know because I didn't want you following me like that. Because I had your complete loyalty and I feared that if you did, it would end up the way Kirby did."

"So I guess with everything else I did. Donovan was supposed to be my replacement?" Silas looked away. "Was he?"

"NO BABY! Donovan was just a fuck. I wanted to fuck him so bad. He wasn't even a good fuck. But, I wanted him."

"And doing him behind my back, literary?"

"The thrill of the fuck! Have you ever wanted to just do something to see if you can get away with it?"

"And what if I would've woke up and saw that...in mid action?"

"Oh I would've have convinced you to join us for an awesome three-some. When I'm on that orgasmic high, I'm very convincing. You should be happy that I didn't know about the other guys in the bed. Can we say Mosh Pit?"

"And the whole family relations thing?"

Silas didn't want to answer any more questions. He kissed him so hard, Mallory couldn't catch his breath. Between kisses, Silas said, "Mallory, I don't know if I can be faithful to you like you want me to be. I'm not built that way... but the last thing I want to do is hurt you again."

"Silas, you're the closest thing to perfection I'm going to have. You have never rejected me or made me choose between you and my family. You've given me more than what I could ever imagine. More importantly, you don't fear me and you let me be myself. I guess I can't have everything I want."

"You should. You deserve the best."

"Fine, I deserve the best, but I want you. I need you. And if that means that I have to deal with your million-man campaign, then so be it. I just need to know that I come first." Mallory grabbed Silas by the neck and pulled him down, "Make love to me," he whispered. He began tearing off Silas' clothes and inching up in the bed. Silas sat up to quickly remove everything else that Mallory couldn't get to.

At that moment, three soldiers walked in and startled the two. One soldier announced, "Pardon me, your Graces. Silas, the board is waiting for you."

"I'm in the middle of something," Silas protested.

"Permission to be blunt, sir," the soldier asked.

"NO!" Silas waved his hand. Everything around them stopped. "I fear this one is gonna really be a quickie." Silas whispered softly. As much as they tried to control their urges, both men forced their climaxes in a massive rush.

"Silas, I need to talk to you about something." Mallory wanted to confess to the reason why the board was calling him.

"Baby, can it wait?" He grabbed Mallory hands and gently pushed him away. He jumped out of bed. "I swear I won't be long at the meeting. Although they called an emergency session, I'll make sure they make it quick. They know my attention span." Silas dashed into the closet.

Mallory lowered his eyes, "Not really, it can't."

Silas dashed out with a pair of jeans and hard body form fitted Henley. "I'll be home in no time and you'll be ready for me!" Silas kissed his cheek and marched off with his soldiers.

Mallory grabbed his robe and sauntered out of the bedroom. As he closed the door, he felt a presence behind him. He looked over and Michael was standing on the patio, watching Silas leave in the helicopter.

Mallory approached Michael and stood next to him. "Well he's off," Michael observed. Mallory took a deep breath and walked toward the bar. "I see that you two are back together. Can you make me a Scotch and water?"

"One or two ice cubes? Or shall I say Heaven or Hell?" Mallory asked. Michael looked over in confusion. "I'm only asking because if I end up wearing this drink, I need to know if you want to be with your lover or not when I kill you."

Michael laughed, "He told me about that. You know, he didn't even drink Scotch then, he was a Vodka man," he huffed, "and Gin made him crazy."

"Crazy or crazier?" Mallory dropped several cubes in a glass.

"I heard Silas claim that he loves you. He's incapable of that, you know. He's all about possession...what he owns."

"Well, he owns me," Mallory handed Michael the drink. "I just don't know if he's gonna want me after this meeting."

"I was going to ask you about that board meeting. You had me kicked out."

"It's his issue, not yours."

"You know, I will let you in on a secret. You're stronger than he is. Your problem is control. How did you put it? You're fucked. You're very fucked and you don't know how to control it, so you suppress it. He knows it and that scares him. So he treats you with kid gloves."

"I would never hurt Silas."

"Not intentionally."

"If I wanted him dead, he would be."

"I don't know why he attached himself to you," he paused, "but I'm glad he did. He can take his place. Now all I need him to do is convert...transform."

"I take it that you're the only one who doesn't know he's done that. We wouldn't have binded if he wasn't the real thing."

Michael froze in a pondering thought be he finished his drink and handed the glass to Mallory. "He doesn't love you, you know. You need to leave him."

"Why? I'm a bottom feeder and once he takes his rightful spot as the true Satan, I won't be enough for him."

Michael didn't want to tell him the truth; that Silas would be the one to get hurt and that if Silas had to choose between the empire and Mallory – the choice would not be apparent to him. "I like you. You did right by my boy. Now do one more thing for your own good. Leave him."

CHAPTER TWENTY SIX

Everyone gathered in the conference room waiting for Mallory.

"Did Mallory give an agenda for this meeting?" Marek motioned for Marlon to move over.

"No and that's unusual. He's Mr.-Have-an-agenda, Mr. Follow-the-agenda and Mr. follow-up-on-the-agenda." Marc twirled around in the comfy conference chair.

"He said he had a big issue and he needed our advice. It must not be money-related." Uncle Mal walked in the room and looked around.

"It bet not be sex-related," Marek added.

"He wouldn't have us here if it was sex-related. He would have his kind give him advice for that," Marc chuckled.

"His kind? That's sexist," Marlon scolded.

"It's not sexist, but it is derogatory," Monty snapped while moving over two seats to allow MJ and Mallory to sit at the table. "MJ, is he coming?"

"Yeah, he's right behind me. Hook up the laptop," MJ threw the adapter across the table to Monty.

"Why does he need a laptop?" Marc fussed.

"He has a presentation he wants to show," MJ answered back.

"A presentation, but no agenda? This is crap." Marc resumed twirling in his chair.

"Leave him alone, Marc. This is his first day back. He said that it was very important," Marlon defended his brother.

"Sorry, guys, I'm running late." Mallory handed large brown envelopes to each of the men. "Okay, I know I don't have an agenda, but this issue came up so quickly that I called one of Marc's 'flash in a pan' meetings. Put this in for me, MJ." He slid the flash drive across the table. "I called everyone here so that I can get a broad consensus on how I should structure my next course of action. This problem is grave and very sensitive, so please bear with me." Mallory grabbed the mouse and clicked on the presentation. "Marek, I want to start with you first. How would you handle this?" Mallory advanced the slide and a picture of Marek and Stacy engrossed in a very public kiss displayed boldly on the ten-foot screen.

Horrified, everyone looked at the screen in their own time. Uncle Mal started coughing and Marc's mouth flew open. The boys were wide-eyed and fixated on the photo. Marek finally looked at the screen and his mouth dropped. He was busted. Mallory advanced the presentation slowly. There were several pictures of Marek and Stacy in intimate situations, all displayed for his embarrassment. Everyone's eyes were glued on the screen, except for Mallory's, who stared at Marek the entire time, but Marek couldn't force himself to look at Mallory.

"I don't know what to do. I'm at a loss for words. I wish my father were here so he could give me insight on how he handled the situation. Maybe you can tell me, Uncle Mal. What did he do?"

Uncle Mal couldn't speak.

"Marc, how would you handle this?"

Marc shook his head and looked away.

"Is this a gene defect? I mean, my father had this problem and now I have it. I guess it is a good thing that I don't have children or this would happen to them." Assorted pictures flashed of

Marek playing with a little girl while Stacy was sitting down, looking on with a swelled belly. "Do I pay child support for this? How did you handle this situation, Uncle Mal?"

He was still speechless.

Denise walked into the conference and announced, "Mallory, you have phone call."

"I'm in a meeting. Take a message." He continued advancing the slides.

"I said that, but he said that it was an emergency," Denise answered with an attitude.

"Fine, I will be right there, thank you." He grabbed Marek's brown envelope and ripped it open. "Boys, beware. There is a defect in your genes." He pulled out more graphic pictures of Marek and Stacy in sexual positions. He threw them across the table. "You may end up on both sides of the fence, right Marek?" He leaned over to Marek and added, "If you're asking, yes, I took the pictures personally. This is sex-related, but my kind wouldn't do shit like this."

"Fuck you, bitch!" Marek shouted. "What? Yo' faggot-ass gonna—"

Before Marek could finish his statement, Mallory grabbed his collar and pulled him over the table and down to the floor. Marek fell on his face. Mallory grabbed a conference chair to throw onto Marek's back, but Marc jumped on the table and attempted to wrestle the chair from him. Mallory took several steps back and threw the chair at Marc. It threw him off balance, so he fell off the table. Marlon slid to the other side of the room to avoid being hit by Marc or the chair. The boys stood up to stop the fight, but Mallory turned to face them and his eyes flashed blue. Once they caught a glimpse of his eyes, they sat down.

"Dad always said not to take an unnecessary ass-whooping." MJ recalled, rolling his seat away from the altercation.

Marek finally got up and positioned himself for an attack. Marek swung at him but Mallory deflected his blow and drove into a wall. Marek wrapped his arms around Mallory's body and squeezed him with immense force. Mallory squirmed, but he couldn't break free. He finally collected his strength and delivered a head butt to Marek, forcing him to let go. They both fell on the floor in pain. However, Marek quickly recovered and pulled the bookshelf down onto his brother.

He jumped on the bookshelf, adding weight to it and leaned over Mallory's face. "Now, bitch! Whatcha gon' do?" he yelled.

All of a sudden, the building shook and two windows shattered in the conference room. The bookshelf moved and Marek fell off it. Mallory threw the bookshelf aside and stood up. He grabbed Marek by the collar, lifted his body and dragged him over to the window. Marek kept hitting him the face, but none of his blows fazed Mallory as he lifted Marek above his head and threw him out of the window. Marc finally came to and looked around the room. Everyone was paralyzed in shock and fear. Marek was dangling outside of a 22-story window, desperately holding on to Mallory's coat sleeves.

Marc looked back and saw Silas standing in the doorway dressed in battle fatigues and holding an automatic gun. "Do something, Silas. He's like crazy mad now."

Silas huffed and slowly dragged himself over to the broken window. He grabbed a conference chair, rolled it up to the window, sat down in the chair and surveyed the scene. Marek was hanging onto Mallory's coat sleeves because his hands were too cold to touch. The threads from Mallory's coat were beginning to unravel and the sleeves began to tear.

Silas huffed again and said quietly, "Hi baby, what's going on?"

"He needs to die," Mallory answered in a dark tone.

"I feel you on that, Boo. But if you kill him here, won't that go against your Violence in the Workplace Policy you just passed?"

"I don't care about policy now."

"I can tell, Baby, but if you break that policy, you can't work for me anymore 'cause they will kill you."

"They can't kill me, I'm an emperor. It's treason."

"Shit, you got me there." Silas hunched his shoulders. "I got nothing."

"Silas, make him stop!" Marc shouted.

Silas got up, shifted the gun from his hip to the front, and cocked it. "Baby, remember I said I love you...and that I would kill for you? Let me do it. Let me show you how much I love you." He aimed the gun at Marek's head. "But I can only kill one person a year for you...and you know that Marc is going to do something to piss you off and then you're going have to wait until next year for me to take care of him." He leaned closer to Mallory, using the gun to caress his hand softly, "Besides, you know he ain't worth it. And you're gonna miss him when he's gone. He's your favorite brother, remember?"

Mallory finally grabbed Marek's arms and lifted him back into the room. Once Marek found his footing, he lunged after Mallory, but Silas knocked him down with the butt of his gun and decked him in the face.

"You have a strange way of saying thank you, motherfucker," Silas snarled, standing over Marek, who was hunched over, holding his face.

"Stop fighting you two, please!" Marc shouted.

Silas stood in front of Mallory and suggested, "Let's consume something, control your anger."

"I'm not angry."

"Oh, those baby blue eyes of yours are telling a different story. If we don't consume something to transfer that built up power, Ima hafta calm you down and you don't like that."

"No...NO!" Mallory shouted and stormed out of the room.

"Oh, this is great!" Silas flopped down in a chair. "I come home from a hard week's work of battle to this bullshit. All I wanted was a hot meal and a horny, naked man waiting for me. BUT NOOOOO! I gotta pull motherfuckers out windows like they're kittens in a tree! And I'm not getting fucked tonight 'cause I gotta go to Hell and fight his ass so he can calm down! Shit! I should let my helicopter blade catch yo' ass."

"Aunt Sile, you went to the battlefield and didn't tell us?" Mauryn asked.

"Damn, I forgot. A fight broke out in our camp and I had to clear some stuff up. I really needed you guys. Either I'm getting old or they are getting stronger."

"You took our sons to the battlefields?" Marc asked, watching Marek slip out of the room.

"YES! Many times...and Hell too!" Silas snapped. "That's what aunts do!" He winked at the boys. Maxwell went to hand Silas a bottle of water, but he shouted, "Don't give me no damn water, I want a Coke!"

"All we got is Dr. Pepper!" MJ shouted back.

"Well, gimme that!" Silas sighed. MJ threw the can. Silas sat back in the chair and continued, "And check on your uncle, see how pissed he is. Come back and tell me how much I gotta whoop his ass tonight. I hate when we fight."

"Since he's working for your ass, you gonna pay for these got damn windows," Marc informed him in a matter-of-fact tone.

"He's doesn't work for me anymore, he's back with you. This is supposed to be his first day back."

"Well, he's fired again!" Marc shouted. "I don't want his ass back here. I don't give a damn who hates it. I run this shit!"

"You run this shit!" Silas mimicked him. "And you think you're gonna charge me for these two little windows?"

"Yeah, motherfucker! He's YOUR fucking emperor!"

Silas slowly sipped his Dr. Pepper. He eventually got up and grabbed his gun. "I'm paying for the windows?" Silas squeezed his eyes shut and took a deep breath. When he released it, all of the glass in the building shattered. "Then send me a bill for that, bitch!" he laughed and sauntered out of the room.

Marek ran into Mallory's office to get a sword. He burst through the door and rushed to the shelf, but it wasn't there. He suddenly heard the door slam shut. He turned around and Mallory was standing in front of him with his sword in hand.

"I take it you want to complete this fight in private?" Mallory said.

"Kinda!"

Mallory threw the sword and it landed inches from Marek's feet.

Marek thought hard about his next move. "I know we're both angry...and that I have no right to be."

"But?"

"There is no but," Marek huffed, "I love her Mallory, I really love her. I tried not to. I tried to stay away from her...but I really love her."

"Why didn't you just tell me?"

"I dunno." Marek bowed his head in shame. "I became the hypocrite. And you have every right to beat my ass down."

"Do you realize what you have done?"

"I caused a rift between us?"

"A rift? You think I'm upset about a bloody rift? A rift is what Marlon and I have because he keeps stealing the new shoes I buy every season and stretches them out with his bloody fat feet.

No...you...you set the wheel in motion for my demise. Marc has been trying to eradicate me since you left. He had me kicked out of the family, had the board sanction me from the company and he even upped the ante by hiring Matthew to kill me. But he always acted alone...until the board got wind of the babies. They found that Phillip wasn't mine and voided my marriage. Now I am a walking corpse."

"Mallory, we can fix that. I'll talk to Marc and we can—"

"We can DO WHAT? My life is over. The board is trying to find out how to kill me. They have been hounding the future generation for any clues. Some even attempted to strip my Death powers." Mallory laughed darkly, "Well, those board members are not alive anymore."

"I'm sorry!"

"Was she worth it?"

"Look, let me talk to Marc. We can fix this."

"Let's fix this now." Mallory picked up the sword and shoved it into Marek's hands. "How about you take that sword and plunge it through my heart? NOW!"

"Mallory...look, let's talk about this."

"NOW, MAREK!"

"I'm not going to do it." Marek dropped the sword.

"Either you put me out of my misery or I kill her and your children...your two beautiful daughters and the twins she's carrying now." Mallory picked up the sword and forced Marek to hold it. Then he whispered in Marek's ear, "I'd rather die by your hands than by anybody else's."

Marek dropped the sword and fell to his knees. "I won't do it!"

"You know what's funny? You people put the wheels in motion and have ample opportunities to eradicate me, but when you have the chance, you crumble. I hate being a Haulm. You're weak. At least Matty was man enough to fuck me before plunging a sword into me." He leaned down and grabbed Marek's face, "Maybe I should fuck you...then you might muster up enough anger to kill me."

"Then I'll be mad," Silas interrupted, waiting at the door.

"He's a mad man, Silas." Marc rushed through the door, raving wildly. "You not gonna to do anything about it?"

"Yeah, I am! I'm going to save him from his psychotic family. Something I should've done a long time ago." He motioned for Mallory to come to the door. "You really had that contract on him? You really had Matthew trying to kill him...after everything you told me...everything we agreed on? You were still planning on having him killed?"

"Silas! He's unstable. If you weren't here, he would kill us all."

"That's amazing. 'Cause I haven't done anything to stop him. I have no power over him. I'm just reasoning with a man that is on the edge...and rightfully so. Marc, if you go after him again, I think our relationship is going to be a little different." Silas walked out of the room.

Mallory stretched his hand out for Marek, who quickly grabbed it and helped himself up. Their eyes connected and, for a moment, they were brothers forced to make amends. Then Marek bowed his head in respect because Mallory was the emperor. During that moment, Mallory knew that he had lost his brother. Refusing to relinquish any pain, he walked out of the room with his head forcibly held high.

CHAPTER TWENTY SEVEN

Early Sunday morning, Mallory stood over a hot stove making Silas' favorite Tex-Mex omelet. Silas had been working extended weeks between LTC and the Abaddon. Sundays were his only free time. Mallory begged Silas to let him help, but he politely refused. Deep inside, Mallory felt that something was wrong. Silas and Mallory always talked about work and the companies, but since the altercation at Haulm Industries four months ago, Silas had become mute. He never talked about the company, the brothers or anything related to HIC, LTC or Hell. The only thing he would do was come home in the wee hours of the morning and hold Mallory tight for the few hours they had together.

Mallory also knew that something was wrong because his company cell phone stopped ringing, he couldn't get access to his Chroniclesations or network access to Towneson Financial, HIC, LTC, or the Abaddon. He was cut off. The loneliness, as well as the guilt, was beginning to eat at him. Mallory felt guilty because he'd been holding on to a secret. He never told Silas about the last board meeting he'd had – where he practically denounced the throne. Deep inside, he knew Silas was aware of the board meeting. The uproar of activities kept him away.

Silas finally made it out of the shower. He sat at the island table and watched Mallory slave over the stove. He finally turned around with plate in hand and walked over to him, serving him with a smile. Silas' face was so guilt-ridden that all he could do was to hold him.

"You know I've got to get use to this, aye?" Mallory confessed. Silas smiled, sat down and picked at a piece of bacon. After a long stint of silence, Mallory finally grabbed his hand and said, "I'm Death, remember? I battle with Heaven's army and I fucked the devil. I saw the dragon and lived to not talk about it. There is nothing in this world that I'm afraid of...so talk to me."

After a long silence, Silas finally broke. "The seven seals have been broken," he confessed darkly. "There are Earthquakes and fires erupting everywhere. Strong hurricanes are hitting the states back-to-back. War has broken out in many places, the global economy is tanking and people are dying from the strangest diseases. I went to my sources and it looks like Armageddon. I even spoke with God, but he didn't start this – it's not time. I have been running around trying to put out fires and wars, but it's too much."

"Let me help you."

"You've done enough." Silas blurted out before thinking. He realized that he didn't mean to say that and he gently grabbed Mallory's hand. "You're helping me, baby...by staying here. I can protect you here."

"What? I don't understand."

"Well, ever since your fight with Marek, there has been threats and attempts to take you out. And since you denounced the throne at that board meeting that you never told me about...your shield of protection is gone. I don't know who's directly behind it. It could be Matthew or your brothers, but Heaven, the Board and armies on both sides are out to kill you." Silas sulked, "And my army has been compromised. I had to sanction a special security team to watch you. There are many who see you as a bounty and..."

Mallory fell in a chair, overwhelmed with emotion.

"But baby, you're safe here. As long as you don't leave Hell, you're safe." Silas grabbed his hand.

"I'm in Hell now?"

"You can't tell?"

"I guess I should have...every time I try to leave, I blank out."

"Yeah, there's a force field around the penthouse. I had it lowered to Hell so no one could get to you. There's only one way in and one way out!"

"I can help you. I can protect myself."

"Baby, if this is Armageddon; you being by my side will complete the formula. You know and I looked...and beheld a pale horse..."

"And his name that sat on him was Death and Hell followed with him. And power was given unto them over the fourth part of the Earth, Revelations 6:8, I know."

"So if you're not with me, it really can't start."

"You think this is the only way?"

"Yeah, it will blow over. Some of these humans need to die anyway. They lost sight of God and think they control the world. There needs to be a little reset."

Mallory bowed his head and his tears hit the countertop.

"Oh, baby, it'll blow over. I promise you that. I will never let anyone or anything harm you." He cupped his face, "Contrary to what my father said, I do love you. You're not my possession. You're my heart." Silas kissed his soft lips.

Four soldiers appeared and waited for Silas. "Sir, it's time."

"I'll be back, I promise. This will all blow over, but I need you to stay here until I say it's okay."

Mallory shook his head.

"**DO NOT** come to Earth for any reason." Silas held Mallory's chin up - forcing him to look in his eyes. "Do you trust me? I mean it! For no reason do you come to Earth."

Mallory nodded his head. Silas kissed his lips, his forehead and then he rushed out.

Thirty-seven days passed since Mallory saw Silas - or anyone for that matter. Being cut off from the world proved too much for him. He gathered all of his old medication bottles and poured all of the pills on to the floor. 6,938 pills. One pill for each day since he came back to the family. 6,938. Mallory laid each pill side by side until all they spelled out the words 'DUMB ASS' And then he lied down next to them, daring himself to start taking them.

He finally built himself up to commit the suicidal act, when he heard the pills crushing. He buried his head, because he knew what was waiting for him. Once the last pill was pulverized, Mallory's heart sank and he wanted to cry. The threatening noise stopped and he felt a presence hover over him.

The presence kneeled down and in an ominous, condescending tone said, WELL, WELL, WELL! Fancy seeing you in this state again. It was Mallory's Ego. I DON'T GET A HELLO? The Ego raised Mallory's face from the ground. He could tell that Mallory had been crying. Melor! We had an agreement, didn't we? If we were in this state again, I would get full control.

"I'm sorry. I tried, but I..."

I-I-I...The Ego mimicked him and then shouted, I DON'T WANT TO HEAR IT! We had an agreement! The Ego stood up and scrambled through his pockets. He pulled a small pill out and kneeled down again. I know that you don't remember, but we did have an agreement. Remember, in the midst of your lovemaking...that passionate wild sex with Silas. You promised me that you would always be happy. And if not, I would take over.

Mallory finally broke down.

The Ego raised his head, Don't cry! Succumb. He handed the pill to Mallory and stood over him.

Mallory grabbed the bottle of Vodka and toyed with the pill. Taking the pill would be the end of Mallory's existence and all the promises he made to Silas would be broken. Mallory took a deep breath, popped the pill in his mouth. Then he washed them down with a half a bottle of Vodka. Streams of Vodka and tears ran down his face and throat. Mallory laid down and waited for the damage to take place. Once his eyes flickered closed, the Ego smiled. Mallory's time was over and it was his time to reign.

Bye, bye love.

Mallory took the elevator down to his winter closet. The one thing that temporarily pacified him was rearranging his closet and rotating his clothes. When the elevator doors opened, he and Tanic, who was now his best friend, walked out. Mallory pushed the button to bring down his winter coats. "What shall we wear, Tanic?"

The dog barked.

"Really? You think? I really like the grey."

The dog barked again, ran to the bench and sat down. Matthew appeared next to Tanic on the bench. He picked up the dog and they rubbed noses. The dog feverishly licked on Matthew's face and fingers as if he was a tasty meal. Mallory sensed a presence, paused and then returned to arranging his clothes.

Matthew broke the silence by saying, "You know I always loved your winter white ensemble with the black Papillion. So crisp and clean."

Mallory didn't respond.

"I've been missing you on Earth. Why are you cooped up? Or shall I say down here?"

Mallory still didn't respond.

"Is it because Silas said so?" The dog finally took her opportunity and bit Matthew, drawing and licking the angelic blood from his finger. Matthew was so engrossed in the conversation that he didn't notice that the little dog was turning rabid. Matthew stood up and put the dog down. "That's right! You're a loyal servant. I remember when you used to follow me faithfully."

More like aimlessly. Look where it got us. Mallory never turned around.

"We would have been happy –"

If what, Matthew? If I allowed you to kill me and tuck my soul somewhere? Mallory finally turned around and shouted, WHY ARE YOU HERE?

Matthew was taken aback when he saw Mallory's eyes turned an ice-cold aquamarine. "Oh my...I'm in the presence of the man himself...the original Mallory Haulm. Is my Emerald gone?"

For all practical purposes, yes. You have to deal with me now.

Matthew took a few steps back. "I guess I owe you an apology for trying to separate you two."

Don't you think it's too late for that?

"Emerald...Mallory. WOW! I haven't seen you since...you were seven." Matthew returned to the bench and sat down. "You looked so helpless and lost then. Boy was I wrong. You were neither one of those things."

I was lost...but I wasn't helpless. You weren't helpful. Not only did I have to protect myself from all those men...I had to protect myself from you. You should've killed me that night when you had the chance.

"You're right, I should have. I was sent down there to do that...but..."

Mallory leaned down and whispered, But what?

"I truly regret that night." Matthew bowed his head.

Why? 'Cause you craved human flesh? Mallory crawled in his lap. You laid down with a little naked boy and allowed me to perform acts on you.

"STOP MALLORY!" Matthew turned away.

WHY? You were no more innocent than I was...I guess I wasn't that innocent being that Daddy taught me everything I knew. And you enjoyed EVERYTHING he taught me. Mallory could tell that Matthew was tormented, so he stood up. I asked a question. Why are you here?

"Why are you not on Earth?" Matthew collected his thoughts.

I'm on holiday.

Matthew looked around. "And a lovely holiday it is."

Why, Matthew?

"Your family is in disarray?" Matthew stood up.

And how is that my problem?

"They need you. You're the only one that can diffuse this situation."

That's interesting coming from you! Aren't you the one that wanted me to stay away from my family? Didn't you say that they would cause me nothing but harm? Now you are the spokesperson for my family! Are you serious?

"You sound just like Silas. 'Are you serious'?" Matthew mimicked Silas' voice then huffed, "Honestly, they need you. This situation has gotten out of hand. The family is divided. Marek is...guilt ridden and he wants to apologize."

And Marc! Mallory rushed up to him. Is it true about you and Marc? He set you up to kill me?

"He didn't set me up. He just asked me. I wasn't really gonna kill you, but you pissed me off and I got angry - like I often do." Matthew grabbed his arms. "I know you keep hearing this, but I'm sorry that I got angry with you and lost control." He pulled him close, "You know I love you."

Yes, I know you love me to Death! Mallory slapped his arms down. I can't believe you. So, now what, you're coaxing me to Earth because you want to kill me officially? You want to start Armageddon and you want all the players on the team to be there? You already broke the seals.

Matthew was shocked. "Is that was Silas told you?"

You think I don't know?

"You don't know. Silas lied. There are no seals broken. Only God can break the seals."

Aren't you my God?

"You stopped worshiping me a long time ago."

Gods are not supposed to break people's hearts. You promised that you were going to protect me.

"Mallory, I tried everything I could to protect you, but I told you that I wasn't a guardian angel. I tried my best. I got you with a good family. I watched you night and day and..."

And you let my Dad kill the one man that was there for me. You stood there and did nothing. Just like you did that night my Dad raped me. You did nothing. When I needed you the most, you did nothing! Mallory roared.

"What did you want me to do, start Armageddon to protect you?"

Silas would. Mallory snapped back. So now you're pissed 'cause he protects me.

Matthew laughed eerily, "Now you're down here trapped while Silas is on Earth fucking away. He doesn't want you to leave him, so he lied to you about the seals. Mallory, don't you get it? Angels don't share. They don't like their possessions roaming around."

Why would he lie?

"Why would he lie about the MMC? 'Cause he could and you believed him...like a FOOL!"

Damned if I do and damned if I don't. I either believe you or him and so far, he hasn't tried to kill me. Mallory stormed away.

Matthew followed closely behind and pushed him against the wall. "What makes you think the first time he tries he won't be successful?"

I like to think that you're a better angel than he is and you ain't been successful yet!

"OH, YOU AIN'T? Those are pissing words," Matthew taunted. He grabbed Mallory's arms again, flipping him and pinning him against the wall. "Baby, let's not fight. I love you so much." He kissed him. "I want you so much." They got lost in their kisses. Matthew whispered in his ear, "Let's go to Earth and make love."

Why wait? Mallory pulled his shirt off. There's no one here. We can have each other now for as long as we want.

"I'll enjoy you better on Earth."

Does it matter where we are?

"Yes, it does. I'm not supposed to be here."

Silas is on Earth, fucking around. We can fuck around in Hell and he'll never know it. Mallory grabbed his belt and loosened it.

Matthew grabbed his hand, "Let's go to Earth now, before we get caught up."

Mallory hooked his foot behind Matthew's leg and made him fall. *I'm already caught up. Damn, I wish I had a sword...I-I mean a condom.* Mallory kneeled down, grabbing Matthew's neck with both hands.

"Déjà vu! This was really our first time, you fucking me and looking for my sword at the same time. You stabbed me in the heart that night, thinking that you killed me. And when my blood touched your skin, you couldn't get rid of me. You might have been seven, but you were a warrior and you stole my innocence. And the more my blood coated your body, the more you started losing your mind." Matthew rose up. "We are one. I will always be in your system. I will always flow through your veins. As you take your breaths, they become mine. You can't live without me!"

Mallory moved to kiss him, but he dematerialized into thin air, leaving Mallory longing for his touch. *Well, that went well.* Mallory sulked on his knees. *What am I supposed to do, Tanic?* The dog barked and ran away, only to return with a silver leash. *I can't leave, Tanic. I black out, remember?*

The dog kept barking until Mallory got up. He switched his closet to formal dinner attire. The dog watched as Mallory was deciding on which outfit to wear; his favorite midnight empire purple Brioni dinner coat with his Midas gold dress shirt and matching papillion or the white ensemble that Matthew suggested. He fussed and primped himself for what he thought would be the last time. Mallory mused, *If I'm going out, at least I'll look good.*

CHAPTER TWENTY EIGHT

Meanwhile, the uncles, brothers and the new generation were just released from the boardroom with news that the Seven Seals had been compromised. They were planning survival strategies when they got word that Mallory was making his return to Earth. They believed that Armageddon was just moments away. The brothers were instructed to prepare their armor and join Matthew in the fight. As they left the boardroom, the new generation stayed together, however, the three brothers went their separate ways.

Marc couldn't fight back the smile that was exploding on his face. He had finally won and Mallory was going to be eradicated. It wasn't long before his joy was interrupted by Uncle Mal, who bee-lined for him after the meeting.

"Marc, go back to the board and stop this!" Uncle Mal shouted as he pushed him against the wall.

"Why would I do that?"

"This is Mallory we are talking about, your brother. Don't you—"

"MY BROTHER DIED WHEN HE WAS SEVEN! Just like yours died at seventeen. You think I don't know the history between you and Dad. Unexplainable and sinister things happened to him when he was seventeen. You've tried to kill Dad ever since and you failed every time!"

"You don't understand what happened!"

"I don't care what happened. This is my time to get rid of Mallory. I want him eradicated. If I had my way, he would be stripped from our history books."

"Marc, why?"

"That man that stands before us claiming to be Mallory is not MY BROTHER! He does NOT deserve the love and respect that my little brother Mallory earned. He is a mockery! To think that Dad abused us both and he parades around like it is OKAY! WELL, IT IS NOT OKAY!"

Uncle Mal was in shock. This was the first time that he heard Marc confess to being abused. No one confessed to Malcolm's abuse, although everyone suspected that it happened. No one discussed it out in the open. He grabbed his arms, "Marc, there's another way."

"I'm happy with the way I'm taking. You failed...only because Dad had a child. Well, Mallory doesn't have children. I will NOT FAIL!" Marc pushed Uncle Mal away, "Say your good-byes now," he suggested curtly and stomped away.

"God help us." Uncle Mal bowed his head, but before he could grieve for Mallory, a clerk ran up to him and told him that Quincy's body was found in an abandon car.

When Marc walked into his office, Marek was perched at his desk, waiting for him. "Marc, this has gone too far. We shouldn't be doing this."

"It's done." Marc walked behind his desk and turned his computer on.

"We can stop this."

"I don't want to!" Marc shouted. Marlon walked into the room and sat on the couch, observing the fight.

"What has he done to deserve this?" Marek stormed up to Marc.

"Other than whooping your ass?"

"That was justified. I'm with his wife. I threw you off the roof for fucking mine. Dad threw Uncle out the window for fucking his... It's a family thing," Marek retorted, leaning over Marc.

"He's a joke. He brought undue shame to this family." Marc walked from behind the desk.

"I think we all have done that at some point."

"I want him dead, okay?" Marc hunched his shoulders. "I got the board to agree that he's a danger."

"I don't agree and I won't fight on your side."

"I don't need you." Marc walked over to the couch. "I got the board and Marlon." He patted Marlon on the back.

They both looked at Marlon, who was frustrated with the whole situation. "I hate being the rope in your tug-of-wars."

"He is not our brother. He's an imposter. Our brother died when he was seven," Marc reiterated. Marek walked over to the couch to join them.

"Only you believe that shit. No one else believes that bullshit, but you." Marek reasoned.

"Marlon, do you think this-this guy is your brother?" Marc asked.

"Yeah, I guess." Marlon hunched his shoulders.

"You guess? What do you mean you guess? That's our brother. He has our bad temper, our exotic taste in women and our receding hairline. And you two have a fetish for expensive shoes!" Marek fussed at him.

"He's gay!" Marc shouted. "If he was our brother, he would NOT be gay!"

"I don't see why not. We have one brother who is a dick and one who likes dick. He fits in perfectly!"

Marc's voice turned dark. "He fits so perfectly...now that he's passing down the family curse."

"MARC!" Marek's eyes bugged out. He knew where this conversation was going.

"What? He needs to know." Marc sat on the coffee table in front of Marlon.

"Know what?" Marlon asked.

Marek stood over Marc, trying to intimidate him into silence. "If Mallory wanted Marlon to know, then Mallory would have told him."

"Know what?"

"He has the right to know," Marlon grabbed Marc's hand and faked a look of concern. "...that his only baby boy was molested!"

'WHAT!" Marlon jumped up from the couch.

"FIRST, he was NOT a baby when the incident happened. He was an adult!" Marek shouted. "Second! We promised that we would not tell his dad." Marek reminded Marc that Maxwell, not Mallory, made him promise. Maxwell knew how protective his father was and he didn't want to cause a rift between the two brothers.

"I don't keep promises when violence is involved," Marc snarled.

"I'll remember that when I need someone to confide in," Marek answered sarcastically.

"Max was molested?" Marlon shook his head and flopped on the couch.

"NO! Max was not molested." Marek kneeled down next to Marlon. He took a deep breath and said, "It happened during the time when Mallory was having his breakdown. You know how the boys love to hang out with him. One night, he was so drunk that he couldn't walk, so he asked Max to help him to the restroom. While he was pissing, he grabbed Max's hand and..."

"Made him jack him off!" Marc crudely finished the statement.

"How tactful," Marek snarled back before returning his attention to Marlon. "Mallory apologized immediately and he wanted to tell you but..."

"He threatened Max!" Marc interjected.

"NO, HE DIDN'T. Max didn't want anyone else to know."

"How did you find out?" Marlon turned to Marek.

Marek huffed, "Mallory confided in me. He really wanted to tell you...that is what sent him over the edge."

"The fact that he was becoming Dad sent him over the edge!" Marc shouted. "You know how Dad made us jack him off." Both brothers looked at him harshly. "He was becoming the same way."

"I have never jacked Dad off." Marek gave Marc a disgusted look.

"Me neither..." Marlon was shocked. "I never even saw him naked."

Marc looked at both of them as a flash of embarrassment plastered on his face. "HE MUST DIE AND HE MUST DIE NOW!" He screamed.

Mallory stood in front of the doorway to the penthouse. He looked down at Tanic, who was all too eager to leave the house. The dog barked again and pulled him closer to the doorway. He opened the door and a blank wall was in front of him. *There's only one way in and one-way out and I don't know the way.* The petite dog pitched a monstrous growl that shook the room.

Rut-Ro Reorge! Mallory breathed his best Astro the Dog impression. He watched the tiny platinum Shih Tzu morph into a massive, shiny black three-headed Rottweiler. The name on the dog's gold-plated tag read 'Cerberus'. The echoes from the dog's bark shook the wall until it began to crumble. The dog made a pathway through the crumbling the wall and dragged Mallory through it.

Against Silas' command, Mallory returned to Earth. An Earth-shattering crash echoed throughout the world. Mallory looked around and noticed that he was on Earth, but the sky was dark grey and cloudy. Buildings were on fire. The blood-drenched ground was shaking and the wind was stifling and thick. Mallory leaned down and removed the dog's collar. He patted it on the side and said, *Get it! Go, baby.*

The massive dog charged off in a thunderous flash. As Mallory stood up, he saw three shadows in the distance waiting for him. He took a deep breath and walked toward them, twirling the silver leash in his hand. As Mallory walked, a destructive tornado a mile wide surrounded his presence. When he approached the three, he noticed that the shadows were his three brothers. They appeared to be armed and angry.

Waiting for me? Mallory asked, looking into Marek's eyes. Marlon stormed up to him and drew his sword.

"Marlon, wait!" Marek shouted, but it was too late. Marlon hit him with the butt of his sword several times until Mallory fell to his knees.

"This is your day to die," Marc replied, drawing his sword.

And you're my executioner? Mallory asked, still looking at Marek.

Marlon couldn't contain his anger any more. He hit Mallory in the face with the sword, "How could you betray me?"

What are you talking about?

"Molesting my baby boy!" He bitch slapped Mallory across the face again causing his nose to bleed.

You have the right to be angry, but I won't deal with you now! Mallory admitted, wiping his nose. Mallory entangled his feet with Marlon's legs and tripped him. Mallory quickly jumped up, holding the silver leash, which quickly transformed in a double-edged sword.

Marlon attempted to take a swing at Mallory, but failed. Mallory swung his sword to knock Marlon's sword out of his hand, but he lost his footing. To stop himself from falling, he pitched his sword into the ground. Unfortunately, the sword went through Marlon's side before piercing the dirt.

Marc tried to attack, but Marek held him back. Mallory pulled his sword from Marlon's abdomen and started walking toward Marc and Marek with his sword elevated. He asked, Are you next? We do have an issue that was never settled...a wife issue.

Marek finally turned around with Marc at his back. He raised his arms and said, "Mallory, stop this. We can settle this another day, but not right now and definitely not here."

Why not? Mallory asked. He walked toward him, but stopped when he saw Marc's sword protruding underneath Marek's arm.

"Mallory, you're the sensible one here. I'm counting on you to help me work this shit out!" Marek reasoned.

Which hand are you counting on? Mallory quickly clashed his sword with Marc's, but unfortunately, Marek's left hand was in the way. He fell to the ground, holding his wound with blood gushing from his arm. Marlon quickly crawled to Marek, which startled Mallory, so he turned and defensively stabbed Marlon in the side again. He reacted, thinking that Marlon was going to attack him.

With his back turned, he felt the cold steel blade Marc was holding against his neck. Mallory calmly said, If I were you, I would do it now. As soon as he felt the blade lift from his neck, Mallory swung around and clashed swords with Marc. Too slow!

Marc held his sword with both hands. The two fought back and forth for a bit, but Mallory had more skill and better tactics. At one point, Mallory lowered his sword and said to Marc, It took me some time to figure out why you hate me so. It's not anger, it's hate. I don't think that you hate me because I'm gay. I think you hate me because you think I escaped from Dad all those years....and left you to endure his pain and suffering.

"Mallory gets a gold star!" Marc replied sarcastically, charging at Mallory, swinging and clashing his sword.

Mallory lowered his sword again and bowed on one knee. Then I owe you an apology.

"More than that, you owe me your life." Marc swung, but Mallory ducked and plunged the sword in his side. He quickly pulled it out and decapitated Marc.

I may own you my life, but the one that's losing his life is you. Mallory smirked. He quickly turned and headed toward Marek. With the tip of his sword, he raised Marek's head. Now about that wife issue, he began. Suddenly, Mallory felt a blow to his head and he fell to the ground. Afterwards, he felt a sharp sword slide across his neck and he soon passed out from his head injury.

Marek glanced up and saw Matthew. "Yeah, motherfucker. It's me. Thank me later." Matthew rolled Mallory's body over with his feet. He leaned over Mallory and slapped him on the face several times to wake him up. When Mallory finally responded, he was pissed. Matthew smiled, "Hey, love, it's me...your angel...your lover...your executioner." He leaned in to kiss Mallory's lips then asked, "Should we fuck now before we fight?"

Mallory never parted his lips. At that moment, he felt a heavy breath of brimstone above him. He looked up and saw Cerberus, his three-headed Rottweiler, holding Mallory's Final Death Sword in his mouth. The dog dropped the sword and growled until Matthew got up. Mallory quickly jumped up to his feet. Before he grabbed his special sword, he dusted himself off and watched his all-white formal attire transformed into a deep red. He leaned down and patted the dog on the back. He quickly looked around and saw a mound in the distance. He took off running with Cerberus following closely behind him. Once he reached the mound, he turned and aimed his sword.

Matthew was close behind. He walked up to Mallory and said, "You always wanted to be on top." He raised his sword to Mallory. As they clashed, the Earth shook underneath them. The Heavens opened up and poured brimstone down upon them. With each clash of the swords, Earthquakes and volcanoes erupted. The wind grew violent and thick with hot ash. As they fought, Matthew spotted a black cloud moving quickly in the distance, but he paid little attention to it. Mallory never saw the cloud. He only had one focus – Matthew.

As the cloud grew closer, Matthew took his eyes off Mallory; who found the perfect opportunity to stab Matthew. With a wicked grin, Mallory looked deep into Matthew's eyes, which were horror-stricken - but not because Mallory stabbed him. He was fearful because Silas and his large army were moving in close. Matthew gasped when Silas stabbed the dog without hesitation.

Mallory pulled the sword out of Matthew's body to stab him again, but Silas grabbed Mallory's arm and swung him around. He plunged his sword deep into Mallory's chest, piercing through his heart. He avoided eye contact with Mallory as he pushed the sword in and twisted it several times. Silas was so close that he would smell the breath of life leaving Mallory's body. He closed his eyes and softly kissed Mallory one last time before pulling the sword from Mallory's chest. In one swift swing, he decapitated his lover. Mallory's head hit the ground and began rolling, not stopping until it hit Marek's foot.

Mallory Towneson Haulm was dead.

The Earth stopped shaking as the last of the brimstone ash turned into rain. The wind stood still and the sun crept over the ruin city. Silas' army vanished in the in thin air, as Silas walked away, never looking back. Matthew fell to his knees at Mallory's body - silent and broken. His greatest love, his obsession, his meaning for human life was now gone. Matthew, along with Marek and Marlon watched Mallory's head and body engulfed in flames, turned to ashes then melted away in the raindrops.

EPILOGUE

Since Mallory's death, Silas was haunted by his soul. When they bound their life forces, Silas promised that they would be together for eternity and that included death. However, Mallory's physical absence proved more than Silas could handle. Every night for a year, Mallory would come to Silas and would not allow him to sleep. He even interfered in his Million Man Campaign. After being so close to his goal, Silas stopped his campaign at 999,999. He started to grow weary and disturbed as Mallory's visits became more violent.

On the eve of Silas' 40th birthday, Mallory appeared to him. As always, he cried and begged Mallory to leave. Silas got drunk to drown his sorrows and Mallory would disappear, but this day was different because Mallory announced that he would always love him. He also apologized for being a nuisance and promised that he would leave Silas alone. Silas was so disturbed that he didn't hear the confession.

"Just leave!" Silas shouted to an empty room. The apparition that haunted him suddenly disappeared. Mallory's spirit was gone. *That was strange*, he thought to himself. Silas laid back down in the bed, nursing his head that had been aching from the tears he cried all night long.

As he calmed himself down, the smell of peppered bacon floated in the air and noises from downstairs bellowed up to the bedroom. Silas finally mustered up enough strength to crawl out of bed. He opened the door and eased down the stairs to discover Mallory's nephews were making themselves at home. He studied each of the boys closely. Maxwell and Mauryn were in the kitchen laughing and cooking. Monty was sitting at the island reading the paper while MJ was on the couch. MJ was the only one who appeared to be despondent.

Monty looked up and shouted, "Aunt Sile, you finally got out of bed."

Silas nodded his head.

"I guess you're wondering why we're here?"

"Among other things...how did you get in?"

"Duh...Uncle Town use to live here. We have keys, cameras, passwords, remember?"

"Right...I'll make note of that."

"Well, we noticed that you have been bothered by a certain soul that's not been called yet."

"And?" Silas looked at MJ who wasn't involved in the conversation.

Monty also realized that MJ was showing emotions that were not consistent with the group. He walked over and stood in front of him. "So we thought we would help you with that. Given that Uncle Town...Mallory, if you don't mind us using his name, was an Emperor. It is only fitting that we get your permission to collect him."

A breeze flew around the room, knocking down pictures and vases. Silas was disturbed once again. He grabbed his head and screamed out, "Please stop it!"

"We can take care of it, Aunt Sile." Monty turned to MJ. "Ready?"

MJ stood up, took a deep breath and began chanting. The breeze zoomed around trying to escape before it lost the battle. MJ took a deep breath and inhaled the escaped soul. Silas saw a tear escape MJ's eyes before he retreated to the balcony. Monty smoothly moved and sat in the wing-backed chair closer to the balcony. Maxwell took MJ's place on the couch. Although they were causal movements, Silas saw through the causal coyness for what it was - a strategic military positioning. They were taught very well to realize that they were stronger, maybe even invincible, in fours. They all watched each other. Silas recognized Mauryrn and MJ were the vulnerable ones because Mauryrn had his back turned cooking and MJ was in an unstable emotional state. Once Mauryrn sensed that he was only one in the kitchen, he quickly finished the bacon and began putting everything on the table, moving everything closer to the other two. Now, only one was vulnerable, but very well guarded and protected.

Mallory taught them well... He would have been proud, Silas thought. "I guess a 'thank you' is in order."

"Among other things. So, there's going to be some changes and we just want you to know that you will be going along with it. We will send the details of the changes in a memo," Monty announced.

Silas was still looking at MJ who completely shut himself off from the rest of the group.

"Are you listening?" Monty eased out of his seat, as not to draw any attention to his cousin and slowly walked over to MJ. It would only be visible to the trained eye, but the other two made chess moves closer to MJ. "With Mallory neutralized, we will be officially taking over."

"I guess that's easy now that Marc's gone too." Silas pointed out.

Monty laughed, "Dad was never the threat. We needed to eradicate Mallory. He was the powerful one. When he fell, they fell like dominoes. Even after moving over to TAE, he was still a strong and powerful force to be reckoned with. We thought him working for you was a bad move, but we were wrong. It was exactly what we needed."

Silas was speechless.

"It was a perfect setup."

"You broke the seals?"

"We worked the system. We figured that neither of us individually, or even collectively, would be strong enough to take Uncle Town out. Apparently, he had dominion over Heaven and Hell and ran the family, unbeknownst to Dad. So we just turned the powers against him. His alliances, his powerhouses and his lovers took him out and we didn't have to lift a finger. All we had to do was sit back and watch."

"You know you could've killed all of humanity? Creating Armageddon is irreversible!"

"That wasn't Armageddon. That's just us working together like a family should." Monty huffed, "That's what the past three generations failed to do...work together." Monty gently placed his hand on MJ's shoulder and asked with sincere concern, "You okay?"

"Yeah, I'm fine." MJ mustered up strength in his voice and delivered a weak smile.

"I know it hurts but it was necessary to do." Monty patted him on the back. "Well, we're leaving. We got what we came for." He motioned for the others to join him. "Breakfast is in the kitchen. I hope you have an enjoyable life." They walked out in single file. Before Monty walked out of the door, he turned and said, "Be looking out for that memo."

And the Millionth Man is...

A week passed. Silas was lost and empty since the nephews stole Mallory. Yes, they stole him. He missed the nightly visits. He tried to find comfort at his old stomping grounds, but they rendered no relief. In fact with one remaining man left, he denounced his Million Man campaign in honor of Mallory.

He stirred in his bed and remembered how soft and sensuous Mallory's touches were. He remembered how they would spoon together and Mallory would nestle his head between Silas' shoulder blade and the pillow. Silas often wondered how he could breathe being so smothered, but Mallory was comfortable. The closer Silas' heat-exuding body was to Mallory's cold frame, the better they both slept.

As Silas stirred more, he felt a warm and somewhat familiar presence. He hoped it was Mallory, but deep inside he knew that his hope would not be his reality. His eyes flicked opened when he felt an arm draped over his body. He tried to remember what he did the night before. Since Mallory's death, he had started to drink heavily, something that he never condoned. He would drink, pass out and wake up alone. But last night, he decided to go to the bar across the street. That was all he remembered. He touched the hand and flashbacks of an erotic night played in his mind. He tried to focus on the face, but the pain from his hangover started to throb in his head.

Who did I come home with? Silas thought. He began to roll over and tried desperately to remember the night before. Once the roll was completed, fear struck beyond his heart, down beyond the soul and permeated his bones. Pain from his hangover did not compare to the pain he felt when he saw the face of his millionth man. Silas flew out of the bed, screaming and covering his mouth.

It was Matthew.

His gut-wrenching screams finally woke Matthew. Frowning, he slowly opened his eyes and focused on a naked and panic-stricken Silas. He quickly looked under the sheets and realized that he was naked too.

"AH, SHIIET! THIS IS BLOODY FUCKING PERFECT!"

"Ah, this is why I don't fuck drunk! I'm going to Hell for this! Wait, I can't go to Hell, I run Hell! I wonder is there a place worse than Hell!" Silas panicked and shouted.

Matthew slowly sat up in bed and bowed his head. This was the last thing he wanted. He had lost his lover and his way back to Heaven. He just wanted to escape. He'd been living out of that bar since Mallory's death. Even though it was across the street from Silas' penthouse, he never saw Silas there.

"I can't go back now," Matthew sighed heavily. He crawled out of bed and walked into the bathroom.

Silas finally calmed down long enough to see that Matthew was just as panicked and hurt. He followed him into the bathroom and watched Matthew get into the shower.

"I guess it could be worse," Silas paused, trying to convince himself. "I can't think of anything right now...but there has to be something else worse than this."

"I can't go back home now." Matthew kept repeating.

"Yeah, you can. God will forgive you for this...I...hope."

"God is forgiving to humans, not angels."

"That's not true. God forgives all his creations." Silas walked into the shower. "He loves us all. I know that now from being around humans. You feel the infinity of His greatness, power, and love. He's too big to be jealous, too big to be petty, too big to be small. He's forgiving."

"I can't go back there being this heartbroken."

"YOU CAN'T STAY HERE!" That statement flew out of Silas' mouth before he thought about it. "I-I-I mean, you can hang out a little bit...Like an hour or day or ...but let's face it, Earth ain't big enough for the both of us."

"Then why don't you go to Hell?"

Silas laughed. "If I didn't know better, I would take that as an offense." He tagged Matthew on the shoulder. "It'll be alright. We'll be okay. Let me get you some clothes. So I can stop focusing on you being naked and hung..." Silas walked out of the shower while completing his thought in silence. *And somewhat irresistible.*

"I want clothes from your closet, 'cuz I don't wear suits!" Matthew shouted after him.

"OH BITCH YOU GOTTA GO HOME." Silas opened the door to his closet. "I don't care how sexy yo' ass is! You gots to go!"

"It's been a while since you spoke with Me," God said, sitting on the bench inside the closet.

"Why should I speak to you? You let this happen! You killed him!" Silas shouted in anger.

"Did I?" God answered coyly.

"DON'T FUCK WITH ME!" Silas shouted back which took God by surprise. "You made me promise something that you knew was going to hurt me. You saw this coming and you did nothing. You created this fight! And with the adrenaline built up, you hardened my heart like you did Pharaoh and made me kill the only man I truly loved since Adam. The only man that would have made me give up this fight with you. I LOVED HIM!"

"I made you? The way I see it, you had choices. Free will, like the humans...you could have chosen differently. For all I know, you could've chosen to kill Matthew."

"Kill an Angel... one of your highest? And then what? Be slated for execution, stoned to death, my privileges to return to Heaven revoked? Those were my choices?" Silas' voice cracked in anger.

"Silas, you could have chosen not to act at all."

"And disobey you! Who do you think I am, human?" In anger, Silas rushed around in circles. "I know what you want...you want me to become that hateful, vile, tormented—" Silas was so angry he couldn't stop the tears from falling down his face. "NO! NEVER! I will NOT become that monster that is written in that hate-drenched, small-minded, homophobic crap, doctrine that YOU BLESSED and called YOUR WORD. No, I won't. I knew you before THE WORD! I loved you and followed you before you crated your blessed humans. I KNOW WHO YOU ARE! I VOWED to follow you. I will always follow you. You can harden my heart, weaken my soul and do whatever you want to me to do. BUT I WILL ALWAYS FOLLOW YOU! ALWAYS!" His voice possessed a thunderous echo.

"Silas, son. Let's talk." God saw that Silas was truly broken and for the first time since their first fight thousands of years ago, God saw and felt that pain exuding from him. "Satan my son. My love, my first creation before man, I don't want to see you this angry again. Please talk to me before this gets any worst. We've come so far—"

"I'm done talking to you." Silas took a deep breath and forcefully wiped the tears from his eyes, "In Jesus name."

"My son, don't," God pleaded.

"I SAID, IN JESUS NAME!" Silas walked out of the closet. "AMEN!" He slammed the door.

The Complete Saga

Other Titles

To learn more about the author or to read other excerpts from these books, visit www.authortljames.com.

PLEASE LEAVE A REVIEW!

ngramcontent.com/pod-product-compliance
g Source LLC
burg PA
507260626
00004B/1227